**A STORY
ABOUT TWO ACCIDENTAL REVOLUTIONS**

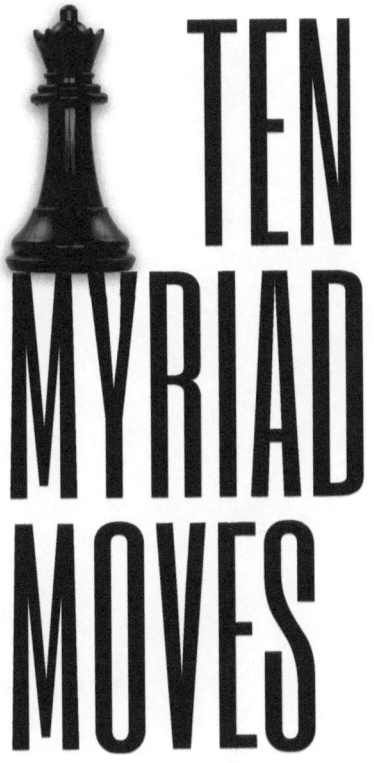

TEN MYRIAD MOVES

MILA ILKOVA

*Oh, Well. F*ck It!*

New York

For M

who can do anything

Ten Myriad Moves
© 2021 by Mila Ilkova

First Edition. And most likely the only edition, because the author hates redoing things.

Design © 2021 by Mila Ilkova

MI1.club
New York
ISBN 979-8-9877558-1-5
Library of Congress Control Number: 2023907901

With only a thousand dollars and an existential crisis Mirra Vladi manages to buy property in Big Sur, write and sell a movie script, found a growing international company, and cause a state revolution. But the latter is totally by accident.

With the moonlight to guide you
Feel the joy of being alive
The day that you stop running
Is the day that you arrive

And the night that you got locked in
Was the time to decide
Stop chasing shadows
Just enjoy the ride

So maybe tomorrow
I'll find my way home

© Morcheeba feat. Stereophonics
"Enjoy The Ride"

ENJOY THE SILENCE

Manhattan has a very specific odor. It can't be confused with anything. Manhattan mightily stinks of money. The city of contrasts combines in itself a drink for twenty-five dollars and a good pizza slice for one.

A pair of high heels and a backpack are completely different worlds. When you wear both, it's like you're stuck in between, where on one side is worry free fun and on the other—a monthly prepaid MetroCard. The two things that run New York are greed and fear.

I was on my way to a movie screening—a writing gig I was promised fifty dollars to forget about my dignity for. I swallowed my pride like the cum of someone who'd been eating hot chicken wings for months. It stank. The worst feeling is when you lie to yourself. The aftertaste had lasted for two years. I let those two years be shitty because I thought I was worthless piece of shit. Everything becomes so easy when you're accepted. I still remember how good it felt. And therefore, here I was, writing a meaningless story about a meaningless event for meaningless compensation. Before, I wouldn't even bother writing twenty-five words for that price, yet I was supposed to compile five hundred words now?

People in New York judge you for a minute and a minute later they forget about you. They think about you for one minute. And that one minute makes you feel so special. Almost like a minute of fame. You can really feel at ease only when you realize your importance. New York can easily make you feel your unimportance.

The movie screening lasted for two hours and the interview with the director afterwords for about the same, which completely burned me up and wiped me out.

I could definitely use a happy hour now. Or two.

Even though I agreed to write that story for fifty dollars, the whole thing really bummed me out. It was my professional rock bottom.

Money leads to power, power is sexy. Power in not having to deal with people you don't want to deal with and not having to do the things you don't want to do. In my early twenties my high school classmates created a closed group on Facebook to discuss me and my life. A bunch of losers... I haven't been willing fame but power is really what I need. I like power; I suffer without it.

Money itself can't be the goal, not even the means to achieve it; it's an attribute. The goal is what you want in life. And the amount of money isn't that. The amount of money determines the level of power. And the possibility of free communication with those who have greater power, and thanks to it, have everything else. Money doesn't help you achieve the goal—money comes on the way to your goal.

I was way too far from power while my ambition

had already named a street in Manhattan after me; the street where my ex lived—a constant reminder of me for the rest of his life. Dream until it's your reality, right? I knew vanity, and therefore despondency.

You can't buy happiness with money. You can buy experiences and opportunities though. And having an opportunity already makes you happy. Saying yes to everything and anything anytime, looking forward to something, makes you happy. Money is just energy that allows you to increase the importance of your actions, for yourself and for everyone around.

Money as a physical object doesn't cause me the slightest emotion. I remember the times, my better times, when I was counting money, organizing the bundle bill by bill, in ascending order, putting it in a safe. That's it. No emotion involved, no excitement, no satisfaction of the moment. Nothing. I remember spending it though. Those emotions are recorded in my memory—it was a very expensive and fun trip to Zurich.

For years, I haven't found a reason to force myself to want something tangible. Most people have a material goal or even a dream: Louis Vuitton, Jimmy Choo, Cartier, Bentley, penthouse, and a golden dick of a husband in their mouth to complete the status. Consumption society. It is incredibly difficult to explain to them that one or two or three or ten cars in their garage in their same penthouse for decades, in the same city, surrounded by the same luxury goods that everyone else has, will not bring emotions. Experiences will. Always. Sure, shoes as well as accessories indicate your wealth, but at the end of the day it's just a bag and just shoes. It has no value if it has no meaning. You're just serving overpriced pieces of garment. Jimmy Choo means nothing in comparison to sharing a joke. Money has no value if there are no people who care about you. The best things in life aren't things. Everything else is marketing.

I guess I'm a weirdo. Instead of dreaming about fame and money, like everyone else, I dreamed about creating something really valuable and significant. That's why I wrote books. My power, so I thought. It was my way of creating something big. It's just it wasn't my big, apparently? Though during the writing process I discovered things about myself I never knew. And that was quite a lot to find out.

Right after sunset, when the sun is gone and the sky is not completely dark yet and the street lights are on, the reality gets its glamour layer, shiny coat, glowing throw. It becomes purple—the color of happiness. Every good social event has its very distinctive lights. When yellow light mixes with all other colors in the room, it reflects back as radiant violet. Oh, that color of a fancy party mood. It's small Italian patisseries and cozy French cafes and A-grade restaurants that serve this color. Dive bars can never have an immaculately violet reflection. When the beer glass hits the chlorinated bar counter, it reflects the color of frugal hopelessness. I was not yet over all the good things in life. I was still very much hopeful, an optimist, a searcher and researcher of the joyful scene of blithe today.

"I don't recognize you," the Wallet app notified before payment. *No kidding? It's because I haven't been myself lately.*

I was looking for myself so I went to the Plaza hotel because I might be there. Instead, I found something I had not looked for—the perfect "Gimlet." The loneliest drinking is not at home behind the closed doors when no one else is there. It's at the bar in a fancy hotel in New York City, when no one acknowledges that you are. At the Palm Court of Plaza I found the perfect cocktail and a friend—James, the bartender, who was kindly entertaining me and even brought me a free chocolate macaron.

English is a very interesting language. A friend is called friend, an acquaintance is called friend, a fuck buddy is called friend, a person you just met is called friend. Your ex during an awkward social moment is called an old friend.

Like a typical New Yorker who knew her way around the city enough to call herself a New Yorker, I complained a little to the stranger slash my new friend, bartender James. He found out what it was like to be a professional writer and not be able to make a living on it, how my books didn't sell as well as I wanted and yada yada.

"Oh, fuck it! Pardon my French," he reacted to my complaints.

"It's ok. I did my Master's in France so I speak that kind of French fluently," I replied.

"You look like you might need tequila shots," he said.

"Thanks, but I'm not into shots. I prefer getting intoxicated slowly, in a sophisticated way. I'm lazy, after all."

"Every time I drink tequila I can't remember that day. It just makes me pass out," he noted.

"I wonder how many shots I gotta drink to forget a bad year."

He filled my glass with a white-girl-who-doesn't-know-what-she-wants-and-looks-sad rosé so I didn't have to think about thinking. This type of wine is very popular in New York City. My intention for the night was to spend my fifty bucks like water, or like wine in this case. And I did—on Whispering Angel from Côtes de Provence. *Maybe the Angel will whisper something nice to me*, I thought.

Making plans, getting ready, dressing up and going out to a nice place on the weekend is like a mini holiday each week. A week almost worth living for. New experiences, new people, new outfits and new stories. It's the best!

Fifth Avenue...more like old financial Filth Avenue. Who wants to get dirty?

On the train, a homeless person, asking for money, said, "excuse me" and kicked everyone on his way passing by. He smelled like a mix of lemongrass and soap. I didn't smell that fresh. God I love New York!

When I came back home, a guy I had went on a date with two blue moons ago sent me a message. He wanted to come over. I was drunk, with unshaved legs, and I'd had potato chips for dinner. I was not quite ready for company per se. I'd be refreshing my make-up for nothing. Besides, he was not a mood enhancing kind of a guy. If there was a contest for complaining about minor problems he'd totally win it. It was so boring listening to all that. A smart and funny man at the base of his penis is what I am very much into.

So instead, I had a very precise idea for the night: write the business plan for a startup and plan a completely new life, and then bam! Feelings...

Usually, you can determine the level of wealth by just knowing the residential zip code.

My life wasn't going exactly as planned. I lived on the Upper East Side, but not where doormen in their uniforms and coats with cape look like a caricature of "Pride and Prejudice" and follow you everywhere like a needy chihuahua; and where the majority of the neighborhood population is in their early one hundreds and looks like a question mark. Their whole bodies ask how is it possible that they managed to survive all the smoking and drinking and still be alive?

No, my walk-up building wasn't even pet friendly yet was full of constantly migrating cockroaches and old dirt that was called fresh paint. Once there was even a mouse in the kitchen, which took the most important of a human's well-being: a sense of security in my own home. Even Henry Miller wouldn't agree to live in this pathetic building, or year.

The neighbors above me were in some kind of always wear stiletto heels challenge or in a late night Ikea building club. And outside, at the building across the street, 520 The Mad House was its address, once in a while, without any schedule, someone vacuumed asphalt.

Every time I went down to the basement to do laundry, I got stressed out being reminded that I shouldn't live like this. My inherent attitude of a Soho House and Friars Club member combined included a doorman in the lobby, not fauna. It also didn't include an old cell phone, five generations behind, with a cracked-in-half screen. Yeah, I was one of those people. Although, my bathroom always smelt exquisitely like Bloomingdales's cosmetics section, because I used various women's perfume samples instead of an air freshener.

My professional career was somewhat successful, and by somewhat I mostly mean that I was able to pay monthly rent for my shit-hole place and buy a pizza pie when I didn't feel like cooking. I didn't have a savings account yet was constantly saving on everything. Oh, and online banking seemed to be a nightmare because using it, any time of the day, pissed me off. I could've just called it the Anxiety App. I wasn't really sure what my account balance was—so not enough for anything anyway. My medical insurance was free of charge, paid in full by the state of New York. Frankly speaking, it wasn't the kind of saving you wanted to brag about. I had nothing to be taken from me, not even my dignity. I was broke, in anguish. And in a deep existential crisis. And thirty-three years old, Jesus fucking Christ. You know, the second fun stage of life after puberty. The stage of major confusion and extreme haircuts. On my birthday, someone wished me longevity. Longevity! Yeah. It's like when one of my exes once wished me to find real love. We were still in a relationship at the time. Or it's like my dentist who, when my new book came out, asked me to sign it so that, as he said, when I was gone, he could sell it for a more expensive price on eBay. By the way, he's about fifteen years older than me. Sometimes it seems to me that the stork dropped some people along the way.

Because of all this (or thanks to it?) I started to actually feel like an adult and spent a lot of time thinking about food, the future, real estate, investments, the difference between pleasure and happiness. I came up with some personal wisdom or whatnot.

That I value humor, humanity, kindness, honesty, intelligence, audacity and, of course, big dicks. You know how they name house communities: Oak Trees, Meadow Views, Sunnyside Cottages? The Big Dicks Village would've been a great name. I support it. I should patent that. I will film the video for it.

That you can explain anything, but nobody canceled the good and the bad.

That movies, books, and men have to be good in bed. The rest I can do myself.

That nature has endowed people with many individual qualities: intelligence, memory, logic, fantasy, a penchant for art and sciences. Just leave people alone so they can develop their best skills.

That there's no such thing as fairness or nemesis.

That you should behave the way that you'll be able to live acknowledging your own behavior. Good luck.

That a movie is not good if you have to google what this movie is actually about while watching it.

That when we cum we all look like retards in pain.

That any jeans three sizes up can become boyfriend jeans.

That an anthem is never a happy song.

That Transylvania is an actual region in Romania and not a fictional country where Dracula lives, like I thought before.

That Patagonia sounds like a made up place too—a place where you go to in your mind when you have a panic attack or obsess about something.

That when someone tries a meal and says it's horrible and suggests you try it too to prove how horrible it is indeed. That's fine; if you say it's bad, I don't need to check that myself. Your review is enough. Thanks.

That the things one person finds disgusting and acceptable might be very surprising. For example, smoking hookah at a public place is ew but eating ass is okay.

That we're so well-connected today and everybody's lonely.

That you always want a female massage therapist. Somehow men's hands are too sissy for true deep tissue.

That saying something stupid and then adding "kidding" at the end of it doesn't automatically make the dickish comment funny. Some men think women confuse these things—we don't. If fact, all women hate this. So if you happen to blurb something like that, the best way is to say you're sorry instead of adding "kidding" at the end. Well, the best way is not to say or even think dickish things at all.

That it would be cool to have a smoke detector that recognizes a voice and would instantly turn off if you yelled, "I'm cooking!"

That there's selfish, and there's self-care.

That God is the absolute of a judgmental person.

Yet someone being judgmental is immediately judged by the society. But man is created in the image and likeness of God, no? Early in life I learned that whenever I judge somebody, soon enough I get to experience exactly what I judged. I keep judging filthy reach people so I pretty please get to experience a mile in their shoes. Ironically, it keeps not happening to me. Stupid rules of the universe existence.

That even idiots in New York are the best.

That if I could give an advice to my daughter, besides everything it'd be do not, under any circumstances pluck your eyebrows. They are very hard to regrow, sometimes barely possible. Just don't touch your eyebrows. You're welcome.

That people don't name their children Dick anymore, but there are still so many of them. How does a Richard call his penis: dick junior?

That you can't expect more than somebody can give.

That it's called stalking to follow a person's life on social media—everything they put out online themselves, publicly. Makes absolutely no sense. It's like you walk in the street naked and sure people look at you and you accuse them of harassment for looking.

That DMV doesn't require an applicant for driver's license to bring a proof of sanity from a psychiatrist, unlike in Ukraine where this document is just as important as a road test. Perhaps, that is why there are so many crazy people on the road?

That when someone says "Please don't be mad at me"—you're about to be judged.

That we are the generation that is the most self-aware of our feelings and the most indifferent to feelings of other people.

That I'm living in a reverse universe: I now use my vibrator as a back massager whenever I have back pain. Clearly, thirties rock.

That you should love people and use things, and not vice versa.

That in movies a troubled lad is always called Danny. Usually, he has a lot of issues and is adorably cute. But since he's sort of disturbed, he looks like Hugh Jackman on crack. Sometimes he goes by Dan. But it's never Daniel.

That it gets so hot in Russian banya like it's a franchise of hell.

That people are not perfect, with their own vices, and that's just fine. I appreciate small banalities, precisely why they are more valuable. It's not easy to surprise me, but an interesting conversation goes a long way.

That I actually don't judge people, at least not intentionally. Once, I read about a woman who named her new dog Cuni, short for cunnilingus. Another one named her cat Mouse. She must call it Mouse, kitty kitty, come here? We all could be friends—I named my vibrator Matthew.

That a money tree at home is supposed to bring you money, but people I know who have it are all broke. What if the money tree actually works the other way around and sucks the money out of its owners?

That a man's height doesn't really matter. Suppose, I fall in love with someone who's a hundred and sixty centimeters—I'd still date him, but not in public.

Within age, a woman loosens up with a man's height choice not because she's desperate but because she barely cares about wearing heels anymore.

That the book's cover does matter, both metaphorically and literally. First of all, nobody has time to read anymore, both metaphorically and literally. And second of all, what are the chances that you get a book with a crappy cover, both metaphorically and literally, and the content is brilliant undiscovered treasure? Nah. Not even in movies.

That once you think how great it would be to accidentally run into someone you would not mind running into at all—it instantly becomes impossible. If you're thinking about it, it can't happen accidentally.

That a meeting without food should be an email.

That any sex article for women starts with "Light a candle". Ugh...

That time doesn't go any slower when you're doing plank.

That every hipster has issues; but not every person with issues is a hipster.

That people who aren't sure about their sexual orientation or identification should have a gender reveal party.

That there's no point of feeling sorry for your emotions, and expressing them publicly too. You can't be sorry for what you feel or don't feel.

That badasses are sexy until they are not.

That Americans understand metric system only when buying drugs.

That we always try to justify those who we love. Whereas you trying to convince yourself that "oh, okay, this is nothing" is a clear sign to getting ready to leave.

That people do change. But it doesn't happen as much as we want them to.

That chapsticks and umbrellas are meant to be constantly lost, otherwise it's the most boring serial burglar in history.

That if you set up your favorite song as an alarm tune, very soon you start hating it.

That no woman in the history of life answered the text "What are you wearing now?" honestly.

That life adventures you get into for a future memoir book for your grandchildren are usually not supposed to be told. First they are PG-13 and then it's your own embarrassment that stops you from telling the stories out loud.

That there are only a few truly disgusting things about people: sweaty palm at a handshake, a spot of hair right beneath a man's lower lip for beard and no more facial hair at all, letting a dog lick your face, when someone's talking and a drop of saliva is seen in the corner of their lips throughout the conversation.

That it's okay to miss someone and not want them back.

That common sense is idle and not as common as you think. If it was common, everyone would have it.

That the sky is different for everyone. All reality, any reality is only in the consciousness of the one who perceives it; just like reality on Facebook. But what a great idea it was: to connect all people in the world.

Being a grown-up woman, I rethought a lot of things in life, understood how it all worked, and what it meant to be an adult besides not pooping on the go and feeding yourself so you don't die. There was only one question that still remained unanswered: hair on toes, why?

I got a chance to rearrange everything in my apartment multiple times, even my thoughts. It made me feel so tired after not doing anything for five hours. My elbows started to hurt because I lied on my stomach because my butt hurt from sitting so much. I was looking for new surfaces to sit and lay on. Next in the list: bathtub without water and fire escape stairs in my kitchen window. I was extremely busy working on my dozen favorite problems.

When people have a lot of free time to think about their lives and reflect on them, it gives them anxiety. So far SimCity was the only big city where I could afford to buy property; but I wasn't anxious about tomorrow—I was just lost, in a very uncomfortable pretzel position, unsolved Rubik's cube.

Crisis in your thirties: you create a podcast or found a startup. Midlife crisis: you buy something red —a dress or a convertible. Everyday crisis in New York City: go out or order delivery?

I was so bored. I was so fucking bored I'd say yes to anything at that point. Thoughts create reality; but only actions, and not words, define it. I had yet to define my reality, because what I had what so unreal.

The other day I saw a dude smoking crack in the train. I'm a New Yorker—that didn't excite me even a little bit.

Getting more stuff always gives instant excitement that lasts for only about five minutes—another version of crack but for health-conscious people. My mood was somewhere between I need to update my wardrobe and where the fuck am I even going. So I said no to the dress. Thought about getting a poodle and naming her Puddle, or putting up the Christmas tree, in August...why not at this point.

I received an email with a new job posting: "Weather Executive Producer—Storm Team 4." What happened to the other three teams? Or were they like astronauts of all the Apollos before the one that actually made it? Gone by the storm?

I googled "yatts" because I like boats but also because not everything needs to have a reason. Then I figured that if you can't spell yacht correctly, you're probably not ready for it.

I was in a constant battle of either trying not to feel anything or trying to feel at least something.

Though, I managed to entertain myself even when things were super annoying. For instance, there was a dental office that kept calling me daily because they were too stupid to delete my number. I trolled them trying to get an appointment for February the thirtieth. In return they asked what time would work for me. Morons.

Every other Saturday or so I was in Bushwick dancing sober at the *House of Yes* night club, which was filled with themed decorations and handmade garbs. Above the entrance to the dance floor were two giant eyes, opening and closing, which could contribute to me opening my eyes too, I suppose. I was looking for a sign that wasn't even there. *House of Yes* felt like social media—super crowded yet still very lonely. But it was my version of meditation, a place to think and make decisions, dissolving in music. When you're feeling lonely, remember that you're not alone —you always have music with you.

In my defense, I could've used big words like retired or artist, but the truth is I was jobless. Looking for work was my full-time occupation. A while back, I had all that: an extension number and my own personal scotch tape. And a "cannibal" cake, open human flesh with exposed internal organs on Fridays, because we had a bakery for a client, and always someone yelling, "Do not eat the whole cake yet! Leave some brain for management!" The office was located in Long Island City. There were like no pretty people in the neighborhood at all. They fell on the loser end of the spectrum—the spectrum of ugliness and mutation disorders. At work I was asked how you create a spreadsheet. I thought it was a prank... nope. And there was very hot water in the restroom that couldn't be adjusted. I couldn't even decide *that* in the building. And the lights in the restroom were so bad that in the mirror I looked like I belonged in Queens. My time spent on spreadsheets was compensated with the chessboard. And then someone took it and I had no reasons to come to the office anymore. My role was to manage expectations, provide solutions to help realize the ambition and add value to the idea within the scope of projects. In other words, to fluently speak the office language. It wasn't easy to do something significant when you lost the answer to *why*—the major sense of doing anything after money and "I just like it." At that point, even my existential crisis had an existential crisis, and a breakdown.

I couldn't sell consumption needs to others because I myself found those products and services not better than any other products and services of any other brand. They were all the same. Socks, hair salons, law offices—no difference. You do not need to over-consume today because tomorrow there will be food and clothes and people and experiences too. Marketing for me wasn't more than just a creative idea described with good words in short. Futile words, better to be kept in the dictionary. But they wanted sales, leads, and more spreadsheets. That day I said: "If I have to do this job permanently, please kill me." It got me fired.

"You gonna be omg," my friend Frank sent me a message to make me feel better. And then one more right away, "Ok not omg."

"Don't underestimate me! I'm not just ok. I can totally be omg."

The truth is, at the time I wasn't omg, not even ok —k at most, on a good day.

"What are you gonna do?" Frank asked.

"Planning on taking care of my health."

"Gym?"

"No. Licking all my pocket change to build up viruses tolerance."

"Which ones?"

"All of them!" and I licked a Canadian quarter for international health insurance. I heard their system was good.

And again, I needed some structure, a schedule, stability. Sit in the office for eight hours a day to be able to buy stuff with the remote control to be able to continue sitting. And then, to manage more sitting, go to the gym to ride a bicycle that doesn't go anywhere. You know, stability, so that I could frivolously order more things than I could track to feel like I'm getting surprise gifts when they arrive. Thank you, me, for thinking of me. As if sitting on a butt and life according to the schedule somehow legalizes your existence.

Once, I had a brain fart and spent about three minutes trying to spell sincerely in an email. It was weird because I'm a very sinsere I mean sensere I mean sensare person. I surely wasn't looking forward to silence in response. It's like in the era of applications all of my emails were sent to the Black Hole. I would really appreciate if companies gave you an email saying, "Congratulations...you didn't get chosen!" I like New York—it lets you be the way you want to be; it just didn't have time for me at that moment. One day I'll write a feature movie Spy Indeed—a goofy comedy about a girl who happened to get into spying career by applying to a job posting on indeed.com. While she has to deal with international problems, she also has to deal with her crazy mother, from whom she regularly gets thirty eight missed calls; and if she continues to not pick up for whatever reason, mom calls to the secret agency to the top secret number. She's just worried and wants to know her daughter is okay, she says. I wouldn't mind being a spy myself. This way I'd have the perfect explanation that my dating life sucks because I'm too busy saving the world. Although, I hate running and according to movies this is number one requirement.

I was so damn tired of trying to be successful, as well as acclaimed, accepted, and liked. Successful was very stressful as well as full of shit. I was done. I didn't want to get better or get engaged in intense rivalry. Competition is illusional. I didn't want to play hard or die trying harder. Fuck vanity fair. I was so done. Oh, and fuck visualizing too.

Application. I hate this word. Its synonym is frustration and its remedy is still illegal in New York State.

Not landing a job with two Master's degrees was my new extraordinary skill that could be added to the bucket of my useless personal skills—like having the ability to drain a pot of pasta using just a spoon and not dropping a single noodle into the sink. I know. Hold your applause. Just a trophy will do.

For ten years in a row, I've been trying to make it as a full-time writer. I did journalism, delivering daily news under deadline pressure. I did integrated communications management, delivering news for those who deliver news. I changed countries and languages. And I wrote five books. Only the first three hundred rejections from book agents and publishers are upsetting; then you understand—such is life.

There should be an hourly service "Nana." An old lady comes to your place, feeds you homemade food, covers you in a blanket of kittens, hugs you, and praises you in every possible way. Occasional support once in a blue moon is fine as a business model, but not a monthly membership; that would be like publicly declaring you're pathetic and don't wish to do anything about it. On the bright side, I learned typing with ten fingers. I used to write with four fingers and those books turned out pretty funny. I can only imagine how awesome my writing is going to get when I start typing with all of my fingers. That's one hundred and fifty percent more better. Though, the books won't be longer—it's ten fingers, not magic. If only they were published. No-no, if only I got paid for my novels: full-time-writer-can-afford-a-living paid and not one-grande-latte-at-Starbucks paid.

I used to look like a less successful Rose Byrne. Now I look like a less successful Audrey Tautou. Why don't I look like a famous writer? A writer is not known by their face.

So it was about time to call writing an expensive hobby, move to Williamsburg, buy a hat at a thrift store, and convert a crazy idea into a real-deal business. Isn't that how Fedora was invented? And maybe find a garage. Any big success in America starts in a garage.

When it's raining in the city, you see broken umbrellas all the time, just like shards of broken dreams. The good news is it always stops raining, eventually. The rain is always live broadcast, no repeats. And even if today you feel like a wet cardboard on a rainy day, no one remembers the rain from even last month. This too shall pass.

For quite some time I was trying really hard to lose my umbrella—kind of needed a reason to get a new one, because why would I have two if I just bought another umbrella? It was perfectly fine, it worked well, but I wanted a new, better and bigger one. Every time I intentionally left the old one on the subway or on a bench in a park, people returned it to me. And they say that New Yorkers aren't nice.

When I was sad and wanted a cheer up, I turned on YouTube and watched cats and dogs videos, while eating apples with peanut butter or my special treat— O'Doul's with carrot cake. If only carrot cake was as healthy as it sounds.

What did I want to be when I gave up? I had to figure it out. "Figure it out" was the most used phrase of that year. There were nineteen-year-old kids who were inventing stuff, ruling companies, competing at the highest level and I was still pushing doors when it says pull. Millennials just eat avocados and ass. But there's gotta be something else out there. I felt exactly like I was in a genius joke I read on someone's Instagram: *Sometimes I just want someone to hug me and say, "I know it's hard. You're going to be okay. Here's a coffee and five million dollars."*

Of course, my personal life wasn't any better, full of weirdos and meaningless strangers that I had for some reason attracted into my life. They were too alien to be my darling. All year, I was single but still went through relationship problems. My birth control method was correcting someone's grammar. Getting into a serious relationship? Ha. I couldn't even get a long-term partner to do a podcast.

I'm going to die alone. Why is this the fear of fears? I'm going to live alone sounds way worse. I was alone, and couldn't turn off what had turned me on. I was looking for shared intimacy—a friend and a lover all in one.

Still, I was giving dating apps a shot because my

strategy of whispering "I love you" to strangers wasn't panning out so well. I was tindering for so long that I was about to get to the very last level of this game, like in GTA, and win it. I swiped through all kinds of characters I wish I hadn't. Once, a guy from the app suggested I be his sugar mama. I wasn't sure whether I looked old or successful according to his suggestion. Backhanded compliment. On the app, there were guys who constantly asked me whether I wanted to have fun. By your thirties you should know that sex happens in your head first. I felt sorry for them: they have no clue what real fun is. There were so many men who, having read *Fifty Shades of Grey*, suddenly became an experienced dominant looking to collar and train a submissive. Why don't they try to share intimacy—that can be real torture!

Within time, I completely changed my opinion about dick pics. In fact, instead of asking how my day was, send me one right away so I know what I'm getting, because I hate surprises. There should be a course available for dudes "How to take a good dick picture." Or maybe even a degree—Bachelor of Penis Seduction Photography, because let's face it: most dick pics are not good, from both artistic and anatomical points of view. Lightening is essential, you DIY photographers! I have a bin for compost, paper, plastic, and a bin for recycled dick pics. The latter is usually scheduled for pick up on Friday nights. However, if I'm being completely honest and they're still willing to send a part of their body, I'd much rather a kidney and make a profit off of it.

I remember the times where there were only heterosexuals or homosexuals. Now it was a whole new dictionary: akioromantic, akiosexual, androsexual, aroflux, bisexual, demiromantic, demisexual, gray-asexual, grayromantic, gynsexual, heteroflexible, pansexual, recipromantic, reciprosexual, sapiosexual, skoliosexual, transsexual, questioning. It was kind of hard to memorize who liked to fuck whom. All new sexuality terms sounded like a complex Starbucks order: tall hot non fat queer demiromantic with cream pumps of honey aceflux extra frapp chips no dick no sugar no spit. And then they called the name—volunteer self-identification.

Also, I had reached the point in my life when going on a weekend trip with a complete stranger didn't seem scary and the worst that could happen was a menace of boredom. Can boredom be considered as charity? Like if you're bored as hell, will it reduce hunger in the world or something? That would make me the biggest philanthropist of New York City. Okay, fine. Fine! Is boredom at least tax deductible?

There was one guy who looked like a peeled Idaho potato. He said he spent a lot of time wondering how many princesses he had to kiss and still remain a frog. I sincerely laughed to his jokes, but his self-confidence was below zero. He didn't love himself therefore he couldn't love anyone and sabotaged any relationship he had. Plus, he was not a good kisser, like diner level. You can eat at a diner and you won't die from hunger, but your taste buds will not feel the sensation. It's always three out of five stars—no diner has an exceptional rating. And you'll be like: yeah, I should just cook at home by myself.

A twenty-eight-year-old told me how nice it was to meet a woman and not a girl. He thought it was a compliment. I felt like I was gazillion years old. I beat him with the imaginary Yellow Pages. Thank god he didn't say I reminded him of his mother. Such a saving on botox. He also sent me a picture of his penis with the caption, *"Here! I made you a present!"* A present usually involves a box and a gift receipt, no? Young males...for that reason, I don't understand pedophiles. How would anyone want a twelve-year-old? They have to be terrible at sex! They know nothing! They're twelve!

Me from before thought that it was so cool if a guy graduated from Harvard. Me now was trying to calculate his proximate student loan debt and how it would potentially affect me. Although, I'd still prefer a guy with a degree. We should have approximately the same amount of wasted years in common.

It was so hard to date men who said they intentionally avoided periods in sentences for simplicity or didn't know the difference between spelling they're, their, and there. I can easily digest dairy but I have stupidity intolerance. One who can't even use chopsticks doesn't know shit about life.

Here's simple math about men: big penis equals poor, small penis equals rich, small penis plus poor equals handsome, big penis plus rich equals ugly, big penis plus rich plus handsome equals gay.

We all have our own value system and reference group. Dating someone who falls under your value system and passes the face control and the dress code of your reference group is the same as brand marketing. I'd easily date a bus driver; the question is: where would I meet him? I don't take a bus. And if I ever will —it'd mean I've given up on life so please kill me. At a vintage store? I'd get allergies from all the second hand clothes and minimum wage payroll. Financial independence, wit, erection. Each ingredient is inter-changeable. If a man has none of the three—maybe he should not leave his house.

"I'm a pervert," a semi-celebrity, whom I met on Instagram a while back, messaged me.

"Yay! Great! Finally!" I was probably the first girl without armpit hair to find him attractive.

He was back into the dating game, he thought, he was back on the market. The dude was fifty. He was not back on the market. He was back at a thrift store. But he was a somewhat celebrity so I was up for an adventure. We went to his place where he told me he actually wanted to get to know me first. Why? Why would he want that? What's wrong with you? What are you hiding? Small penis? ED? Can't find a clitoris? Asexual? Tell me now! I hate Schrödinger's cat. Hon-estly, I could not care less how many siblings you have. Tell me something dirty instead.

It became impossible to get laid without an emo-tional investment. It's like by talking to me they were trying to save on therapy. Ugh, I didn't want to listen to somebody's problems before they would put on a condom. No Sex and the City anymore, it's I-Want-To-Get-To-Know-You and the City. Pure blah. The world has switched upside down: he was interested in seeing my personality first and I was interested in only showing my pussy.

So we were drinking tea. Decaf. And we were talking. About sex. And I realized: there it was—promised perversion.

Sometimes I feel like I don't say, "fuck you" enough. Sometimes I also think that normal relationships are like sparkling soup—technically possible, but sparkling soup?

To me, everyone looked the same and had no name. Besides, I had noticed that being the little spoon, they all felt the same from behind—well, more or less. These stay-over-souls couldn't do enough for me.

I'd been willing a long-term relationship for so long that this wish of mine totally lost its value and importance. But it's not like I could cancel lust and switch off my libido. *Okay, why don't I just have some fun*, I thought. At the same time I was so very much tired of sucking, literally. Why? I'd entered the era of my peers approaching occasional erectile disfunction and mild substance abuse normalization.

"Wanna have sex tonight?" I texted the French guy, and we met at his place.

"I want to abuse you," he grabbed my hair...and lost his erection.

The only thing he had successfully been abusing for quite sometime was wine, enormous quantities of wine. And being French was not enough of an excuse for drinking all day every day, with consequences. Plus cigarettes, plus cocaine, "because, sweetheart, you don't understand, everyone else does it in my industry."

I was in my thirties and constantly horny. I liked

different sex but a soft dick was not my fantasy. I blew him twice. He lost his hard on three times that night. You might fool yourself competing with better pictures on Instagram. Competing with blood vessels influenced by numerous years of wine and spirits consumption makes no sense. Nature always wins. A human body has its limit of capabilities, like any other machine. And blowing once again, for the third time, won't really solve a problem. Perhaps detox will.

Marquis de Bullshit. First drink.

"I'm gonna fuck you all night!" he said.

"Yeah, baby!" *Um, about fifteen minutes is more than enough though.*

Thirty minutes and a cocktail later.

"I'm gonna fuck you hard!" he said.

"I really look forward to that!"

After an hour and a half and two more hard liquor drinks.

"I'm gonna fuck you so hard!" he said.

"Can't wait. Will you please, finally?"

Sometime later.

"I'm gonna f..."

"Yeah, yeah, yeah. Whatever."

More and more guys, at least the ones I happened to cross paths with, tended to choose sex when morning erections occurred. They fucked not because they wanted but because they could.

One guy I've known for years sent me a picture of his soft dick, with a caption, "It needs help."

"Remind me of your address, please?" I replied. He and I had literally just one thing in common — we both liked his cock. *That's a cool bathroom sink*, I thought next as I kept staring at his picture. *I wonder if they sell those at Home Depot.*

"Oh, I can't. I'm tired."

It's all talk. Action is character. What a person does, and not what he says, is who he is. I'm a writer. I need more action, not dialogue.

As much fun as sexting can be, if it doesn't eventually lead to an actual meet up, doing the things you'd talked about in texts, what's the point? It's like watching porn and not masturbating. For the same reason I'll probably never understand stripping. You get turned on for nothing. Like pressing the gas pedal and not going anywhere. Meh, not that big a fan of just the engine sound. Vroom, vroom. Yes, there are multiple ways of making someone orgasm. Yes, there's a variety of toys and dildos and vibrators: robotization of the best, the most natural, yet the only analog process in today's digital era — sex. But still, what the fuck, man. And with weed gaining more and more popularity, taking more and more of our energy and willingness for effort, I wouldn't be surprised if within time humankind will stop fucking for good. We'll just go to museums. On the bright side, sex toy manufacturers must be making tons of dollars in profit.

On a Sunday, I texted my ex. Frankly speaking, we didn't have a lot in common. I'm a stand up comedy kind of person. He is more of a sit down drama kind of guy. I was looking forward to my future, he was afraid of losing his past. Clearly, not having unneeded drama with an ex is better than continued drama with anyone. But I wanted to get laid and he was well-known and comfortable—like memory foam. We agreed we should meet up but neither of us was excit-ed enough to actually make plans with each other. Oh, well. I don't wish anything bad for my ex. Though, I don't wish him anything good either. I wish he has everything so-so.

I once had a pineapple as a pet. No need to feed or walk it and you can always eat it or leave at a pineap-ple shelter. It's called a fruit market. Then I figured I was ready for a serious commitment—so I got a plant. Since I already had Fedya and Sandro—I named my plants after my exes—I should also get a new one, a spiny cactus, and name it Dan. It'll be a reminder to stay away from it unless I want to get hurt. I decided to go with plants—it seemed a safer variant, because I already had a transgender parrot who killed itself. Sorry, themself. It was supposed to be a he when I got it. I was hoping I could teach him how to talk, all the bad words obviously. But after a while he turned out to be a she when one day I saw an egg in the cage. I guess she was suffering from postpartum depression, because a couple weeks later, after coming out as a female, she seemed to be having so much fun on the swing in the cage, but had actually hung herself on the swing's hook.

If someone painted my surroundings, the prevail-ing mood in the artwork would be annoyance. I lived not the way I should have, not where I should have, not with whom I should have. Incongruously. And I was too old to blame my parents for all that. I could've watched the TED Talk "To Help Me Stop Procrasti-nating" and still procrastinated it. The only thing I was definitely successful in was a lazy-fat-cat sleep for twelve hours a day—a defense mechanism of the brain to frustration. I laid there like a dead battery, with my non-sparking eyes and the facial expression of an animated character that was still on paper, not brought to life. I've always been an extrovert, but this time I had the charisma of a wet noodle. I didn't have a rebellion in me. You can have all the drive you want but if your gas tank is on empty, you ain't going nowhere. Newyorkoma. One night I had a great idea right before passing out and was way too sleepy to grab my phone and write it down; then the next morning I couldn't remember it, of course. But horoscopes said I was gonna get book deals in a few months, so I shouldn't worry about anything. If it's in horoscopes then it's definitely going to happen, right? Heretofore, I was binge dating, running around the city like crazy, looking for love. It's like the app "Nesting" was installed in me but the settings weren't activated. I was lacking that feature update. A few times I was asked how long I had been single. Most of my life, with a few breaks for relationships, frankly. So I kind of gave up on dating. On the bright side, I grew out thicker eyebrows, which the first couple months looked like they had been in a cat fight. Some days I drew them to fill in the gaps, some days I embraced natural beauty...and laziness; but eventually they became the centerpiece of my resting sad face. My days looked like this: Netflix and chill or CNN and panic; not necessarily in that order. Then I stopped caring about democracy conflicts, what he said she said in the White House, and even the weather on the East Coast. Binge watching Netflix became my everything. Simultaneously, I was binge lying while living a fictional life on the screen instead of my own. I've learned a lot from it. Here's a few.

That I don't like movies in which women sleep with their bra on and men with their watch on. I don't like lies.

Or that they make characters throw up with disgustingly realistic vomit yet women wake up already with fresh makeup and a hairdo.

Or that characters in the movies act really surprised after having found out about a (whoopsy) accidental pregnancy. Haven't you heard about protection, people? Pulling out is not an actual contraception method that you can rely on.

Or that if there's a Russian President involved in the story of any American movie, he will certainly look like Brezhnev and his name will always be Boris.

Or that the most used word in *Suits* is "Bullshit!" And when someone comes into the office and throws a bunch of papers on the table, the solution of the case is always, always, always on the first page.

Or that every documentary about drugs has such cool soundtracks that you almost want a career in that industry yourself.

Or that even animation can make you cry. I almost got myself dehydrated because of the amount of tears I had at the final episode of BoJack Horseman. But then I realized how stupid it was—the creators just stoped drawing the horse.

Or that stand up comedy in movies always sucks. Usually, we see an aspiring comedian who behaves on stage way too confident, like he's been in the business for at least ten years. Not so much authentic. And he's always shown as a badass confident guy who kills on stage, gets a hot girlfriend and yells at his boss.

Or that characters in shows intended for mature audience don't behave mature at all.

Or that in movies set in the nineteen seventies people were very physical: lots of touching, pushing, kicking, even with strangers. Or maybe it seemed a lot because I haven't touched anyone in months.

At some point I was out of good shows and movies so I turned on porn. The plot development was meh.

One night, I was scrolling through Netflix and saw a show with a description that went something like: "A nun discovers that the pope is corrupted and her body is found the next day." Is that it? Oh, this plot could be developed in a much more interesting and exciting way, something like: "A nun is going though personal drama and decides to quit the nunnery. During her last night, the pope meets her in a church for a ritual but instead ends up comforting her and they have sex during which the pope dies of a heart attack. His body, with a steady boner (God's miracle), is found the next day. Forty years later, a baby boy conceived in the church becomes the first youngest pope in history. His mother is a retired lobbyist of opioids by now, living a happy boring life. But a tiny software mistake in delivery creates a big problem—a revolution of nuns, because they are hooked on Oxycontin, an official sponsor of the Church. She comes to visit her son, the pope, to solve the problem with angry nuns, but instead finds him in the exact same spot, just like his father, with the exact same miracle. Now she has to find that one nun who killed her son and....and someone has to get married at the end, for sure, but I don't know who yet. It's only the first season after all. I mean, it does sound like a pornographic soap opera with elements of a thriller, but c'mon, wouldn't you watch that?

I've reached the kind of ennui that I started spending money on reality TV, episode by episode. It's worse than crack. Then what? Gathering in dangerous reality TV houses with strangers for a week-long binge-watch? Probably, worse than reality TV can only be a love story movie during Christmas time; and there are children involved, and even a dog. That night, I ended up watching the reality show *Intervention*, which reminded me that my lease was about to end and I had to decide whether to renew it. It's a pity I'm not an addict. I wouldn't mind spending ninety days in Florida or California, all inclusive. But there are no rehabs for idiots who put up with a lot of unnecessary shit. I just wanted relief. Even the CBD oil "Drops Relief" did not give any relief for me. Not even one drop.

In the window, I saw a crazy person walking in the street, yelling, and talking to someone only she could see. With all of those voices in her head, she'll never feel lonely and will always have someone to talk to. She doesn't even need a streaming service—she's got a show of her own going on.

Sometimes, being a woman in New York City, you've got to make a very important life decision: order pizza delivery at midnight or go to sleep. I had cereal. If only American Express knew that about me, they'd never approve my credit line.

At the time, I just didn't want to be bothered and wanted to be left alone. My wish came true—I was alone. Wishes really come true. The universe is a bitch. During the flu season they recommend staying away from socializing. Ha. I was living like the flue season lasted for two years. Basically, this is how long it took to finish Netflix. Not sure whether it was good or bad, but I didn't even have anyone who I could call *that person*—a unified nickname for a new ex or someone you generally don't like or someone you had a nasty argument with or someone you have strong feelings for. Feelings are amazing, even the bad ones. But a feeling of someone's indifference towards you is the most painful of them all. It makes a person forget your birthday, ignore asking how your day was, leave a text message unanswered. To relieve sunburn pain and help it heal, you can spray thermal water all over your booboo. What is there to spray on something that feels like sunburn from the inside?

The worst feeling in New York is when no one and nothing awaits you nowhere. Silence has a sound too. The sound of your breathing. Silence can be happy, sad, disgusted, fearful, surprised, angry, prideful, shameful, embarrassing, exciting. I could have a whole album of social silences. Once Upon a Time LP produced by Loneliness Records. Everything was on in my apartment: TV, radio, coffee maker... Social media streams make you feel lonely, so to feel that void you turn on content streams. Why do you think TV shows and podcasts are so popular? It all gives a simulation of a conversation, an impression of companionship, tuning into socializing, whether you're alone or lonely. It's hip to be successful, but not happy; and free, but not happy. Successful in happiness is not even promoted. Happiness, paradoxically, means unfreedom. Unfreedom from people you love and responsibilities that make you feel needed. It has become a trend to have no house ownership, no meaningful relationships, no deep conversations—no affiliation of any sort. Everything's superficial and sort of easy. Nomadic couch-surfing individuals with childhood trauma and a passport. The only acceptable affiliation—affiliate links on your blog. The only attachment is a picture in iMessages. Once you are free —you become successful. But within time it looks rather predictable: you, so smart and beautiful, in a white coat, in sorrow and in deep emotional shit. One is the best for success but it's the loneliest number of all. What is life? A fatal sexually transmitted disease. And the whole point of life is to be happy. Love can make you happy. But can power and love be together or are they mutually exclusive? *Ugh, don't go there. It's too much for you right now.*

And then Netflix really surprised me. There was a show *Fireplace for Your Home. Birchwood Edition.* Not a history of fireplaces or famous fireplaces of famous people or fireplaces-Santa Claus killers. Literally just fire burning on the screen to some tunes. Season one! Really excited to see where they go with it in season two. As it usually happens, the second season might be worse than the first one. By season four they'll change writers and will be nominated for the best editing on the Golden Globe. By season six it won't even be a fireplace. I had Christmas lights on my window—I am so pitching Netflix.

Being alone, especially during the holiday season, feels exactly the same as when you accidentally hit your elbow: it's stupid, it hurts, and you can't help it but to wait for it to pass. Moreover, I was having not just a bad hair day but a whole bad hair season. The left side of my hair looked like a celebrity's older sister that no one knows about. The world of Christmas lights and disappointments. I wanted to color myself like a coloring book with bright felt pens just to feel better. I'd be so much happier if I could feel every day the way I do when I'm ovulating: prettier and sexier. But no! Only a few days a month at most, if lucky.

Yeah... For a while, I was existing, functioning, not living. Two of my favorite words were ass and shit; kind of difficult to create a story "Happiness" with them. I wrote to Mozart and walked to Eminem a lot, to the point that Eminem kept showing up in my night dreams; we constantly went on dates and hung out but he kept bringing his bodyguard with him every single time (yo, kind of annoying, Marshall). Then suddenly it was just the two of us, no security, so basically we were in a committed relationship. Thank god Mozart was out of my subconsciousness— he's not as cute and nobody likes rejection. My second life, dreams, was much more exciting than real life; and I kind of stopped wanting things at all, slowly sliding down to the basic physiological needs, numb from wistfulness, becoming a certain je ne sais quoi. Yet somehow, with only a thousand dollars in my pocket and a little bit of persistent patience, I got the things I forgot I even wanted. I managed to buy property in Big Sur with the ocean view, write and sell a movie script, found a growing international company, and cause a revolution in one of the Eastern European countries. But the latter was totally by accident. Ironic, considering that one of my name's meanings is peace. Mirra. Mirra Vladi. Where is my license to kill boredom?

PIZZA 2000

Cutting your hair pixie short and then growing it out again to your lower back takes a very, very long time. That's how I've felt about going to Upstate New York. By the by, I felt that way about going anywhere that wasn't a walking distance from my home.

My friends, Sonia and Ricky Brand, invited me to their housewarming party. They recently bought a house, which was automatically a good occasion to host a party and take out the family plastic.

Sometimes it's impossible to meet with certain people because their Mercury is always in retrograde or it's not a good day in the Malaysian chiropractics calendar or the Queen of Spades is upside down or it's a full moon or their Aquarius is full of shit. Unfortunately, I had none to excuse my absence from Sonia's party. I faked disappointment at not being able to make it, but Sonia was persuasive and said she had a surprise for me. Besides, she kind of knew that nothing was going on in my life and thought that hanging out with a bunch of married people in Westchester would be fun for me. Pfff... I couldn't wait. I was looking forward to this party with as much excitement as a root canal.

Sometimes I feel very annoyed with people and just want to yell. I call it my Bill Burr days. When I'm old, I'll most likely be that lady on the Upper West Side who yells from her apartment through the window at pedestrians to shut the fuck up. Wouldn't be hard—I already have that quality. Ladies on the Upper East Side don't yell—they suffer quietly.

When I was wandering around, tired of the city noise, craving more coffee, and thinking what to buy for the Brands that wouldn't make me miss food, I saw a homeless person at Thirty-Fifth Street and Broadway. He sat leaning against the wall of his sublet residence—Macy's Department Store—with his legs spread and some shabby wrap covering his crotch. I wasn't sure whether he was jerking off for pleasure or because he was trying to warm up.

It doesn't matter how sophisticated you are or how much money you make or who you're with. When basic instincts aren't fulfilled you can't do anything, can't think of anything, you aren't even anything. Try to concentrate when you're hungry or sleepy or horny or when you want to take a leak. My basic instinct in that moment was to get more coffee. At Starbucks, I put my first, already empty Starbucks cup on the counter and asked for a refill because they do that.

"You have to be at the store for a refill," the cashier said but what she actually meant was be at the store to drink the first cup.

"I am at the store right now..." People are horrible at communication so I gave the cashier the time to process. She didn't get it.

If you say your name as That Bitch, the barista will

have nothing but shout "Coffee for That Bitch" when it's ready.

The Starbucks on Thirty-Sixth Street and Sixth Avenue is the shittiest in the city. The coffee shop is so dirty it seems that their lattes come with hepatitis instead of pumpkin spice. Immediately, I wished to wash my hands and when I did, I knew exactly what to buy for my friends. No-no, not hepatitis. Can't buy that on Amazon. Yet. I got them a large-size penis-shape soap that had a suction cup to attach to the bathroom wall. The most sterile Caucasian cock ever. It was the perfect gift to momentarily make people laugh and happy and dirty-clean. I'm one of those people who gets something for like ten bucks in an online store and adds a bunch of crap up to twenty-five dollars to get free shipping. Paid shipping is four ninety-nine. No wonder I was broke.

It was the nineteenth of December, only twelve days before I have a new life starting the new year; erh, cliché but true.

At the subway entrance, there was a new announcement. This time not about construction or schedule change. It was an announcement of a predator who harassed a woman on the train and was now under investigation. A senior lady read the announcement together with me and said, "Ouff, scary." *Lady, you are in your sixties. You've got nothing to be scared of. You're safe. Especially in those Uggs.*

The train from Grand Central took forever to get to Westchester. It was not Bestchester at all. Walking from the train station to the Brands' house I saw a street full of nail salons, just nail salons. Around the corner there was a gym and a pizza joint right next to it. Very convenient. Genius business idea actually: cooking fat and burning fat—non stop production.

Right away, I knew that time machines worked because the name of the pizza place was *Pizza 2000*. It had probably been there since the eighties and back then, two thousand seemed like a magical number, almost unreal.

Sonia is from a tiny little farm town that produces cows and corn and football players who peak in high school and have beer bellies by twenty-six. Such is the way of small town life. Ninety percent of people never leave and the ones who do never go back. In her town chances are you are somehow a second cousin twice removed from a person you are thinking about dating. A lot of these people had parents, grandparents, great grandparents that lived in the same house they grew up in. It was so...suffocating once she got older. She had a pretty perfect movie-like childhood, but the "best" job in town was at the bank. Her town seemed like a small brothel. Everybody had already fucked everybody twice and started the third round. You could always find a mutual friend of a friend and could rest assured that at least one of your girlfriends had already sat on the face of every bachelor worth paying attention to. However, it was still somewhat embarrassing when Facebook offered to add to friends exes of your exes. And when your posts were being liked by the ex-girlfriend of your ex-boyfriend as well as by his sister, all you wanted to do is to sit down and have a drink all together. There was no "Oh, don't worry I will never date your ex. Us girls have to stick together!" because literally you would have no choices otherwise. So Sonia moved to New York.

Sonia is a pretty positive, can-do-attitude, healthy-yoga-lifestyle kind of a girl. I hate her a little. She's too damn perfect, with her black tights. I can't figure out her vice or if she has a perverted secret of some sort. Like, maybe she has never had an orgasm—that'd do too. But no, nothing! It's driving me bonkers. The worst thing she has probably done in her life is not floss before going to bed one night. Unlike the bad girl me who at Whole Foods always enters through the exit doors. Nothing, absolutely nothing is wrong with her. Tame, beige, vanilla. Her secret is that she's trite and very normal.

Ricky is a physically attractive fellow, a warrior, who'd be able to make it on the cover of a men's magazine, but not a feature interview due to lack of sense of his words. Well, maybe only in New York. He has read a couple of how-to books and now quotes them, sure those are his own thoughts. He's The Captain Obvious of all captains. For example, he says: "The secret of chess is to not let your king get checkmate." Or once I heard him asking Sonia: "What are we doing about my lunch?" Ricky's greatest skill is breaking things—kind of like reverse engineering. He is half German, half Italian. Recently, he did a genealogical research and found every single paper ever registered on his German ancestors. His Italian side of the family has almost no official evidence of existence. Lots of information missing, a bit of a mess of who's whose second great grand cousin in the family tree, three marinara sauce recipes. As if instead of a birth certificate, they were like: "A baby is born! Fantastico! Let's have a meatball!"

They met in New York City. Prior to that, they matched on Match.com. They are also the only people I know who still have their email accounts on AOL, which automatically defines you as a fifty-something-year-old. Sonia and Ricky are both thirty-four.

At their date, Ricky yakety-yaked some men's ready-witted phrases for charm. He wanted a family so badly that he sweated boiling water trying to impress Sonia. Then he was silent for so long, like in an art-house movie, that Sonia somehow decided—destiny. They are the only couple I know who are genuinely happy and truly complete each other. Like they really found each other and proved it was worth waiting for.

In any group of friends, sooner or later there's always a person who gives a dildo as a joke present. And I don't think that person is appreciated enough. This time I did it. All I know for sure is a good dildo, especially given at the right time, is so worth it. They both liked my soap dildo. I knew it because when you don't like the present you repeat its name a couple times, slowly saying it very clearly, with uncertain question mark after each repetition, usually up to three, tops. They both looked a little embarrassed, but I could read between the lines of what Sonia was thinking: if you put a condom on the soap, is it okay to multi use it? I know I thought that for sure. But I'm not as perfect as Sonia. The dirtiest place in New York State is my mind.

"I love your face!" Sonia said. "What product are you wearing?"

"Natural exhaustion," I replied. "How are you doing, Sonia?"

"Very good. My life is such a blast," she smiled like she was happy for real and couldn't even describe it in words. "How are you doing?"

"I'm doing. Spent some time at Barnes & Noble the other day, got a funny book by David Duchovny, saw Sean Penn there. Apparently, he's a writer now, too."

"Oh, how interesting. What's he written?"

"I have no idea. He looked so annoyed and bored, so I figured his book is just like him."

Sonia said something else but I wasn't listening because I saw a bottle of wine, all by itself, waiting for me. *I'm going to a pretty place where flowers grow, I'll be back in an hour or so,* I sang Eminem's song as I was pouring wine in my glass. Nokia is connecting people. Wine is tolerating people. I was about to lower my soft behind when Sonia said the chair was for Anton, then pointed in his direction and winked at me.

Oh, okay, I guess this chair is only for his royal ass. I took a look at Anton: the guy had a face of a killer.

Molly and Felix Acker, a married couple in their mid thirties, were there too. And they brought their newborn baby with them. For fun, I guess.

Molly, star of bitterness sea, queen of rebelliousness logics. You'd think that Molly would make you feel better, altering mood and perception of surroundings, increasing pleasure and emotional warmth; you know, like hanging out with good friends does. But no. She represents the type that lives a facade, very Instagramable life and secretly complains on Scary Mommy website. Oh, mama! The things that people confess to there are indeed scary. This is the same absurd type of people who buy a used item for five dollars on eBay and then write a bad review, complaining it's not Saks Fifth Avenue quality.

Those guys who identify themselves as down to earth have one major issue—they can't dream big. It's not their dreams that come true but schedules. Though, someone has to live the simpler life of colorless individuals who form respectable mass citizenry. They think that Instagram is what's going on in the world. And hence have an account, thinking of themselves as web influencers, fashion stylists, life coaches. They document every moment of their mediocre lives, adding a selfie stick to a chapstick and chopsticks as essentials; and a dolly shot of breakfast, pretending it's their reality show. Please don't ever photograph your food unless you're a professional food photographer. Otherwise it's such a washout. Maybe a filter can help your face, but whatever you eat and want to brag about on the socials—it always looks like porridge an old teddy bear vomited. No filter can fix that. Also, they constantly ask for style advice, life advice, and whether or not they're boring online. I don't know why they can't decide on their own.

"We don't believe that smoking cigarettes causes lung cancer, khe khe khe," Molly said for both her and Felix, lighting up her second cigarette in a row.

Hm...you'll be lucky if you make it to your sixties, my friends.

Molly kept showing everyone pictures from her wedding, calling it the best day of her life. She had already posted tons of them so I guess these were her social media leftovers that she was too greedy to delete. In the meantime I was looking for the unsubscribe button from this real-time boredom. There will be no equality as long as women keep calling their wedding "the best day of my life."

Sexism on the highest level is when newspapers don't capitalize first lady, unlike the President. I bet if Oprah ever becomes the President, and she totally should, her husband will be capitalized First Man.

Alas there are always double standards applied when you're a woman.

You go to a guy's house on the first date—whore. You don't go—what are you, a little girl? Your clock is running, how many more dates do you want?

You get more than one college degree—don't be too smart, men don't like that, especially those women who are smarter than men. No higher education at all —don't be too simple, men don't like that. You have one degree and have a decent career—don't make too much money, men don't like that. You don't make a lot of money—loser, she must be a gold digger.

You lose some weight—she should put on some weight, men like curves. You gain a couple kilos—she is so fat, men like small-size girls.

You care about your career—she's a feminist. You care about your boyfriend's/husband's achievements—she doesn't have a life of her own. So boring.

You don't have children—when is she going to have children? You have children—is she going to have

more children? And what about her career? She's becoming a boring housewife with no self-realization in
life at all.

You don't take care of a man—she's too cold. You
take care of a man—she's too intrusive.

You don't wear heels and dresses—she's not taking
care of herself. You wear heels and dresses—oh, she's
a slut looking for a man.

You're being initiative—stop it, men like chasing.
You're not being initiative—is she a lesbian?

Perhaps when a woman's self-esteem won't rely on
what men think, we'll actually be independent and
have other best days besides a wedding day?

"What is he doing? Where did he go?" Molly asked
about her husband.

"I don't know. You should know. You're married to
him after all," I said.

Apparently, he got annoyed while looking at his
wedding pictures too so he went to the kitchen, perhaps searching for some testicles, because his were in
Molly's purse.

Later on, Molly started complaining. She manages
a law office remotely.

"I hate clients. Stop calling to check in on the
progress of your case. Nothing has changed because
your case is not a priority right now. I haven't looked
at your file in four months. Goodbye. There's a reason
I never made it in the world of customer service."

"You're way too smart for customer service. That is
the reason," Sonia said.

"Okay, yeah, that too."

"God, I am lucky I don't have to deal with that! I

work by choice," Sonia looked as if she was sharing a top secret.

"Of course you do, Sonia. Otherwise it'd be called slavery," I grinned.

"Let's all take a picture!" Molly suggested.

Oh, we're having a good time that I want to remember? Okay. This was one more social event that made me think I should've stayed at home instead.

"Smile! Baby, smile! I'm taking a picture of you. Smile!" Molly yelled in excitement to Felix.

"I am! Can't you see? That's my smile!"

Poor Felix. He's a nice guy. It's like good fortune and success had a day off on him. His name is the only luck Felix had.

"Mirra, you look so fit. Do you exercise?" Sonia asked when we got to our plates.

"No."

"Yoga?"

"No." *My life sucks.*

"You know, intercourse is kind of like exercising too." Ricky started giggling and waggling his eyebrows.

"Yeah, I remember it feels good." *Thanks for reminding that my personal life sucks too.*

When someone says, "Don't take it personally," you're about to get offended. When someone says, "I'm going to be honest with you," you're about to hear something nasty.

"Please don't take it personally..." Molly said.

And there it goes. Molly figured she could give relationship advice once she was the married one. One day they will unite around the world and then that will triumph what always triumphs when crazy bitches unite. Yikes! She quoted Instagram: "Stop searching for happiness in the same place you lost it." Dumbass. That was enough to set me completely off the handle. I hope all her taxi drivers always talk politics with her.

Moses said everything was from God. Solomon said everything was from the brain. Jesus said everything was from the heart. Freud said everything was from sex. Einstein said everything was relative. Conclusion: an opinion is like an asshole—everybody has it. Though, you don't show your asshole to everyone, especially when not asked. Why not apply that rule to expressing an unwanted opinion? Whenever you feel the urge to express your opinion, why don't you shove it up your opinion. Or share your comments where they're supposed to stay—on the social media platforms. Hey. Hey! Stop being an opinion. One day I'll write a book titled "The Annoying Shit Of Humankind."

"Do you ever wonder how bodybuilders, who can't put their arms close to the sides, wipe their asses?" I said, changing the subject of my love life to the life of shit and powerlifters and taxes and hookers and social security in Europe. "Or whether prostitutes in Amsterdam can deduct expenses on condoms like office supplies and if their clients can't bring their own condoms, like alcohol to bars. And if a prostitute loses her job, does she get unemployment benefits from the state?"

If anyone choked at that moment, it'd probably save the awkward situation I had created. Well, what?

I was kind of curious about the bodybuilders.

Sometimes, when I meet some of the people I know, I'd like to say *what are you* instead of *how are you* because that implies I believe them to be an alien creature not of this world. I like to think this is true in some cases because there are some seriously whacked out people out there.

The show wasn't over. Apparently, Anton was meant for me and all those talks about me were nothing but my social profile for him. Setting up two single people is like dogs mating. Couples think that all it takes is leave the two alone in a room for some time and things will happen eventually. Anton told someone's terrible joke: "Threesome? No thanks. If I wanted to disappoint two people in the same room I'd have dinner with my parents." Then, he mentioned that for him holiday pressure was more about producing tips for the doormen and super. I did not give a rap and felt achy just from the sound of his voice.

"Let me refill your glass. What would you like?" he asked me.

Ibuprofen.

Anton smelled like cab drivers, bums, and athletes' feet at the Olympic finals gathered in one drop of some French fragrance. I don't like men's cologne, any cologne. It is always way too intense. Or perhaps, men wear about half the bottle all the time? I'm an animal—I like natural essence a lot.

He talked to me like he was trying to find a template in his brain to apply on me that'd work. As if he was dead inside because the juice was cut off and he just wanted to fit in and pass for a nice guy. He was actively trying way too hard. It was so fake and he knew it. His mood swung. He now acted as if his phone was on silent and vibrated and he couldn't pick up right away and that made him neurotic, because things went out of control. I also thought he was high on something. Watching a sloth piss chocolate milk would be more attractive. I felt like I was wasting my words on him.

The food was terrible but the hosts looked happy. There is no greater disappointment than food that tastes like the sole of a shoe. In a Pizza 2000 town! What do you usually endure from an uninteresting meeting? Full bladder.

No matter where I went and what I did I had this irritating feeling, like when you're about to sneeze but can't, that something significant was always missing. Better, faster, stronger—it's never enough. Family, children, career, apartment, fashion bags, friends, gratitude, love, recognition, appreciation, money. As if everyone but me had all the things I've ever wanted. As if anything I did was never good enough to reach those achievements. I wasn't good enough, was I? I couldn't enjoy a moment, any moment, to the full extent. There was always fucking something. I was not in harmony with my environment, my world, myself. All I did was defense, just like in chess, anytime I played. I know that sometimes the only thing that is wrong is to ask what's wrong too often. But asking or not, something was very much wrong.

Married couples and to-do lists and planning everything for tomorrow. They lack some spontaneous behavior and flexibility, and have got nothing to do except put on fat. Oh, and buy a bigger, flatter, screener TV. What can be more annoying than boredom? The world has much more to offer than home made penne alla vodka.

The leftovers of annoyance followed me back home after dinner at the Brands'. On the subway, a mad lady was talking to herself. I've seen her on my train multiple times. What was annoying was not that she talked to herself but that her story was always the same. I've heard it seven times already. *Hey, lady! Yeah, you! What happened next after he kicked him and left the building?*

In fact, the train car was full of characters, as always though. There was a very smiley artist who looked like the grandfather from the cartoon "Up". He drew pictures with felt-tip pens and tried to sell them right away. Two stops later the host of the Entertainment Tonight replaced him. He desperately craved attention and forced the audience to listen to him by being rather loud. Headphones could not save some lucky passengers, neither earplugs could. Todays episode was about Aziafrika, the geopolitical structure of the world and who brought gangsters to Italy; as well as about the Jersey people—a small but very proud nation. And where else if not on the train talk about politics, right? "The dutch, the french, the jersey people went to Africa for natural resources in the eighties. If it wasn't for the natural resources, there would not be industrialization. Europe wouldn't even go to Africa. There's no Eurasia, it's Asiafrica. Who opened Italy for example? Criminals! They came to Europe and discovered Italy!" One woman and her son accidentally nodded to the proposal to use pizza as an alternative fuel, which only made the man talk more about it. She already began to look at the world with a painful gaze and her son, poor boy, almost caught dementia through airborne droplets.

Clearly, drunks, crazies, and other down-shifters claim to know it; but imagine if they all actually know politics better? Doing nothing obliges you to have tremendous theoretical knowledge. Someone has to do nothing too. And they just do their job well.

Many issues remained unresolved on the political arena but it was the speaker's stop thus is was the time to sum up the world results. He wanted to be called for an encore. Statistically, there are not so many masochists, even in such a crazy city as New York. The audience breathed out with relief; many still did not remove their headphones to not frighten off luck.

The train car remained normal, well, New York normal. There was a young woman with an electronic ankle tag. I immediately wondered what she had done. And there was a moped. I bet you can easily fit a MINI into the train. The only difficulty would be getting a MINI into the subway, because not every station has an elevator.

The train driver was very talkative, behaved like an aspiring airplane pilot. He yelled stops, thanked for riding with MTA all the time, and even tried to crack a bad joke couple times; someone was already eating stinky chicken from the container, so only announcements of weather forecast and how many meters we were underground differed that trip from some local low cost flight where people don't mind standing in coach.

I was sulking over every little thing.

Why is it always people with a terrible voice who sing out loud all the time? Why can't I see a guy or a girl in headphones on the subway who'd open their mouth and it's Lady Gaga's voice. But no! When did people start to feel the need to sing out loud publicly. It is fantastic that they are so open to the world and willing to share their joy but that off-Broadway musical coming out of their throat is like the screaming of a horny cat in March. And why do I always have to have a list of things to do in the upcoming new year and know where I see myself in five years? It makes me so anxious and lost and anxious again. I don't even know what I want for lunch tomorrow. Each day brings its own bread with it. Things will turn out all right somehow. All I have on my list for the upcoming year is to start making lists maybe?

As I walked home, I saw an illuminated sign on a building "Face Gym." *I have to train my face too? Squats for eyebrows, plank for lips, which is basically duck facing.* And then iBooks notified me of their new feature: reading goals. *Ugh, great. Now they want me to be anxious about not having enough entertainment too?*

How easy it would be to feel happy every day without accomplishing any goals; without any conditions; just be, you know. Especially for women, whose fears are thriving every fashion week season. Adding to that so many industries that rely on women's insecurities and cultural decisions to please men, otherwise there'd be no sales at all. Well, first they form an opinion that there's something wrong with us and then immediately slip the solution with a monthly subscription. One industry serves another industry through our minds. The obsession with photoshopped magazine's images, portraying the impossible female anatomy is insane. We have cellulite and bellies and all kinds of stuff sags due to gravity. Those standards that you are supposed to follow are unrealistic and frankly exhausting; and it makes no sense to even shame anyone for the physical force that's way stronger than Botox. We choose to believe in all kinds of nonsense that has nothing to do with reality: Santa, Jesus, Equality... We objectify ourselves by agreeing there's something wrong with us. And once it seemed like marketers of happiness have already used every single fear trigger to boost sales, someone came up with a new, absolutely different level of goal: you're not glowing enough, woman!

You can tell the anxiety level of the city by the number of people who run. And when they don't go for a run, they run metaphorically. "Gotta run, gotta run!" Where do they all run when they gotta run? To buy illuminasers for more glowing?

I was tired of a city raped by tourists, always being nearly crushed in the crowd on bustling streets every time, everywhere I rambled. Even headphones at maximum volume didn't save me from the annoying endless buzzing, including my own thoughts. It's like the whole New York was my roommate. I was on "I hate New York" mode which means only one thing: you've got to get out of the city for a while. So out of sight is literally out of mind.

I needed a circumstance that would switch my life for the better. Randomness is a combination of facts we don't know about.

Wandering the city streets, searching for silence,
But sirens distract from guidance to find balance.
Your guts ain't science, yet still the best reliance...
Time to issue your mind riots a happiness license.

WORDS THAT SELL

The next day, at three pm in the morning, I turn off the TV that's been on all night long—my faux plus one —and call Val Zironka, my sanest of insane friends whom I love tremendously.

"Have you ever talked to someone at a party, nodding along, and in the meantime try to figure out whether that person is on meth or molly or just naturally fucked up?"

"Oh, absolutely, darling! Once, a guy told me he was Lucifer and could speak to dogs. Although, he was on molly," Val adds. "What, darling, the married couples grabbed you into their cult?

"They're not a cult—they don't want me to give them my credit card information and donate my life and attention to the leader. There's not even a leader. It's more like a club. They let me watch, take a tour, but will accept my membership only if I bring the damned plus one with a certificate of proof."

"Want me to create a horoscope for you to see what's coming?"

Val believes in all that.

"Thank you, I'm good. Hey, can you create one for yesterday? I'll tell you what coincided with the truth.

That should be fun."

"So, those married motherfuckers dragged you into anguish?"

"I get it—they live in ways that can be explained. In their pursuit to follow up with my personal life they actually acted extremely rude. I decline to understand why I have to broadcast updates of my love life especially if there aren't any at all, why I have to justify being single. They just made me feel like I'm broken, with a factory defect, fucked up, you know."

"Mirra, you are fucked up! In a beautiful way! And being single or not has nothing to do with that! You have an artsy aura. By the way, you know what your name means, right?"

"Yeah. Peace." *Ironically, I don't have my own Mirra.*

"Mirra is a true cross-cultural name, a *peaceful* meaning in several Eastern European languages, a well-used name in Arabic cultures meaning *queen-like* or a *female ruler*, and a nature name in Sanskrit. You are peace. You are prosperous. You are wonderful," Val says.

She always knows how to cheer me up. She's always there for me, no matter where she is in the world at the moment. I use her for spiritual comfort, she uses me for sarcastic remarks and straight-forwardness. She says one day I will ghostwrite a book of her life for her because things like that need to be documented and saved for her descendants. When we meet up, we end up having fantastic, fabulous and incredibly funny stories together. It's inspiring to be able to share moments of happiness and joy.

Val is thirty-eight, single, and lives in London. She scouts models for men's magazines in Ukraine, couches and performs lectures on how to marry an oligarch all over the world. She calls herself a producer. I suspect she's a high-end pimp. Very possibly, she's the one who puts models and other pretty girls under millionaires and billionaires and then we find out in the press that some rich man got his girlfriend an engagement ring the of a size of a melon in exchange for her pretending that his penis is not the size of a peanut. Her clientele is literally any girl who posts deliberately sexy photos on social networks and then gets offended when she is considered depraved. The girls usually speak English, but only nouns. Val takes care of that. It happens that a girl is beautifully immaculate, expensively dressed, speaks coquettishly but her hair is pinned with a light green scrunchy. Val takes care of that too. Val's hair stylist does the necessary makeover for each girl. At the end he spins her around and puts his face near hers and looks into the mirror with her and says, "Now you have a chance, kid." Mine never does that. Just overcharges.

For me it remains a secret how Val does all that and pretty successfully.

Val is like a New York cab driver—within twenty minutes she knows who you are, what you do, where you come from, where you studied, how you got here, and what you want.

"How are your new book sales?"

"Meh. I've had better."

"You have to be active on Instagram and post more sexy pictures of yourself," Val says. "Any form of sex branded and marketed well can sell."

"Val, I know that. That's why I always make sure to have my topless selfie on social media, but they keep blocking me for sharing child pornography cause my boobies look like a twelve-year-old's."

"Oh, shut up," Val giggles.

"But I figured there're at least ten ways to annoy a writer."

"Bring them on!" Val says.

"*My book is published.*
'Congratulations!'

To congratulate a writer is the same as clapping your hands when your plane lands, regularly, without any sort of emergency whatsoever. Next time I talk to a software developer I should cheer, right? Because, oh my god, he's doing his job—let's celebrate.

'My book is published.'
'Can I get a signed copy?'
'Sure. Buy the book and I'll sign it.'
'Oh, I meant a signed copy from a writer.'
'So you want me to buy you my book?'

'My book is published.'
'Do you have a discount coupon?'

'My book is published.'
'Is it available on torrents?'

'My book is published.'

'I know how to promote your book!'
'Great. How?'
'You gotta come up with a marketing plan.'
'Any specific ideas?'
'I don't know, I'm not a marketer.'

'My book is published.'
'I know a guy who's done something with book publishing. Come to a party tonight to meet him.'
'Share my number with the guy.'
'Oh, he won't call. He's a very busy guy.'

'My book is published.'
'Is it a true story?'

'My book is published.'
'Is that you on the cover?'

'My book is published.'
'I think you should've gone with the black font instead of white.'

'My book is published.'
'I hope to see it on the NYT's best seller list soon.'

This one is really a slap in the face for an indie writer.

You know, being a writer kind of subconsciously makes you look for drama. It's exhausting. I'm not sure why but whenever I say I'm a writer people always tell me they write something too, be it short stories or poems or a memoir they plan to start after turning fifty. Sure, people just want to find commonalities to connect. Although, it's kind of rude to say they could easily do my job too. No, you fucking can't. I don't mention my knowledge of the Constitution to a lawyer or that I floss to a dentist or that I know the exchange rate of US dollar to Euro to a banker, or that I built stuff with LEGO to an architect. Gah! I can't tell you how many times I was asked if I use a type-writer. Instead of a perfectly ergonomic keyboard? Hell no! That would be like going on a road trip on a horse instead of an SUV. According to stereotypes about writers I have to use a typewriter, compile a novel within one night while chain-smoking ciga-rettes, be a drunkard, oh, and a man. My personal fa-vorite is when one guy thought that all books are called novels and used the words books and novels interchangeably. I laughed so hard." I take a deep breath. "One day I'm gonna write a memoir and call it 'Erh.' Val, you still there?"

"Yeah, I'm here. Let me guess: everybody wants you to write about them because they think that get-ting pissed on a Tuesday night is an extraordinary story worth telling and throwing up in an Uber on the way home makes 'em an interesting character. Not every blackout story is the 'Hangover' movie, you people!"

"Val! How did you know?"

"You told me that. I listen. Any more stories of yours that I can listen to? Maybe dating stories?"

"Nah, Netflix is my boyfriend. Though there're two easy steps to find out whether a guy is really interest-ed in getting to know you. One: write a book; two: ask if they've read it. If they haven't—we have nothing to fuck about. I have a whole bunch of how to's that help save time and energy."

"Hit me," Val says.

"I'm allergic to miser. There is no worst quality in a man than being a cheapskate. I get that some men had a difficult childhood with wooden toys nailed to the floor, and in worse cases if they weren't born a boy they'd have nothing to play with and so on but come-the-fuck-on! Grow up already, would you? Once I had an amazing date with a guy from San Fransisco who was visiting New York. We spent six hours laughing. It was so much fun! And we actually agreed to meet again. So I asked him to get me an Uber home. The extra thirty bucks spent on a taxi can tell me everything I need to know about a guy's relationship with money. In an instant, an adorable Californian guy changed into someone I didn't wish to spend six minutes with. He jokingly called me a gold digger. I heard enough. Did I mention the dude was on a payroll? Score for a gold digger!"

"That's a good one," Val says. "Next time I'm unsure about a guy's stinginess, I'll ask him to get me a private jet."

"Everybody has their own level of gold digging."

"I think you need a vacation. Come to London, darling!" Val suggests.

"Val, I'm sorry, I can't: I'm scheduled for an orgy."

"So do your seven o'clock gang bang and come over after it."

"You know I was joking right?" I am actually confused.

"Well, I wasn't. You've got to live a little, darling!"

"Actually, I do need to move out very soon. I even had the idea to go on a cruise as a temporary sublet."

"So come to me instead. Let's have fun!"

"Let's! Who's gonna pay for that?" I laugh.

"Do you want me to set you up with an oligarch?"

"Thanks. It's always helpful to know in advance whose dick to suck. The rule of a hotel room: first you suck the dick, then you sign a contract. Of course, this kind of money almost always comes with strings attached. I'm not ready for a commitment like that."

"You're in need of sex and money. Do you see where I'm going with it?"

"I do, Val. And I'm ignoring it. But thanks."

"Fine! Will you come anyway? All expenses are on me," Val insists.

"I can only pay you back when I can, which may take a while."

"Oh, money-shmoney. A while is fine by me."

So, it was agreed.

When it is difficult to decide something, you need to postpone the decision, put it on pause in the long run, and the solution will be found on its own. Or not. Well, if not—you'll take it off pause and make a decision and you will find a solution for sure. I need a break, an escape of some sort. But no matter where you go, there you are.

Nowhere do you feel more lonely than in a bustling terminal when you fly with a carry-on, alone. It is important that someone sees you off at the airport. This means that they're looking forward to your return. And it is also very important with whom and where we check in our luggage. On the bright side, it's easier to travel alone than with just anybody.

"M'am, do you have any sharp objects?" the security officer at JFK asks me.

"Only my tongue."

So I'm talking to this guy on the plane and I ask him:

"What do you do for work?"

"Financial advising," he answers.

"That's a very broad area. It can be anything: banking, businesses, consulting, etc..."

"Not really," he says. "That's pretty much narrowed down to what I do. I'm an individual financial advisor. IRA, IRS, things like that."

"Oh, so you're an accountant," I conclude.

He takes offense. He does accounting indeed.

If you add industry after anything, especially if it's meh, especially if you're not proud of what you do—in an instant, it sounds cool and legit. Also, if you talk about something with confidence, people willingly agree with you, even if you actually know nothing. And obviously, you are your number one manager and sales person promoting your own genius and expertise. Sometimes all it takes is confidence and constant repetition of a pitch to sell.

There are so many words that can create a certain image just by using them. They sound cool. They sound serious. They sound expensive. Consulting, contract, management, vice president, entrepreneur, project metrics, CRM, founder and CEO. Oh, the last ones are my favorite. Let me ruin the power of those words.

Imagine you have a pizza joint. And you call it

Joe's pizza. There is no Steve or Mark or David who make pizza. It's always Joe or John or Jack. Anywho, you open a pizza place and you even register a DBA so you can use the word pizza next to your first name. Done. You can call yourself a founder and CEO. You founded your pizza place? Of course! You execute all the office matters on a chief level? Absolutely! Now, don't forget to update your LinkedIn profile with your new job title. CEO and founder of Joe's pizza.

At some point, it's kind of like cheating when you're an accountant but you call yourself a financial advisor.

"Sir, could you give me financial advice regarding my finances. So, I should have more money than less, right?"

"Correct."

"And I should do my taxes every year?"

"Yes."

"Thank you, sir, for your financial advising. One more question though. What should I invest my money in?"

"Oh, I specialize in financial advising only. To help you with your investments, you need an investment advising specialist."

People create a bunch of titles pursuing their main goal: to sell themselves for a higher price. Sometimes it works. Sometimes it doesn't. Sometimes it sounds ridiculous. Pet lover, mother of three, yoga junkie, Netflix addict, world traveler, art observer, learner, social media follower, water drinker, food eater, air breather. Those are not professions! Every time I see that list of useless words, I'm like, so what is it that you do?

There's so much spam in the universe. Words and titles and brands and emails and marketing promotions that are meant to supposedly sell you a feeling of importance, a feeling of happiness, a feeling of contentment by having certain goods. It lasts about an hour. We own so much shit! And we get caught by the big words such as CEO and entrepreneur and luxury. By using those words, we think we'll attract the lifestyle that the words represent. No one knows more about expensive cars than those who can never afford them. They discuss brands, criticize and philosophize the lifestyle behind owning the brands, trying to imagine what it's like. Trying to get one step closer, they take pictures wearing the brands and with famous people, showing everyone that they are "friends," that they belong to the "club." Success.

Nobody is further from success than those who eagerly consume "the truth" at online and offline courses—How to Become the President One-oh-One and Get Rich in Sixty Days; or those who read an autobiography of a successful leader. It all creates the illusion of the path, copying someone else's life, someone else's success, because they can't even imagine their own. They think they're just missing something. So they fork over truckloads of money trying to get to that one little nugget that will help them move forward. They spend hundreds of thousands on that. People are willing to pay for knowledge, especially for the "secret" that suddenly opens the financial flows to please the material needs, so they can finally drink their fresh juice with a disposable diamond straw.

Consumers of the "secret" imagine that suddenly, a wonderful antelope will strike gold coins by hooves, like in an Indian fairy tale. So much gold that it could be reforged into a toilet. Precious metals have a positive effect on the gastrointestinal tract—antelope hunters are convinced. The secret knowledge, generously shared at trainings, is nothing but words, air, zilch.

The truth is same brands can't unite. Same ideas can.

It is very easy to distinguish rich from poor. A rich man diligently pretends that he has less money than in reality. A poor man pretends that he has more.

By the time the plane lands, I decide to push forward the business idea I've had in mind for two years. An online service for professionals who work with information, a club that would connect journalists and experts, because they have something in common—a story that needs to go public. Information for professionals, a club of acceptance. InfoPro.Club.

The need is right on time. Journalists pick up new stories on either Facebook or Reuters. Facebook is not a reliable source, Reuters requires expensive access key. Journalists constantly need expert opinions, trusted sources and new stories. It's not easy to get a database of experts. Experts can't pitch target media unless they have the database of journalists or know them personally. Without an easy access, calling or emailing the official contact of any media outlet is almost never helpful.

InfoPro.Club is a database of media opportunities that serves daily communication needs: endless stories for journalists and killer media coverage for brands. Journalists have fast access to valuable information in one place, get connected with exclusive and trusted expert sources, and can choose the best newsworthy pitch. Experts have all target media in one place whenever required, can easily pitch, and get valuable media mentions as stories, interviews, reviews.

Multiple websites like this, HARO, Cision, PRWeb, i-Newswire, Media Syndicate, Source, Box, PR Newswire, Media Kitty, Pitch Rate, Press Release, Muck Rack, News Certified Exchange, have already existed on the English speaking market for years, though on the Russian speaking market there are literally no competitors.

There's more than four thousand active print media outlets in Ukraine published at least once a year. That's just print. There's twenty thousand journalists who hold membership of the National Union of Journalists of Ukraine; in reality, it's at least three times more of them. Adding to it all media outlets, PR agencies, branding agencies, independent experts and freelance writers—and the market size becomes a million bucks. Literally. And people would pay because purchasing a monthly membership of the private club would automatically make you a part of the elite community.

In the business model, there's two possible rounds of revenue. The first round is a monthly subscription fee of twenty-five dollars per account. The second round opens more possibilities in the future. In the roadmap for five years, the plan is to have major

Ukrainian media outlets and communication agencies in the Club, establish strategic partnerships with media intelligence service, and create an online job board for the media industry. After being actively marketed nationwide, the Club becomes number one InfoPro community in the country. InfoPro Awards is launched. The Club is addressed to all Cyrillic markets in the world and expands customer database to the point that it controls information flows.

This is the new era of information in the Cyrillic world built on trust, integrity, professionalism; and the access to it starts with InfoPro.Club.

I am not delusional about trying to make money on mass media. If you've ever seen the business plan of a magazine, you'd understand what I mean. I don't want to reinvent the wheel—I am going to create a new type of tire. The business model is not just about the revenue. The return on investment in my idea is much broader and global: management of information flows in Ukraine and then maybe even the whole Cyrillic world. Eh, native roots calling, you know.

Right from the airport Val and I go to her place so I can refill the level of "Drilled Cherry," my drug of choice. (After having watched all of the *Intervention* episodes, twice, I talk their slang, like I belong. I've got to lose it or people won't get me right). Val is a fan of cooking and does it amazingly. There's one thing, her signature meal, that is always in stock—"Drilled Cherry" jam. Each cherry is stuffed with a walnut and boiled in sugar syrup. I can eat it forever! I'm addicted to her jam—the fruit and sugar heaven.

This is what InfoPro.Club is like: a cherry-journalist and walnut-expert that absolutely can work separately but when combined, it becomes delicious.

"Why will they pay for the membership?" Val asks flipping through electronic pages of the presentation.

"It is very simple. Let me ask you this. Don't you like the show more because you paid more for it? Don't you try harder to learn something significant in a course because you paid decent money for it? The more you pay—the more you value it. It's a simple truth. Your oligarchs know it like no one else. If you want to be a member of the club full of cool, special people, you're going to have to contribute. Oh, paid content and 'be seen first' feature are another ways to monetize."

"Okay, but how are you going to market it?"

"The good old never-failing method of Henry Kissinger's shuttle diplomacy. It's ugly but it works."

"What is that?"

"Val, I'm not even sure it's true but I really like the story, where Henry Kissinger explains what shuttle diplomacy is.

Suppose you want to marry Rockefeller's daughter to a lad from a Siberian village. Easy. You go to a Siberian village, find there a young man and ask him, 'Would you like to marry an American Jew?'

He says, 'Why?! We've got enough of girls here!'

'Well, she is the daughter of a billionaire.'

He goes, 'Oh! This changes things...'

Then you go to Switzerland, walk into a large bank's board meeting and ask, 'How would you like to have a simple Siberian man to be your bank's President?'

'Oh, hell no!'

'What if I told you he was Rockefeller's son-in-law?'

'Oh! This changes things...'

So then you go see Rockefeller and ask, 'Would you like your daughter to marry a Russian peasant?'

'What do you mean?! Everyone in my family is in banking.'

'Funny you mentioned that. He is actually a Swiss bank President.'

'Oh! This changes things... Susie, come here, my child. Mr. Kissinger found you a good husband. He is the President of a large Swiss bank.'

'Bah! All big bankers are skinny sissies!'

And you finally say, 'Well, this one is a strong Siberian hunk.'

'Oh! This changes things...'"

Despite as easy as it sounds, Val thinks my idea is hardly profitable but like any supportive friend she says she has a friend who knows someone who knows someone who might be interested in investing in a tech startup. And that I better have an elevator pitch and a party mood for that since the next day we go to a night club to sell my Club.

I truly hate going to social events trying to sell a pitch. It's exhausting and sucks out a lot of energy from me, because I have to fight back all the unneeded flirting and dirty ambiguous remarks before we can actually cut to the chase and talk real business. Val lives by a golden rule: "If you treat me like a hole, I'll treat you like a wallet." Perhaps, it makes sense to apply it.

It will never fail to astonish me how people talk business at night clubs, loud and drunk, without getting a throat hernia. Yet there I am, about to talk to someone who knows someone who knows Val's friend. It is hard to pitch when someone you're pitching sees first your boobs and then your spreadsheet. Especially if you're a woman, with a Russian accent, from New York, looking for a startup investor, in London, to do business in Eastern Europe—it is crucially important to keep the balance of an outfit's sluttiness, an attitude's cuntiness, and the advantage of smartness. The main purpose of doing business is money. The main criteria of doing business successfully is power. *Bloody hell. It is actually possible to talk at a night club. Sound proofed VIP room. Very important indeed. I smell deliciousness—illegal financial transactions.*

Dwight and Kellen are in the group of people I am introduced to.

Dwight Hale is a broker. He owns an island in the Caribbean and real estate in London, New York, and Moscow. He's thirty-six years old, visits brothels on multiple occasions, smokes roll-ups, and says "Do you understand" after every other sentence. He also expresses the utmost excitement and astonishment to everything I say and showers me in complements, saying the word insane a lot. When people use *insanely* to describe something good, they're probably insane. A broker usually equals a pathological liar, my guts yell. And Dwight's British accent is confusing and perplexing—the accent itself creates an image of decency, like glasses automatically add to intelligence.

But something is awry about this dude. Hard to explain but I have a weird feeling, so weird like a blazer tucked into panties.

"Have you been waiting for me?" he asks, leering in the darkness of the private club in the heart of London.

I dislike him already, and his stupid expensive tie. We talk about this and that and yada yada.

He says it is important to compare yourself to others. This is how he learned to get better.

"Better? Better for what? Better for whom?" I ask.

"Better than others. Better surroundings, better drinks, better level, dear. If you stop comparing yourself to all the others, what do you do? Do you just sleep, eat, watch porn?"

"I don't know. Maybe compare yourself to others only every other day?" I grin. "When you compare yourself to others you always lose."

"Not necessarily!" Dwight calls the server and orders two glasses of the most expensive cognac on the menu, priced for two thousand seven hundred pounds each. He is about to prove his point. I start sneezing because I'm allergic to bullshit.

"So Dwight, that feeling of being better than others, does it last long?" I ask when our drinks are served.

"I think it lasts only a moment, sometimes never. But I think it's good." Barely looking, he puts his glass on the stool-like table.

"Does it make you happy?"

"It makes me better, dear." Dwight rolls his eyes. "Don't you think?"

In a person's life there're two things that matter: what one does and what one feels. What one thinks is important? Not so much.

I sip cognac and it does not massage my throat while I swallow—the two thousand seven hundred pound drink burns my throat the exact same way as a hundred dollar drink does. Unimpressed, I put my glass next to Dwight's. The server comes to ask whether everything's okay and accidentally makes it the opposite. I watch the glasses falling down from our shaky stool-like table and breaking into tiny pieces like the server's dreams of leaving the hospitality industry.

"Oy," the server whispers and dies for a moment after realizing he just trashed five thousand four hundred pounds. I am really interested in Dwight's reaction. Perhaps he'll feel something now.

"I think we need this mess cleaned up and a refill, same."

"Yes sir, in a moment sir. I'm so sorry." The server is nervous as hell.

"Don't worry about it. Just bring us our drinks, chop-chop," Dwight says and turns to me. "Where were we?"

He was trying to prove me how great it is to be better yet he couldn't feel his own betterness. Money truly can't buy feelings.

Kellen Watz. He says a lot of *whats: What's that? What's this? What's what?* He does it with the intonation of Kevin Hart. Watz is a typical general manager—very pro office culture and mindset, one of those who makes like forty thousand a month. He shows me a new rebranded logo of his company without asking as if it is a picture of his child, and then starts explaining what it means. He probably doesn't know that explaining the logo means either you're an idiot or you're surrounded by idiots.

Kellen is perfect, perfect perfection, smiling twenty-four seven. He's very neurotic and thus his legs shake all the time—they never stop just like his mind. I think he was hired because the company had a quota.

Men love watches with multiple functions. Kellen shares the same model with James Bond, Omega's Seamaster 300—its iconic namesake from nineteen fifty-seven but updated and upgraded. So the watch is a combination of an address book, telescope, and piano.

I can tell the brand of everything he is wearing because his clothes have it in huge letters, yelling to a fault, "Luxury!" Although, something is off. He doesn't have...the quality. I bet he still prefers Popeyes deep fried chicken and soda for dinner. Some habits can't be changed with the new Prada collection. From the back he looks fine, but from the front he looks like he doesn't have a family.

The target audience of luxury brands that are easily recognized is poor people and the middle class. Those who flip through pages of glossy magazines in cheap beauty salons. It's for them there is advertising on busses.

Look at it from a slightly different angle. Coming to a business meeting with a much more successful person, you put on your best suit and your high-quality

Rolex replica and expect to be perceived as "at the same level," don't you? If this is all that you are capable of—okay, no dissonance, continue meeting the people you meet and doing things you do and wearing shiny, like a new stainless steel saucepan, pseudo success that leads to emptiness made of crocodile leather. No questions asked. The big logotype right in the middle of every thing as a sign of status, the main meaning of life—it has been chosen to represent it. Le vulgarity.

Status you want to achieve by climbing the ladder limits your freedom. You can't put on a t-shirt for your meeting with investors. Somehow you have to look your best presentable way to ask for money, as if wearing a suite will guarantee your reliability. It's all made up. True freedom is when you can wear a t-shirt anytime you want, regardless of the board meeting decisions.

The paradox of todays society is everyone wants to be different, avoid bios and stereotypes yet chooses the same attributes and identifiers of specific groups. And marketing of products is stuck so deep in our minds that whenever you hear a specific brand, you automatically apply everything you know about its consumers. iPhone VS Android users is a clear example.

In chess, counter gambit often leads to a complex matching game with mutual chances. Power playing with power—that's the only fun way. What's powerful about brands that everyone else has? Yes, I now know how much you spent on your clothes. Does that automatically make you an interesting person? Sure thing not. It's just stuff—high quality of nothingness.

A brand, as identification of belonging to a certain society, group, or club, is labeling. What you show off is what you value the most, including in yourself. It's what you think is the most valuable thus important. If a picture in front of your car is so meaningful to you, it's odd to expect that your followers will care about it too. If most of your Instagram is pictures of your boobs, why would you possibly think that your followers value your personality?

Your paradigm is what differs you from others. Your standard, perspective, set of ideas is your only competitive difference and advantage. Well, if you have those, of course. If not, then go with the boobs, the bigger the better.

We attract people with the same perception of the world as our own. We get along with people that have the same value system. We meet people that we already know.

Rich is not about pathos, whose penis is bigger and whose car has more horse power. Rich is about ken and the habit of questioning and searching for answers.

If you had to choose one, would you go with a high-fashion purse or a week in Paris?

I start to trust my gut. Finally! My first impression of people is always right. When I try to persuade myself that I was wrong it's almost like betraying myself, because I always come back to my very first conclusion. It's easy to see the truth when there's nothing at stake. As soon as you stop doing what you don't like, when you finally stop lying to yourself, you start seeing incredibly colorful dreams again.

Dwight expresses interest in my business idea, tells me to contact him, and later on never responds to my messages or calls.

Instead of wasting time with "I need to concentrate now on my career", "We will call you back if there's interest", "Send over your presentation", people who are able to say "no" out loud have my deepest respect. Leaving the English way when the actual answer is expected is cowardice. Frankly, only humor is good the English way.

There is only one universal excuse that's ambiguous enough so everyone understands it in their own way: due to the situation in the country.

"Let's partner up? We will give you three times this, this, and this. And you give us only one time this and that's all."

"We stopped any kind of partnership due to the situation in the country."

"We should meet for coffee and talk."

"I can't. Due to the situation in the country, you know."

"Let's hook up."

"I am extremely busy due to the situation in the country."

"Maybe we should have a vacation soon."

"How dare you even think about that? Now is not the time due to the situation in the country."

Due to the situation in the country. Substitute at the end of any phrase at your discretion.

There's a new socially transmitted disease among people, an epidemic spreading all over in economically developed countries: ghosting. It's chronic. It's unpleasant. But it still can be taken under control with proper treatment. (Out of all epidemics, syphilis was probably the most fun because people got to really enjoy themselves first.)

Communication in the twenty-first century is hard. With all these numerous applications that are supposed to connect everyone in the world, it became impossible to talk. Moreover, no one answers their cell phone anymore. When was the last time you actually dialed? In the Jurassic period? And when you did, what did you hear in response? Major confusion.

"Heeey...Did you mean to call me? Or was it a pocket dial?" you hear when they pick up the phone.

Voicemail is still very popular because it gives you an opportunity to ignore it.

I understand. It's hard to pay attention today. You get distracted with like fifteen thousand notifications that need to be processed daily. Facebook, Instagram, Twitter, LinkedIn, Medium, WhatsApp, FaceTime, Viber, MeetUp, Amazon, eBay, Netflix, GrubHub, Seamless, Macy's, Sephora, Barney's, Century 21, Tinder, Podcasts, YouTube, PayPal, Stripe, Google Voice, Amber alerts, text messages, and about two hundred work related emails and a dozen non-work related, mostly suggesting viagra and a merchant cash advance. Newsletters, promotions, special offers, deals and discounts, buy one get one free, refer a friend and get ten bucks on your account, shaving subscription, clothing subscription, food subscription, job board subscription, dating subscription, friendship subscription, Christmas tree subscription, anything-you-can-imaging subscription. Hit auto-ship and auto-renewal, and save five percent—but no worries, cancel any time. Aaa!!!

Not ready to commit yet? Rent it! Rent a brand, rent a company, rent a brain. Knowledge as a service can be helpful in certain situations, but if you don't know how to invoice clients, maybe entrepreneurship is not for you. But rest assured to receive loads of emails that will always have some form of call-to-action towards you.

We all are so well-notified about what's going on in life that we get distracted from actually living it. No wonder so many people suffer from attention-deficit disorder.

Alright, I get it. Sometimes you can't filter everything and you might just forget to respond to a voicemail or an email or a text message. It happens. We spend so much time on waiting for someone's response via texts, it's insane. But the question is what's an ethically acceptable time frame for not responding but still being considered nice and polite? A day? A week? An eternity? Though, no answer is a very clear answer.

The nature of tech makes communication interesting. It's both quite easy which is great but also pervasively intrusive.

The way people use their cell phones is sometimes

incomprehensible. They schedule a call in advance and then don't pick up the phone. They answer the call only to hiss in annoyance "I can't speak now!" On Instagram, they promise to get back with an answer in a day and instead delete their account for good. They answer the "how have you been" text with plain and simple "good" four days later. They must be living an absolutely mind-blowing life. Share the secret right now! And the classics: they say "I'll call you back in ten minutes" and of course never do—not in ten minutes, not that day, not even that month. Wow to the mysterious ten minutes opening a portal into I won't say where, because that cuss word hasn't even been invented yet. It's a shame you can't hang up anymore like you used to with rotary phones, letting out full-blown anger while putting down the receiver. And unfortunately, more often than not, to understand some people's messages you have to put your phone on asshole mode.

What is it with people not responding to texts promptly? Instant messages are called instant for a reason. For other purposes, there's USPS non priority mail. If you claim you don't want to be like those kids who stare at their smartphone all the time—get a rotary phone! If you behave like an asshole, don't blame the big city and say that it's normal for this city. The city is great and you're still an asshole.

When someone ghosts me but in the meantime keeps watching my Insta stories, I want to send them a notification: Hello! I can see you! If you're doing something wrong, you gotta do it right, man.

Kellen, on the other hand, is very active in further

communication, unfortunately.

"Mirra, could you download Telegram for instant messages?"

"We are instant messaging now in regular messages. What's wrong with that?"

"I'm not used to the interface."

"What? It's the same keyboard! LOL."

"Yeah, but could you download Slack for group chats?"

"WhatsApp has group chats."

"Yeah, but we need group chats for desktop."

"What'sApp works for desktops. Unless you'd like to use emails."

"Emails? For what?"

"For group chats on desktop!" I couldn't. I just couldn't. Nothing is worth wasted nerve cells. I don't have the time for that, translation from British English—I am not willing to spend my time on what you're suggesting.

Kellen, I have an equally valuable business offer for you—go away!

Val thinks I am an idiot for declining Kellen. Everyone has an opinion. I'm a highly opinionated person myself. It doesn't mean I have to listen to all of them, and be listened to.

"Val, I hate when people start to argue with me," I say. "If we're not on the same page personally, it'll be extremely hard to do business together. This messenger, or that messenger, or no, better this messenger... Fuck you!"

"Darling, business is not personal. You don't have to like your investor's personal qualities to proceed with work," Val says.

"Everything is personal. The only time it's not personal is when you get a cheeseburger at McDonald's and they forget to put pickles in it and then apologize, and ask you not to take it personally. And you don't. But other than that everything is personal."

"McDonald's?" Knowing me, Val looks surprised. "Really?"

"Feh! No! Geez, Val. How could you even think that. I haven"t been to McDonald's since, like, high school."

"Phew. So no Kellen, huh?"

"No. Besides, I hate people who say *It is what it is*."

"Oh well, what can you do. It is what it is," Val says.

"Oh, fuck off!" We burst out laughing.

"So what are you going to do?" Val asks me.

"There is an old parable about a short-sighted person who lost his keys late in the evening and is looking for them by the light of a street lamp. Another person comes and offers help, asking: 'Are you sure that you have lost your keys right here?' 'No,' the short-sighted person replies. 'But there is only enough light to search here.' Maybe it's finally time for me to start doing something I actually like with people I like," I breathe out. "I'll go see my friend Ange Lanvin in Paris. He's an artist and knows a lot of people, because everybody wants to be friends with an artist. Maybe he'll introduce me to someone."

"Lanvin who created the brand?" Val looks confused.

"He's a cousin of a cousin of the original Lanvin."

"Mirra, darling, you're telling me that you left New York City, the financial center of the world, where there are more high net-worth individuals than trees in the streets, where everyone is investing in something literally everyday, only to visit your creative friend in Paris?"

"Yeah, pretty much. Game rules are the same everywhere. Methods differ. Besides, there's always someone who knows someone who knows someone."

TEN-EURO CASINO CHIP

New York is never more New York than in Paris. The apotheosis of traveling. I am a bit sentimental entering the pavements of love and dirty luxury and fatty livers. And hobos that give the illusion of being a local. Rich people can be from anywhere, poor people are definitely locals. The rule of metropolitan areas. Paris is filthy and green—a perfect place to try to find peace within yourself. Europe looks good on me.

I clearly feel how the world is smaller because distance is conditional. You live where your thoughts are. Where your loved ones are. Where you feel your body at the moment.

All what we are and all that we need is always with us—brain and feelings are the only baggage. The rest is infrastructure.

Home is where people get you and you get them. A bunch of snacks usually makes me feel at home, too. That's why I always feel at home in hotels. Ah, it'd be so much fun moving around the world living in hotels... One day I'll write a book about traveling titled "There you go."

Home is the atmosphere. Not a kitchen, not your favorite sofa, or a morning coffee mug. It's where all makes sense to you, where you're free from things, habits and laziness, where you can expand your horizons.

Traveling does the same—it expands horizons and timezones, cultures and traditions, impressions and clues and beyond. So you can feel at home anywhere, and feel like a queen anywhere. It is quite ridiculous to stay a queen in your small village when the whole world is out there. Though, it is the easiest way for sure. True success is global. Translation for younger generations: global does not always equal googleable. Often times, most successful people don't even have business cards, or if they do, they put something like "Cigar shop" on them.

In Paris, with Ange, I don't have to be regularly in a hurry or show off my intelligence three times a day. I am detoxifying pathos, consumed in London with Val, from my system, and practicing letting go.

I feel at ease with Ange. He has always thought of himself as Jim with a splash of Andy. Turns out he's a male Meredith type of a personality. He is the kind of a person who comes up with a plan to conquer the world and then totally forgets about it in a drunk blackout.

"So, how's life?" Ange asks me.

We are having dinner at a typical Parisian cafe; any of the ones they show in movies—all true. Foie De Veau A La Lyonnaise and Ratatouille are so good that I forget the word "problems" ever existed. Wine's included, too, duh.

"Life is definitely...something," I reply.

"Dating anyone today?" Ange's English is sometimes precious for a writer.

"Not today, darling. Did yesterday, hopefully will do tomorrow."

"Tu fais Tinder á New York?"

"Unfortunately I do Tinder, yes. And guys send me all kinds of questions, like, *Mirra, what's your body like?*"

"Fabulous. Always fabulous." He accents on *ou*.

"They see my profile pictures, full height included. What's my body like? Very rubbable. Two legs, two arms, belly button, eyes that sparkle. Sometimes, almost right away they offer to get me an Uber to come by. Sounds like a sex delivery. Uber eats."

"Ahaha," Ange laughs like a true artist, theatrically throwing his head back, almost in slow motion, and then lights up a cigarette and sips his wine. He says he can't smoke without drinking something.

"Back in my cigarette smoking days, it was funny how someone who did drugs three times a week instead of weights lectured me on health consciousness," I say.

"Lectures are good at a university. Unless I'm paying for your lecture, merde, leave me alone!" Ange hates all kinds of unwanted opinions too.

"Sometimes it seems to me that guys go on dates just to have an excuse for their weakness of hard liquor."

"They've got wiskeyness," Ange notes. "Take me, for instance. I am drinking responsibly as in I am the only one responsible for my drinking."

"Drink responsibly. Ha! The whole point of drinking is lose all responsibilities. Cheers!" He's my inspiration, even though I always say that the creative artist in the family can only be me.

"There must be so many tipsy, incredibly lonely guys with a six-pack in New York," Ange waves his arm, nearly sloshing his wine on his jelly-belly.

"Oh, yeah. You'd be surprised."

"I would comfort them all and cheer them up and show them my...adorable personality. And then we would be so happy all together," Ange giggles. "Especially if they look like Jason Statham and smile, oy!"

"Jason Statham does not look good with a smile. He looks good with a Kalashnikov. I'm not a big fan. He's too short," I say.

"Statham is my height! I take offense!"

"Yes, you can." We burst out laughing.

Ange is one adorable queer boy. I gesticulate more when I'm with him, just like we all do when we spend time with people we love. We start copying them.

"So, no drama with a current boyfriend or anything like that from Mirra?"

"Sorry, darling. No current crazy dating stories. I can tell you my previous boyfriend story once again if you'd like."

"Hell no, that is way too dramatic for a little french man!" Ange drops his head in his hands.

"All of the stories were put together in one of my books. Oh, by the way! I joked in the book that the rock bottom of dating would have been meeting an ex convict and it actually happened for real. I unintentionally wrote it into the existence: I had a date with an ex convict."

"Whole new meaning for 'your ex'," Ange laughs.

"Guess what! I asked Jeremy Leven, the screen-writer of *The Notebook* movie to review my book, so that, you know, I could sell it better. He ended up slut shaming the protagonist of the book. I couldn't even take offense. Jeremy is a man in his mid eighties. He has no clue what's going on in the dating scene now. He dated back in the days when women did not have a right, an opinion, and a clitoris."

"How dare he!"

"I know!"

"I feel like I could piss out a book about art in two days, especially with a ghostwriter," Ange says.

"...I hear literally from everyone. We can talk our-selves into all kinds of false ideas. Just because you can text doesn't mean you can write. Same as if you read contents on a jar does not mean you're well read.

"Okay, Mirra, you're right. Writing a novel would be brutal."

"Mon cher, I've got a story for you. Once I had sex with a guy who was very short, like a hundred and fifty-seven centimeters. Do you think I can now delete midget from my list?"

"That'll do. And hey, I'll buy your book, I promise," Ange says defensively.

"Here's how to check whether your family and friends believe in you and will invest in you: try to sell them your independently published book for fifteen dollars, will you?"

"Mirra, now I feel bad."

"Meh, you don't even have to read it—you've heard pretty much every chapter exclusively from the au-thor," I say.

"How big is it?"

"Two hundred and seventy pages."

"I haven't read a book in four years or so. I'll wait for the movie."

"Ha. Good luck with that." I react.

"Why not make a long ass book—give people something to dive into fully to escape their lives?"

"Ange, those who write long books, like eight hundred pages, are either crazy or in prison."

"I don't think Tolstoy was in prison. But by your rubric he wrote like he spent a lifetime in prison."

"Nineteenth century had no Wi-Fi. You ought to kill time somehow." I say.

"What do you do these days? Are you working?" Ange changes the subject.

"Marketing and all that type of writing. Have to freelance just to pay the bills"

"I don't understand. What exactly do you write?"

"I write shit that runs on social media. The more idiocy the better. That's the requirement. Like, anti-aging shampoo, or a new breathable bra. Because, you know, other bras suffocate nipples. Everything has to be breathable these days. Bras are breathable, men's underwear is breathable, and we are suffocating in the era of so much breathable shit."

"That's funny. I don't get it," says Ange.

"Okay. I'll give you a sample promo of whatever to receive a free whatever that usually reads like this:

A great way to enjoy BRAND NAME for free—compliments of COMPANY NAME.

You are just a few steps away from totally loving BRAND NAME.

1. Download the BRAND NAME app from the App Store or Google Play.

2. Access your free account on the app to subscribe to BRAND NAME promo emails.

3. Check your email for a BRAND NAME coupon and next steps.

4. Share the BRAND NAME coupon to your Facebook profile.

5. Share the BRAND NAME coupon with ten close friends in messenger.

6. Pick up dry cleaning for the marketing manager of BRAND NAME.

7. Rate BRAND NAME on Amazon and Yelp.

8. Give a relaxing foot massage to a homeless person and live stream it to Instagram.

9. Also, take a selfie with the homeless person and post it on Twitter tagging BRAND NAME.

10. Enjoy a five percent discount at the online store of BRAND NAME***

*** Discount is applicable only from four to five in the morning on Monday, February twenty-ninth, from a traceable, cookies accepting IP address located in Alaska."

"It sounds stupid," Ange says.

"It sells." I shrug my shoulders, though I agree.

"Do you still write in the shower?"

"Yeah, I do most of my best thinking in the shower. What else do you have to do in there besides think? If only I had a secretary who'd write down from the other side of the bathroom curtain.

"Don't we all want a clone who would do all the

dirty work for us and feel all the bad feelings for us and be our worse version that we could compare ourselves to?"

I stare at Ange—he looks sad and in so much pain.

"How are you doing, darling? For real," I ask. I myself am actually doing great because I'm already drunk.

"The silence is slowly killing me," he says with all seriousness and takes a big sip. Anything to help you not feel alone.

We chew our food in silence, ironically. Ange is still alive.

"Silence is a clear message. It hurts, but if you can't change silence, you need to accept that. Have you tried to date others? Don't get me wrong, but he's not the only man in the city."

"I don't like others," Ange exclaims.

"What's wrong with them?"

"Nothing. Nothing is wrong with them. That's exactly the problem."

"Yeah, tell me about it..." I sigh. "We need more drunk."

Which we get of course, as we go on the loose with another bottle of Pisse-Dru Beaujolais like tomorrow is the end of the world. Well, if it is, then I definitely overpaid for the Persian lamp on eBay.

"Ange, what I don't get is when people don't reply to my messages and calls but view and like my shit on Instagram—what's that all about? They're interested in following my life but not actually talking to me?"

"Or interested in just fucking you, as a plan B. Who doesn't like to fuck an intelligent person?"

"But talking to her is erh, disgusting, right?" I roll my eyes.

"That is why, darling, I choose food—it is more exciting than sex."

"You're thirty-four, Ange! Thirty-four!"

"I recently had a threesome," Ange says.

"Oy?"

"I had three double chocolate brownies and I had them all, in my mouth, one by one."

"Ange... In that case, I'm a true artist of masturbation with a Master of Arts degree."

"Phew. Good. Because PhD sounds like an STD."

"The other day, I was 'practicing my art' and turned on porn. There was some spectacular cock on the screen. Very hot. It picked my interest, so I looked at a guy's face—very handsome. Both his cock and face could have been models for a girl's imagination. I even found and followed him on Instagram. He made me so happy a couple nights in a row. But then I noticed a band on his ring finger...and unfollowed him in all ways," I finish.

"*If you like it, then you shoulda put a ring on it,*" Ange sings. "Sex is being vindictive to me for no reason at all. I recently went on a date with a cute guy. We totally hit it off and agreed to meet again. The only problem is he is crazy busy the whole week and then he's undergoing through circumcision, which is awesome, but like six weeks of just talking for me?" Ange says.

"Oh, poor baby. I'll instantly make you feel better now. Look at me," I point at my oversized long puffer that makes me feel like I'm covered in a duvet in the street. "I'm wearing a sex repellent coat."

Ange laughs and continues.

"I am following this one guy on Instagram. He is so hot that I would very much love to sexually harass him. Maybe I'll send him a direct message sometime."

"Are you really gonna do it?" I ask.

"Nah, probably not. Do I want to do it and regret it or not do it and regret it? I choose the easy way—the second one."

"Sounds like someone has a crush. DM him, get to know him better. The best cure for love is knowledge. Just do it!"

"Don't Nike me!"

"It could be a happy ending," I encourage Ange to be adventurous.

"Oh, come on. It's not a Hollywood movie. He's an actor—it's blackout."

And we laugh hard. You always laugh harder when it's actually a hardcore crying situation—this way you're getting rid of scary boogieman a.k.a. babaika, and then absolutely destroying it with long-lasting hiccups.

"You are adorable," Ange moves over and kisses me on the cheek.

"Pfff, tell me something I don't know," I say and blush a little.

He takes it literally.

"Did you know that women in beauty pageants apply ointment from hemorrhoids to shrink the cellulite on their legs."

"Women put all kinds of crap on their bodies: creams, polymers, unfaithful partners..."

"Men do that too," Ange eye-rolls.

We get more wine.

"You know how women who obsessively want to get pregnant see only babies and other pregnant women in the streets because their focus is currently on that? So I'm just like that but with dogs: I see them, I pet them, I talk weirdly around them. A dog in your life can add warmth, humor and peace of mind. A dog can teach you empathy for others while keeping your secrets," I say.

"So does a boyfriend," concludes Ange. "Let's go to a boyfriend shelter and rescue one for each of us. They'll be traumatized by their mothers, not well socialized, but we'll bring them back to life."

"Nah, let's just wait a bit until Amazon delivers boyfriends. Speaking of which. Don't you think it is very infantilizing to call sex from behind 'doggy style'? Why on earth isn't it 'dog style?' Do you want to fucky wucky like a cutie wootie doggy?"

"Mirra..." Ange rolls his eyes.

I take a picture of him. Or better say fifteen to choose from: it's always nice to have an option.

"Mirra, I would love to see you drunk."

"Three drinks make me drunk."

"I mean like *drunk* drunk."

"That's kind of impossible for me—I start puking after fourth drink."

"I'd clean up after you."

"#truelove."

"Oh my god, that really is!" Ange takes a sip. "What brings you to Paris besides the fact that you missed me and haven't seen me in, like, forever, you curly cunt?"

"I'm looking for dunbing..." I hiccup.

"What?"

"*Funding!* Ange, I'm already so drunk."

"Awesome! What would you like to fund?" Ange, my drunken angel, seems barely tipsy.

It is extremely exhausting to drink with an alcoholic friend. I have no idea how he does all the drinking and is still himself. Those who drink to forget are actually setting themselves up for a tsunami of suffering. I feel sorry for what he's going through, the vicious cycle of obsession and compulsion, the level of which I can only imagine. Unfortunately, he's still adamant, on "don't even notice I am lying" mode—denial. Though he knows that when he's sick and tired of being sick and tired all the time, he can count on my support anytime. Unless you're in entertainment, you have no excuse to be an addict. But even then, still not a good enough excuse. Substances can give a feeling of temporary relief or support, but they can't be the actual solution to your problem. They can certainly add to one more problem though.

And there I am, drunk in Paris, and Ange's not. Or he seems to not be. He's a very good conspirator.

"I want to find an investor for my business," I reply. "Oops, I can't find my napkin. It was right here on my lap. Where did it go?" I start looking around the table.

"What type of business?" Ange asks but I don't listen to him and start saying what's on my mind.

"I know how I can find an investor. I need a casino chip! Lucky ten!" I finish the wine in one big gulp. "If only I had that, everything would be alright. I know it." My speech is slurred and overall it is not pretty at all. Drinking deletes reasoning and just makes me wanna dance. After the third drink the lady in me turns into a college sophomore that shamelessly pees in the street, although manages to collect her dignity.

"Darling, you've had too much wine," Ange says.

"Exactly! And that is why, my friend, we're going to Monaco! Yes! There's a casino in Monte Carlo! I need to get a ten-euro chip from there!" I almost yell.

"What would you do with it?" Ange asks.

"I'll just own it." I'm surprised Ange doesn't understand the obvious. My imagination is already overwhelmed. "Do you have ten euros? Let's go!"

"Where to?"

"To Monaco!"

"Mirra, let's go on a bender instead." He lazily leans back in his chair.

"Ange! Follow me. We're going to Monaco to get me the lucky casino chip."

Ange hurriedly pours the remaining wine from the bottle into his glass, then picks it up and drains it.

"My old stool"—Ange calls his car a stool—"is in repair now. We should take the train."

Thank god. Otherwise we'd be so dead. And even though driving drunk is like a computer game, we probably wouldn't even leave Paris without a car accident.

Because it's New Year's Eve and traffic is crazy, we're late for the last train and stay in Paris, joining Ange's friend Nikki. She's an art dealer and, surprisingly, broke. I've always thought that art dealers are like gays—they always have their finances figured out. A homosexual on welfare is like a jewish policeman— they're only in movies. Some stereotypes actually pay off, don't they?

Nikki's apartment is very artistic. It is small but tasteful. Above the sofa there's a cute painting that grabs my attention: a girl near the window watching the ocean. The mood of this art piece is so calming that I want to hug the frame.

There are other people at the party too, who come and leave so fast I can't even memorize their faces. That's what it means to be extraordinarily social— you're so preoccupied with making lots of acquaintances that you end up barely remembering them at all.

"To my first year in Paris." Nikki raises her glass.

"Nikki's from Germany," Ange says into my ear.

"Hopefully, I'll learn the subway station names this year," Nikki giggles.

"I'd like to know that story," I say.

"Well," Ange exclaims. "I think it was Nikki's second day in Paris and maybe third time in the Parisienne subway overall. We're waiting for our train at the station, Nikki sees the sign Sortie and exclaims: 'Ah! Sortie! I've been at this station before!' I laughed so hard I swear to god a little pee came out!"

"My first time ever in the New York subway I found myself on the train to Far Rockaway in Brooklyn. I was aiming to actually get to Greenwich Village in Manhattan," I say.

"You live in New York?" Nikki asks me.

"Yeah."

"You follow the American dream? I was trying to chase it too when I was down there in New York City," Nikki nostalgically rolls her eyes.

"You see, I don't have The American Dream. I just have regular dreams that ain't connected with location. New York is a city of my choice and my preference to live in. Well, currently. Maybe it'll change within time, who knows..."

Ange gives me a face and I understand that sometimes people ask questions only to answer them themselves.

"Anyway," I continue. "What was your American dream, Nikki?" I ask without realizing we all are about to be dragged into her panties.

Nikki's outfit makes her story a bit surreal because she's in a satin floral mid length dress, knitted socks, and toy puppy plush slippers. She wanted to be an artist and went to New York, where she ended up fulfilling other people's dreams as a sex worker. Nikki was a dominant at a sex club. She's pretty open about it and talks as if it's just another type of a job, like a cashier at Dunkin' Donuts—nothing special.

One of Nikki's regular clients had a Russian accent and a huge nose. Every month, he visited Nikki and tipped her generously for the things you might not even want to witness on even the nights you're most sexually open to experiments.

Then one day she chanced upon gay porn (as a staff training program I presume), starring this same guy, only thirty years back. He went by the nickname Pinocchio; and his movies, plural, were on different porn websites, available free of charge with the keyword Pinocchio. The things he did in those movies, Nikki says, oh mama!

I ask to see a short clip and there—my guess is approved. Pinocchio turns out to be a Ukrainian governor, a powerful oligarch well-known for being homophobic and rude and full of toxic masculinity. Ha. I had no idea he liked this type of fun. BDSM is one thing, I understand why he's doing it—to reverse the pressure of power. But porn movies? Well, that's new.

Nikki also mentions financial domination that was a part of her job. I find it fascinating that people will pay a lot of money to get humiliated and affronted. Financial domination fetish is quite hard for me to understand, because true domination would be a one time thing, "Hey! Give me all of your money and never call me again!"

Sex generates money. Money generates sex. I've always been convinced of that. And I don't mean literally, as a sex worker, although that's obvious. When you have regular sex or your personal life is stable and everything's okay in this area, your finances magically stabilize and grow too—you either find a new job or a passive source of income or get a successful investment. Similarly, when your career is going up or you get an exciting opportunity and you're feeling content having achieved what you wanted—your love life becomes richer or you start dating someone or you find yourself up for an adventure. All you've got to do is fix either one. All I've got to do is fix one to achieve the other.

The party doesn't last long, so Ange and I have plenty of time to rest before our train trip. Early in the morning, we sally forth. Adventures are always better when shared.

In his dream, Ostap Bender from "The Little Golden Calf" by Ilya Ilf and Yevgeny Petrov wanted to go to Rio de Janeiro to walk in white pants under the bright sun. I'm wearing orange pants and on my way to Monte Carlo. The only difference is that I am not a con man and I'm actually going.

On the train I open my laptop to write down a couple of ideas when the computer goes blank and never comes back to life. Most of the trip to Monaco I spend talking to customer support trying to revive it, but one thing is certain: the damn hard drive crashed.

"It is official. Today is January first and it's Monday. When, if not now, to start a new life, because all of my data is gone. Everything! I am so attached to the life I used to have! And now I can't recover my past. Something really awesome better happen like right now to balance this loss. Also, how am I supposed to replace all the dick pictures?" I say after the customer support line stops being supportive.

"You didn't back it up?" Ange asks a pretty logical question.

"I didn't have a precedent to start."

"You should get iCloud."

"What's the point now? I've got nothing to store there." I almost cry.

"Why do we need so much data anyway? I have screenshots of shit from five years ago and I'm pretty sure I wanted to do something with them back then and now who cares," Ange says.

A while back, in the time of my now unrecoverable

past, I used to let myself be sad for up to two days in a row, because after that it was the work week. Now, when I'm rarely sad, it only lasts up to five minutes—a sad song long. I turn on "Je suis malade" by Lara Fabian, I feel it, I cry, I'm over it. Just like in movies, except that there's no five-minute rain. I manage to feel miserable without necessarily getting soaking wet.

"Everything's going to change completely," I declare. "Three sixty."

"I'm not a mathematician but even I find it hilarious. Can you imagine a coach's slogan 'I will change your life three sixty'?"

"Ugh...I just heard it. I meant...You know what I meant," I sigh.

"I know. But it's still funny," Ange teases me.

That silliness cheers me up for a bit.

As it usually happens, one day all the pain becomes just a memory that fades away, like a dream or a book or last year's snow.

A little past two o'clock in the afternoon, Monte Carlo is like an apartment without a TV on—scary quiet. Ange and I head straight to the Casino de Monte-Carlo to get me the ten-euro chip. Inside, it is empty—there're only two dealers, a janitor, and a waiter. My plan to simply exchange ten euros into a chip fails, because there's a minimum required. So I go straight to the dealer and talk to him. At first he doesn't understand what I want but when he does, he starts explaining the impossibility of this exchange right at the table and that there are rules and so on and so forth. I'm still a little drunk because Ange and

I had Mimosas for breakfast. So I start bribing the dealer with a double price. He says no. Ange grabs my hand and starts pulling me away. Then I double the double. He says "no" again. Ange suggests we leave. When I reach one hundred euros for a ten-euro worth casino chip that I'm persuaded will bring me luck, the dealer loudly sighs and asks me why I need it so badly. Apparently he's not sure whether it's a sign of desperation or stubbornness or confidence that a piece of plastic can bring luck. It's all of it and none of it all at once.

"I don't know." I look at the dealer imploringly. "I just think that if I own it, everything will finally be fine in my life..." I'm about to give him a sissy, eloquent speech, like in a movie, when the character gets what she wants because the story is based on The Book of Empathy and everyone is so understanding.

But he just gives me a typical condescending smile, like all French people do, and hands me the chip so I'll leave him alone. And I do, leaving him ten euros. Ange can't believe what just happened. I kiss my chip and we exit the casino. With luck. The year starts amazingly.

We walk for a bit and then head to explore our lodging options in town and end up at a lovely yet affordable hotel that has available rooms due to the off-season. At the terrace, I notice a bunch of candles on the ground set up in the shape of a heart, and "Hunny-bunny, I love you" in the middle of it. Such sweetness makes me throw up in my mouth a little.

The terrace is empty except me and an impeccably dressed stranger at the next table and Ange, who is away at the moment getting us coffee.

"What are you hiding from here?" the stranger asks me.

"New York. Noise. New York," I reply.

"New York twice? Ha. I remember that feeling."

"Ever been there?"

"I used to live there. I still miss the city."

"Then why did you leave?"

"Let's just say, I am not welcome there anymore," the stranger replies.

"What are you hiding from here?" I ask him.

"My ex."

"So technically, you're hiding from the noise too," I conclude.

He smiles.

"You know, sometimes I don't understand what women want at all. What do women want?"

"Two things you should know about women: women with curly hair want straight hair, women with straight hair want curly hair. That's it."

"Now I know all."

He comes to my table, asks for permission to join, and sits down.

"Loris Monti. Nice to meet you."

"Mirra Vladi. My pleasure."

Loris Monti spits his accent like a dry Martini. Manolo Blahnik are obviously the best shoes for women, but their male version is what I call "shoes for pimps." If an animated character played Loris, it would definitely be a drake.

"What do you do when not hiding from noise in Monaco?" he asks.

"I write stories. For myself as novels and ghost-write for others helping share their stories as memoirs. Sometimes I write commercial texts, which I call very unnecessary productions."

"How exactly does ghostwriting work?"

"Here's a very simple explanation of what a ghost-writer is. You want to build a house but you have no idea how to do it yourself. You hire a professional to do that for you. You get the house you've always wanted and its ownership. Same as if you wanted to write your own book."

"I want that. My story is very sensitive though. Do you think you can manage that?"

"I'll make sure I have a handkerchief."

"Not that kind of sensitive." He grins. "The information is delicate," Loris says and excuses himself. "I'll explain what I mean in a moment," he says before leaving.

Oh my... Now he's gonna tell me his life story without paying the advance first. I can't stomach it. I like writing, but not for charity.

Ange comes with coffee and a birthday cupcake for me, singing "Joyeux Anniversaire," the French version of the "Happy Birthday" song.

"Awe, thank you darling!" I hug Ange. "I sort of forgot it's my birthday today."

"I will always remind you of your age." Ange winks and laughs.

"Ha-ha, thank you very much!"

"I got us a double room for one night. That's all they have left and frankly I don't want to go anywhere else." Ange hands me the second key to the room.

"No worries. We're staying here then." I take the key and put it in my backpack. "Now that I have the lucky ten, we both are going to be alright."

"Were you talking to that man who just left the terrace?" Ange asks.

"Yeah, he went to the bathroom. His name sounds very Italian. Linguini, Martini, Sardini, Fettucini, Cipriani..."

"Oh, my god! Loris Monti! I knew it was him! And please stop naming pasta—it makes me hungry." Ange rubs his belly.

"You know him?"

"As a matter of fact I do. Not him personally, but of him. Most of his family is in America. They have a chain of hotels and restaurants around the world. And he had to come back to Italy because of a tax fraud scandal, after which he's not allowed to enter the United States."

"How do you know all this?"

"It's a gift!" Ange pauses. "And gossip magazines."

Europe is not too big: if you sneeze in Spain, they say "bless you" from Portugal; and if you sneeze in Germany, it's rainy in Luxembourg the next day.

Loris comes back and joins me and Ange.

"Happy birthday, dear!" Loris says. "You will probably have a big party in New York."

"Yeah, probably. Though it'll be more like a get together type of dinner," I say. "I'm born on this one particular day. They call it a birth day for a reason. I'm born when I'm born and not on the nearest upcoming weekend when it's comfortable for everyone else to gather. So the time to celebrate my birthday is now."

"Mirra, do people tell you you're very forthright?"

"Some, not all. Because not all people are forthright to tell me that."

"She must be a good friend," Loris tells Ange.

"Definitely. Mirra is a keeper," Ange says, nodding along. "Loris, would you like to join us for dinner?"

"With pleasure. I don't have any other plans for tonight anyway. Unfortunately, I won't have time to buy a present," Loris says.

"It's okay. Forget about the present," I say.

"What? How can you forget about the present? No-no-no! You never forget about the present!" He suddenly throws his arms in the air in disagreement. Very Italian. So I obey. "When are you leaving?"

"Tomorrow at midday," I reply.

"For a present, I'll get you a helicopter transfer from the hotel to the airport. It's very convenient, saves you about an hour. You'll love it. I myself, like a little child, enjoy it every time."

"Thank you, Loris. I appreciate it." It does sound exciting indeed.

It is a pleasant dinner and enjoyable conversation. Ange is absolutely amused with the fact that he's eating in the company of someone he constantly reads about in the press. Loris says once he's ready for a book, he will call me. I take it as a no, which is fine. From now on, everything is going to be good no matter what. Suddenly, starting the new year and my personal new birth year, I'm not afraid and my inner core is as solid as the Earth's.

All day long I've been receiving texts with congratulations and wishes. Summing them up, blossom beauty—will have, find harmony—will do, dreams come true—will make, surprised with pleasant surprises—will be, write a lot—we'll see, be happy—certainly will. And I got a message from a graphic designer who eight months ago promised to create artwork for my book and disappeared.

"Mirra, Happy Birthday! I wish you to be surrounded only by good people and not assholes like me," he wrote.

Wow, things start to come true "prettay prettay prettay" fast.

The next day, as promised, our transfer is waiting. Ange starts laughing as the helicopter takes off.

"Mirra, this is so fucking you!"

"I guess my lucky ten started working." I take my ten-euro casino chip out of my backpack, kiss it and put back into the side pocket.

"How do you even manage to travel if you're broke?" Ange asks me.

"Honestly? I have no fucking clue. I'm lucky? I've got friends everywhere? And now I have one more: Loris Monti?"

"Questioning?"

"I question a lot of obvious things, darling. One thing is for sure—I love you." I kiss Ange on the cheek. "Come visit me in New York sometime. Don't be a stranger."

"Fine, you curly cunt. Will do soon." Ange hugs me tight.

We leave Monaco on a positive note.

"Holy anal! Seriously, Mirra," Ange says. It is

overwhelming even for an artist of his calibre. "How the fuck do you do this?"

"Oh, you mean making arrangements about a start up investment, then befriending someone in one of the richest countries in the world who's persona non grata in the United States, taking a helicopter transfer to the airport where the plane will take me to the city where I have no permanent resident address? Do this? I don't know. Because I don't care? Isn't that the way it works? When you diminish something very meaningful to you, you get it. And the lucky ten-euro casino chip of course!" I give Ange an intentionally fake smile and even believe my own speech myself.

"The thing is, never to be too anxious. Everything comes in due time," Henry Miller wrote. And if it doesn't—oh well, fuck it, I add. This is my golden rule.

Val is right. New York is a better place to find investment. And Steve Jobs was right. "You have to work not twelve hours, and head." It is time to go back home.

How actually great it is to be an adult! I smile fastening my seat belt on the plane. I am an adult.

Memorize the day, memorize the feelings, everything's changing and you are not an exception.

When I land in New York, tired and hungover, with five thousand dollars that Ange lent me and only one thought: rent a hotel, take a shower, and sleep—Val calls me.

"Mirra, is that what you really want to do?"

"Yes, Val! Sleep is what I really want to do now."

"I meant your start up, silly."

"I believe in this project, which is absolutely fantastic—both kind of fanciful and extraordinarily good. And also, what's the worst that's gonna happen if I try?"

"When you left I gave it a thought and went through your business plan again. It makes sense on a much higher level than just selling ads and subscriptions. If used right, it's basically controlling all informational flows in the country—a power tool."

"I know. That's what I said."

"You got it. I'll fund you."

"What, just like that? Easily? Out of nowhere?" *Whoa, Val was right indeed. It is easy to find investment in New York.*

"It doesn't necessarily always have to be hard."

"Fair. I didn't even know you had that kind of money."

"Yeah, I've been saving on shoes for a while."

"Val, if you're willing to invest, maybe you can do stocks or bonds or futures."

"I do futures whenever I feel like losing money. Besides, I don't believe in the importance of rice, I believe in people, especially if they're my friend Mirra. But you have to understand that only quality can make money in the long run."

"Only what's in my own demand basket, same quality I'd choose for myself. You know that."

I am still stunned with Val's proposal and can't find a reason or an explanation for why she's doing it. So I ask.

"Val, why are you doing this?"

"Because..."

"Because what?"

"That was the end of sentence. Just because."

"I'll take that."

In New York, when you see a girl with luggage, she might be coming back from a trip. Or from a laundromat.

While Renat Novak, my web developer, creates the online Club, I write the copy and design the logo. Then I open an LLC and find a beautiful, hardworking lawyer Paul Triggs to compile the most important document—terms and conditions. No doubt he's hardworking—his shirt is wrinkled in the back because he sits a lot, buried in documents and files. There's also Lada Lembas, my very talented sales pro in Kiev. She is so good at talking and presenting the necessity of the Club, besides doing all the leg work, that I feel glad knowing how to recruit personnel. And Victor Maly, a twenty-five-year-old social media marketing artist of God level with the three-kids-in-a-trench-coat personality.

It is super exciting to create something I care about and like, so I work with abandon. Just like with story creation, the business requires zeal. Turns out my depressive mood was very situational—it was a signal about my emotional discomfort, cry for change; and all I needed was to realize my full potential and apply myself to fulfill it. Being content is an incredible feeling. On a sunny day, so sunny I screw my eyes up even in sunglasses, I'm in a car going fast on the highway, a song that I like is on maximum volume, and I sing along. That's contentment in its purity—a natural high. So this natural high lasts as long as you're occupied with what you want. And I start doing

balance exercises on a stability ball. Balance and stability—exactly what I need at this point.

Less is more. Quality over quantity. I switch to
minimalistic lifestyle overall, not only with things that
I use but also with people that are in my intimacy circle. One hundred things and one hundred people—
that is the number you can maintain without losing
the quality of it. Also, I don't make trivial decisions
anymore—it's just a waist of time. I like my coffee
black, water sparkling, shoes Italian, friends decent,
love reciprocal. So when I do have to make an important decision, I do it with a full store of energy and not
impulsively. Also, no more online shopping. Well, almost. I still keep the account in case I really need
something and circumstances don't let me go to a
store. In general, my interest in shopping has faded.
Online shopping erases the whole experience you
could have by making a day out of it. Things start
happening once you leave your apartment and shopping can still be an event with meeting people and socializing and walking (which is always a good idea regardless of anything). But browsing online, going
through endless options is tiring, overwhelming and
very time consuming: you're looking for a new dress
and then bam! Four hours have passed and you forgot
what it is you even wanted to buy. Eliminating things
in your life that don't lead to happiness is generally a
good idea.

We don't create a space of love—we desperately
create a space of unneeded stuff. And then more space
for more stuff. Some rent storage space or even a sep-
arate apartment just to keep their stuff there. No In-

stagram filter applied for hoarding. Love is the only thing that matters. It can't be adjusted at a tailor's. When the very thought of something and someone you love makes you smile, then you know you're on the right path. Love more than even. Love is the best a person can do. You can only give a certain number of fucks. So make sure it's for something that matters. I throw away all the unnecessary stuff in my life to empty space: clothes, books, annoying people. It all is here: bad friends, good enemies, mediocre nothing. Cheers! Thank you. And goodbye. It feels so liberating.

It's been long enough that I do not feel like doing laundry, so I just start buying new shit. I also so do not feel like cleaning. I guess I'll buy new shit, in a new apartment and be the dirtiest girl in everything clean. Which I do—I get lucky with a beautiful top floor apartment in Tribeca that becomes my rented comfort mecca. A pigeon once sits on my fire escape. I wave my hand and say hi. And it lifts its leg and waves it too! Must be a tourist pigeon.

I love Tribeca. It's very neighborly. I have my pizza guy who looks like George Carlin and flirts with me in a sweet way, my deli guy who always asks me how I'm doing and means it, my the-best-in-the-city massage girl who barely speaks English but always understands me. And there's a mystery happening at my building entrance: one ridiculous object lying on the ground and it is changing every day. So far, I've seen a radiator, a wok pan, a book, an apple, and a full pack of cigarettes. Kind of keeps you wonder so you go outside to check on what it is going to be there today, and then naturally you go for a walk. This could be a state program to fight online addiction or loneliness.

Something is seriously wrong with priorities. We went to the Moon and are going to Mars soon yet there are no washing machines in most apartments in this city!

A happy apartment can lack in a balcony or a washing machine, but it absolutely has to have a walk-in kitchen. The most important human issues are usually solved in the kitchen. Myriad interpersonal relationship services can be purchased for money, including empathy (scheduled by appointment hourly), but sometimes even a shrink's office, the temple of sedation and whining, can do nought. Combining the two small spaces, a kitchen and a room, into one large and spacious living room is undoubtedly an excellent design solution. But the kitchen is still where the most interesting things in life happen: from gossip to making big plans for the future. Fate and destiny are decided in the kitchen. Perhaps, for a happy life all you need is a walk-in space with a teapot?

My apartment has minimum furniture but maximum of space and light. The dust has almost nowhere to settle except on the floor. My cleaning lady and my inner Mister Proper are super happy about that. I have a high-quality bed and many bounties. A huge wall clock, that goes backwards to signify the time that never comes back, occupies the full wall. Another wall in my studio is decorated with a vinyl banner of my Instagram pictures posted during the two years that I used the app. I no longer do for a number of reasons. It is so much easier to love yourself without Instagram. I do not need to constantly know what everyone else is doing. And frankly, I could not care less about other people's babies. Living in a constant content flow is like trudging through a locust invasion. I plugged out and now I have more time to do whatever myself rather than watching whatever anyone has already done and bragging about it. I stoped caring about online presence and started caring about my presence in the moment. For me, it is more enjoyable to share life experiences with someone and follow your passion rather than follow and share content online. Social media is like high school on steroids trying to figure out who's the coolest kid. I find it useless to have other people tell me I'm cool. I'm cool despite what others say. I'm my own brand recognition.

Everyone's a brand. What significantly differs one brand from another is confidence. I am a good example of a professional amateur who's not embarrassed to do what I want and enjoy it and have so much fun in the meantime. That's also my way of playing chess. Eventually, I want to win every game, but it is so delightful actually playing that the result does not seem all that important. Not expecting anything from myself makes the process so easy. Ninety-nine percent of the population of the planet is much better versed in everything, knows exactly how to do everything better and clearly sees the mistakes in projects, undertakings, and ideas of others. Their ideas are fresher, newer, more interesting, and more innovative than others'. But only one percent proceeds and gets going, makes mistakes, releases something very raw, a beta version, crooked. Then fixes it, receives critics, gets blown to smithereens and yet the other ninety-nine percent still use it. Because all they know is how to do things right, not actually do them. That one percent are not complete psychos. They too fear failure and lack confidence. But they do it anyway. They make things happen.

Accidentally or not, people-drafts show up in your life. Maybe they are your subconsciousness, maybe they are just crappy people who create nothing but chaos wherever they go. They say you won't make it, they seed hesitancy, they envy your agility and creativity. I ignore them and keep doing what I'm doing.

"No, it's a bad idea. It's not going to work out. You're fooling yourself!" they insist.

"I heard you the first time. But I'm going to do what I want to do anyway. Now will you please leave me alone?"

People-drafts follow you anyway, trying to punch your Achilles' heel—they know everything about you thus try to sabotage you. They tread on your heels, but I'm very ticklish on my feet so I kick the drafts, accidentally or not. It's their fault they started it first. They didn't calculate one important thing in their sly plan: I don't care about what they think. So none of this matters.

Talent can't be without a doubt. That's always a package deal. Suppose you buy a book of Bukowski and the bookstore gives you a literary collection of Lugansk poetry with it for free, but you can't not take it. That's the package deal. Talent and doubt. That's how anything big is created, because it's never good enough so you keep working towards your ideal. Is it neurotic? Absolutely. But that's what moves you, that's how art is created, that's what civilizations were built on. All it takes is one's ego and people-drafts. *Oh, you laugh at me and say I won't make it? You'll see, sweetie.*

Before my London trip, I asked a male friend, who's a pretty successful businessman, which funding option would fit best my startup idea and would actually bring investment in. I was pondering over venture capitalists. He recommended I put on a mini skirt, high heels and find myself a sugar daddy. Scowl. Friendship divorce! According to his logic he did a lot of sucking to get his IT company rolling.

Whatever you do and no matter how badly you do it, there will always be a market for it and your target audience turned consumers. There is no competition—it simply doesn't exist. As simple as that. Your market can be far from you, in a different time zone and informational space. That's it. Change your location services, move on and do it. Right the fuck now.

And maybe, just maybe, disable your social media. You'll see how things magically change after you detox from the endless stream of content, constant hum of voices online. Not everyone needs to know everyone. I mean, we're not even following people on social media anymore—we actually spend our time unfollowing them. Because it is cool to not follow that many of them. Like, who are all these people? Most aren't even people. Just check your Facebook notifications: you have been added to the group Permanent Eyebrows, Sally Microblading, Psychic Madame Bella,

Philadelphia Ceramics, DIY Plastic Surgery, Apartments for Rent in Afghanistan, Laughter Funny Laughter, Women XXXL and Proud, Women With Children XXXL and Proud, Hiking in Europe, Chicago Cowboy, Secret Best Events in Town, Hair Nails And Other Body Parts Extensions, and A Woman Dental Technician.

We all have become digital hoarders. And if you open your phone contact book, you won't remember half of those people you supposedly know. Like who the hell is Christina armchair? I don't even have an armchair. Or Jonathan 34? Must have been some very significant people in my life. No matter how deeply I escaped into a life full of illusions, pretentiousness and virtuality—I can only feel the real me when I'm alone. All social networks are an attempt to distance yourself from reality as far as possible. It is always easier to hide behind the flow of information, just absorbing it and disappearing in it. It is so much easier to live like that—less of yourself, less responsibility for your life. And the illusion that you're living to the fullest. While online, scrolling, it seems you can travel endlessly, get new experiences, and deny loneliness. Scrolling through social media can be harmful because it erases your critical thinking. Everything seems happy on Instagram, doesn't it? The most marketed good today is illusion. Critical thinking is a very useful tool. Unfortunately, life suggests multiple ways to numb this extremely important skill. Alcohol, drugs, and compromises are an ideal way to lock yourself out of your brain; if done repeatedly for a long time, you lose this most valuable brain function forever. Critical thinking and questioning does not mean judgement, which is very much condemned. You can also take the path of least resistance—smoke weed and masturbate, sleep, for instance. You will feel lost. You will look lost. Remember Eminem's face on Relapse album cover? Extremely sensitive, scared, tired, depressed, cautious, out of place. Wake up. Hey. Hey! Wake up! There's a whole group of people in this world who don't think April twentieth is a holiday. You've got plenty of time ahead to be cured of your choices. When you stop thinking critically, you can't figure out what's wrong and what's right thus you become a victim, and easy target for manipulation, be it customized suggestions on Amazon or an artificially-created reality—your personal Truman show. Sometimes, systems have errors; and if you don't have truth to base your reality on, you can go crazy.

Your mind is pretty rational when not influenced by substances and media. It's a machine that can be programmed and you choose your software and your upgrade. Open your eyes. Open your eyes. Your sky doesn't have to be vanilla for that.

Realization of a dream is like the ability to walk—a skill. Try to think about how exactly you take a step, try to control each muscle and you will not move an inch. The ability to walk is programmed since birth; the ability to move forward is obtained when you learn to fall, clumsily stagger, crawl forward, then get up on two steady feet the way nature intended. Actually, nature has created us to be happy by default. It's just that in our attempts to control everything we often interfere with it. Everything, meaning life, people, yourself. To walk, it is important to learn to trust your body and believe in your innate skill. Let yourself be in the flow.

Creating dreams is so easy. Making dreams come true is so easy. You just have to want to want it.

We, humans, are stronger than we think we are, morally stronger. We are capable of changing dramatically, instantly, completely, of rebuilding everything from the decision-making process to lifestyle, priorities, principles, in a matter of moment. Nothing is impossible. When you really want something, you will get it. Like love—you just know it.

Sincere desire is the most honest and, surprisingly, simplest way to set life priorities. Just start doing something!

Money can't buy happiness. True. Although, being depressed in Paris is much more fun than in Yorkville, Manhattan. We easily accept our misery in foreign places but not where we're most comfortable. Mystery of the unknown appeals more not because the grass is greener somewhere else. It is stress and the mechanism of survival in a foreign place that helps us forget about our problems of a higher, emotional level. Therefore, we go back to the easier level of physiological needs. Maslow's pyramid is like a real life computer game: impossible to get to the next level without passing all the previous. And the grass is greenest where you choose to water it.

What is happiness to you? What is happiness for you? How long does it last? Are you happy? I asked these questions to everyone I knew. I was looking for my own happiness, living life with one existential crisis at a time. I used to think that happiness is a moment, like the live photo feature on iPhone. Now I think happiness is a process with its ups and downs but constant confidence in knowing that you can figure things out anytime, because you know you can. Happiness is in balance.

I could never do without the peculiar feeling that things will ultimately work out. It is difficult to write about this feeling. If you have it—you have it, if you don't—you don't, no matter how hard you try to pretend. When you come closer to the real you, you get a chance to deal with feelings, and you give them a chance. You will become vulnerable as you have never been in your life. You will experience emotions that you were previously unaware of. You recognize yourself, you deal with yourself, and you discover yourself again: the new you, amazing and unexpected. Confident.

I know it like no one else: it is very difficult to fall asleep every day with complete confidence that you are doing everything right in your life, despite how incredibly hard it is to be confident no matter what. What do you see when you close your eyes? That itself makes you feel calm and content, and thus a moveable feast. When a feeling of a holiday becomes a habit, you find yourself on a constant wave of luck.

Confidence lives in the shoulders. Your stoop forms in your mind. Straighten up! Anything is possible when you believe in yourself. Just do it. Nike didn't pay me for this. I actually believe in it. Advice for beginners—begin. You are going to want to give up. Don't! You walking in a corn field and someone powerful drives by and throws a multi-million con-tract at you—it's not going to happen that way. But with just a little bit of effort on your end things will get done. Even to mold an obscene word from plas-ticine, you have to make some effort. Though some-times, to get what you want all you have to do is re-spectfully use the magic word "please." It still works, too.

After you figure out something very important about yourself, after you relive your patterns again, you'll feel incredibly strong knowing you're actually in control of your own life, as it has always been, as it is supposed to be.

Health, confidence, mental comfort—these are the main three things we all need to feel content.

The world doesn't owe you shit, but you can take what you want. It's right there—just let yourself have it. And start finally doing something. It really hit me: I've got it all! I can do literally anything I want, any-time, anywhere. Why? First and foremost, who gives a shit. And most importantly, nobody really gives a shit. God bless. A salute. You're welcome.

First thing on the "I can do anything" agenda is my business InfoPro.Club; ironically, in technology while I'm staying away from technology. Contradictions...of course, life is full of them.

Just like anything else, technology can be good as well as bad at the same time, depending on how you look at it and use it. Driverless car, Alexa telling you what you like, catalogs of people online like it's Pot-tery Barn. We already call on a watch, use computer for calls and a phone for anything but calls; and soon will sync bacon with earrings and are close to charging shoes. (They will probably market a new version of roller skates—connect a pair of sneakers with an electric scooter). If you can't force your stupid driverless car to drive over the speed limit, is that really the world you want to live in? What's next? Stop talking and communicate through texts only? We're half way there. Stop it! Sorry, technology. You're great, but the world is more exciting than your algorithms can analyze.

I don't buy things that advertise as more than: "It's more than just a yogurt," "It's more than just a car," "It's more than just a picture frame." No it's not. It's literally just that. No more, no less, just lots of fuss.

Marketing today is reintroducing what has already been created. Uber Pool is just a version of a bus to prove that.

Any new approach to showcase the existing product or service can go from viral to trending to mainstream. What a brilliant marketing move—to write the content of wheat on bakery products. You can also measure it, say how much bigger your ass will grow in a year if you eat these cookies—you know, the actual audience numbers.

Everything is exclusive these days, nothing is regular. Especially in New York, in this impersonal city, everything's advertised as custom-tailored, bespoke, and personalized.

The news are always so exclusive, even more exclusive than jackets of Elton John.

The paradox of the contemporary life is news are exciting and the world is not. Next time you see in the news "according to our source"—know that PR and Journalist bundled up.

"If you can't write, don't write," Ernest Hemingway said. Therefore it's better not to do anything to not regret it.

Journalists form mass opinion, whether they realize it or not. Most of them aren't even professional journalists—they are bloggers, who pass on their judgement, sometimes wrong, into masses. Just because you can use an Oxford comma correctly doesn't mean that your opinion is valid. Some people are not worth listening to. And in the grand scheme of things, some people are not as important as they think they are. Besides, it's not journalists who produce news—it's public relations folks, the bullshit junction between media and people. There's always someone who gives journalists news to report on. And there's always someone who provides public relations professionals with the news to give to the media.

To be a professional journalist now means more likes and views, and not ethics and responsibility. An expert opinion now is anyone with more than five thousand followers on any social media platform, fact check is a Twitter post and two reliable sources is a shared Twitter post more than once. Bloggers can write well but the actual journalistic story differs from a listicle like "7 Reasons Why You Should Eat Apples Everyday", "You're Probably Making These Common Communication Mistakes. Here Are 3 Ways To Fix Them", "30 Products That Won't Leave You Waitin' For Results", "Here's How To Tell Within 10 Seconds If You're About To Spend More Money", "My Friend

Looks 10 Years Younger Than She Is, So I did Her Skincare For 5 Months". I take offense that those writers treat me like an idiot. It'd be so nice to have at least one week when the news doesn't use the word "unprecedented".

All media are owned by someone. It's still a business after all, that needs more readers and shares and likes and followers that convert into subscribers that become ads audience which is cash. The worse—the better is the typical daily news. Sensation, fear, terrifying headlines—that's what sells the best. News on TV follow a specific pattern: hysterical chronicles, historical chronicles, chronic hysterics, and about the weather. Weather is also bad news, always. Hurricane, tsunami, snow storm, strong wind, thunderstorms, humidity, high pressure, and finally air quality. It's a rollercoaster of information. To translate it to something mundane, the rollercoaster of feelings goes from "hey, let's make out" to "everyone leave me alone".

Read the news, get anxious, drink alcohol to feel better, read more news because you're feeling slightly better, drink more alcohol to south your anxiety... you get the cycle.

I once had an argument about inequality in salaries with a guy at my previous office, the only pros of which was a chessboard. Trying to prove me wrong, with a face expression of a winner, he sent me links to blogs! The winner here is the obvious—blogs that have already formed his opinion and will make him buy more stuff than he actually needs.

If you're a doctor with a YouTube channel, I won't

make an appointment with you. Sure, being a go-to med expert, a talking head for the media is also a career. Or, if you want to be famous—go to Bachelor or something. Actual good doctors don't have time for blogging.

So consuming the news, critical thinking and questioning might be of use, unlike a bottle of rosé. Besides, a person with "two double triples on the rocks" in them becomes not pretty at all.

If you suffer from anxiety or suddenly started to feel more anxious than usual, put down alcohol and turn off the news. Both increase anxiety tremendously, thus increase sales of stuff to make you feel better—pay for Prime to get it delivered faster.

I never consume news in the evening, moreover not before bed; only in the morning and not more than five major stories. After that it is very easy to get lost in the endless content streams where you're vulnerable and unprotected from information influence and your own imagination. CDC won't recommend news consumption in moderation, or define moderation. And it's not like you can use a condom from content. Whenever I hear someone states to be a news junkie I conclude two things: the person is subject to manipulation, prone to anxiety.

Professional journalism today is like a virus. The information quickly "heats up" and spreads, and it's not necessarily of high quality; not to mention the websites that rewrite already rewritten news. The message should be the simpler the better, so the masses can understand it, consume it and come back for more. The best way for the media to get traffic is to publish as much as possible. Sensation, extremism, sex, scandal, hatred—this is what's sold best and fastest. So they keep selling it, so the wholesalers of news keep pitching these to the media. Tackle topical issues such as the growing rich-poor gap, racism, climate change, sexual abuse, migration, human trafficking, political polarization and relations among Christians, Muslims and Jews—the never ending news. Professional writers and reporters don't make a lot of money for their work, so it's understandable they are trying their best at writing stories that will create resonance thus more views. It's all done at cost of quality of writing and mental health of a story consumer. Although, some journalists are so lazy that once they receive a press release they publish the exact copy paste of it. Less quality, more quantity. Traffic, traffic, traffic! And lots and lots of reposts on Facebook. Extra scandals, discussions and rumors that excite imagination are always welcome.

If a story was published then the facts in it are true. A news consumer does not check the trustworthiness of the news because the media is supposedly responsible for that. Even media pros sometimes don't bother to fact check. Most importantly, grab the attention and then figure it out. Anytime you see "The story is being updated" it means that their only source isn't reliable and they are waiting for more information to come anytime soon; and maybe then fact check by some media expert who's trying to build their career on giving out opinions.

When we receive conflicting information, which we cannot verify, we tend to give preference to the one

that came first. When we receive consistent information, we give preference to the one that came last. But
media doesn't make mistakes: they make updates—
news about news.

Now self-respected media quote social media accounts of people as the official source of information;
and not the accounts of officials like President or
Prime Minister or Secretary of State, chief of FBI,
healthcare executive or Elon Musk—just random
John Smiths. Facebook and Twitter became the new
Reuters. "Today on the Avenue Street something bad
happened, as the good citizen Smith writes on his
page. He was going to the supermarket to buy some
milk and became a witness of something horrifying,
but we're still not sure what exactly. Stay tuned,"
shares a media outlet on their page. And then, according to the herd principle, office workers and hipsters
with a touch of glamor and those who eat bologna
sandwiches share what the media has shared. They
are a unified portrait, metadata of the mass, that
forms anything: from lines at Starbucks to coups.
More self-aware than before, they are still sucked into
content: producing or consuming it. This is the new
professional ladder of the twenty-first century—you
only consume content if you're a nobody and you first
consume and then produce content if you think you're
a somebody. What distinguishes them among themselves is the amount of their followers online. Leaders
of opinions control the consciousness of the audience
from the page of their account, at the same time being
a resource themselves, ready to perform its function
on demand, even without knowing about it. Regard-

less of their followers number or advertising money, which has made some rich, both content consumers and content producers are equally stupid. Trapped by vanity, they all have common vices, psychological traumas, reactions.

Social networks—a form of socialism making you believe that everyone is equal. You have a voice, you can contact anyone, your opinion matters. Yet the very visible difference is "friends" and followers. It's cruel. Social networks bring out the worst in people. The only equality existing today is the influence of alcohol on people regardless of their status, looks, and background; no exception. Some use substances like they don't care their children might be born with intellectual disability. According to the Diagnostic and Statistical Manual of Mental Disorders males are more likely than females to be diagnosed with both mild and severe forms of intellectual disability, which is funny because there are still some men who think they are smarter than women purely based on their gender. Although, this is a story about different type of equality and not now. Back to the vanity fair.

The more a user spends time online the more comfortable they feel thus the more they believe in what is happening there. And the user themself becomes more trustworthy to others. The news create a pseudo environment, but the person's reaction to it is very real. Internet community is a unique space where everyone thinks they are an expert of something. Online, anyone behaves pompously as they believe they should, as if being a celebrity. They fill up the Internet with their filtered emotions in forms of pictures and advices, sincerely thinking that the high reels of their lives are interesting. They utter droplets of their thoughts with such importance it seems they're about to have nosebleeds and lose consciousness. The caste of likers jerks off at their own personality and value in the virtual society, and participates in speed racing, where a person competes with the cell phone. Moreover, they seriously believe that there are two opinions: objective and subjective. How naive.

Craving a minute of fame, they are chasing long-lasting glamour lifestyle but easily settle for a quick hype—sell their opinion in exchange for a two-minute news broadcast.

Eighty-nine percent of journalists search for stories on blogs, forums, and news feeds of their social media accounts.

The function of a PR professional today is not just to try to make people talk about the PR object but also to provide crisis management in case people talk about the PR object in an undesirable context. There is nothing to be afraid of, if you are nobody for the community, internet, media. But even in this case... who knows. As a satire writer Mikhail Zhvanetsky said: "One accidental move and you're a father." One accidental move—and you're bullied; or a trending star...either one, who knows.

Once journalists and PR pros start using the Club and stick to it, they automatically become its promoters whether they want it or not. Audiences can be converted into profit in different ways.

News is a drug and media space is a drug dealer that influences your life decisions. Hook them on that drug and you can make people do anything, from a movement of the newly created activity, and accustom to any new rule or tradition. Carrot and stick motivational approach, where stick is playing on your insecurities and carrot is making you release dopamine, but not too much so the next day you do it all over again. That's how Facebook works, and a lot of other companies as well.

Suppose, you hate your job so much that you'd rather go finger painting but that activity doesn't pay the bills. Just like Thursday is movies premier night, finger paint should be a new regular activity, say on Tuesday. First it'll be unusual for people, they might even call it a disorder, then there'll be a parade ending at Home Depot with mass splashes. There might be protests down the line, "Yellow Paint Matters" or something like that. And at the end orange and orange paints will get married, kids will want to become paint fingerer, celebrities will promote paint fingering on their Instagram. It will become the new normal and soon enough the mainstream. Habit forming of consciousness. Truth can be adjusted so you stream more ads and do more product placement. It's like a mythical god in action—insanely scary.

It's enough that social networks already make people feel stupid, frigid impotent and loser at the same time. The Internet community of voyeurists and exhibitionists, two in one, in desire to win the rat race (followers)—will trample anyone. Anyone with a different opinion, anyone who doesn't express their opinion publicly, anyone who doesn't express their opinion strong enough, or what is expected at this given moment of what's wrong and what's right. Usually, the internet community creates the idol, puts it up on the pedestal, envies it, hates it, fiercely destroys it. Narcissism 101.

Online bulling and public shaming and cancel rituals have become so common that it's basically pop culture. Becoming (or forcefully pushing into?) pop culture is one of the ways to normalize anything yet unacceptable in the society. For instance, in the form of a song, the lyrics of which are very stupid and actually offensive to women but the beat is so sexy that you want to move your hips, singing along to it; or in the form of a movie, where a man hits the wall next to a woman's face in the middle of a fight. Abuse as it is, ladies and gentlemen, mistakenly taken for strong passion.

Humor is also one of the powerful ways a culture passes on its values. Why silence what's actually important? What values do we have now to pass to the next generations? Ghosting, narcissism, and thrift jeans with high waist? With the development of technology and AI and generally unsatisfactory education level of most of individuals it's almost like people are asking to be told what to do so they don't have to bother and can keep chilling. The principle of a multiple choice test prevents you from creative thinking. Luckily, there're still people who think wider than Shakespeare is A) tractor; B) writer; C) body mass index; D) cupcake.

Mental differences are smoothed out in the crowd. Herd effect. It's easier to manipulate the human mind in the crowd where consciousness of personal "me" become mass "we." Knowingly lie if needed to blend in with the crowd—a natural instinct to survive. One who cannot stand conflicts easily submits to authorities. A crowd online, like in a group on Facebook, also counts. Online can turn into offline within minutes. Although people in a group are not as good as individually, we tend to want to belong to a certain community, be associated with something, be in the caste, for self identification mostly; be it a group of shared religious views, stay-at-home moms, aspiring entrepreneurs, brown-eyed blondes, or fans of parsley. You don't want to be free. You just want to be a follower. Created set of rules to obey helps with the development of the herd instinct. Just not too cruel—nobody wants to suffer, not too much freedom—give three options of choice and call it empowerment. It works on every level of the human rat race. The diet of the cardinals during the papal conclave is an illustrative example: up to three days is no different from the usual, after three days of elections—one meal per day is allowed, after five days—only bread, wine and water. Interestingly, since the beginning of the twentieth century until today, the pontiff is elected within two-three days tops.

We form groups based on shared interested, views, and believes, which is important in terms of community needs but it automatically creates certain demographics, making it easier to use for profit— financial or ideological. Let people identify with something big. And you'll get your following fanbase. Yet, we think we want to be unique and differ, be a little weird, but not too much, a reduced offer, a self-made limited edition so the demand increases; just like the American dream. The effect is everything, an illusion, an impression. Quite awhile ago, there used to be a test on Facebook "Find out how unique you are", the result of which was of course "You are among two percent of people with non-standard thinking and lack of herd instinct. You are free in your choice." The test proved that human psychology is not unique. This is the only field where we are all equal, actually. The total number of people who have taken and shared the test was (ta-da!) eighteen million. Talk about uniqueness...

Someone has to say that something is cool so the crowd will want it too. Why do you think you read reviews for anything before purchase? Who actually wrote them? Or comments about politics on Facebook? Why does anyone ever share news on their page? Ayooo! Exactly. If only the majority of an opinion was always the right one. Freedom of choice. Democracy, you say. Who's behind the public opinion and what's their end goal, I question. Who's programming you and what kind of program is it? Beta version or an updated version of a stable release? Who's the producer today?

AWARD-WANTING WRITER

On a shitty cold February day, I finally decide to do something I have always wanted to try but never did—an open mic. Not that I am thinking of starting my career as a stand up comedian at thirty-four, but getting embarrassed in front of a small audience of not so funny folks has been on my bucket list for sure. People volunteer for homelessness or disability. Apparently, for years I've been supporting depression—twenty dollars plus two drinks minimum at every comedy club. Ha! I learned the history of comedy in this country before the history of this country. So it means a lot to me.

The pedestrian street light near my building has always showed red every time I was at the crossroad, regardless of the time of the day. But it is green right now. Something is suddenly different, a new direction and seems like I need it. Let's see where this goes.

At seven o'clock I enter The Grisly Bar in Greenwich Village, ready to step out of my comfort zone and rush into the anxiety zone. My set starts with the following: "Hi, my name's Mirra. I'm one of those people whose friends said I should do stand up because I'm so funny. Now, let's prove them wrong, shall we?"

Then I mention that I use online shopping—it is called Tinder. And that there is nothing to be ashamed of for using online dating. We all have those apps on our phones. It is like herpes—we all get it at some point.

On the stage, I feel like my eyes are bleeding because of the too damn bright spotlight. I guess I am not ready for fame. I never calculated how many minutes of material I had written, so apparently I go over my time and, by the end of my performance, am not sure whether the audience is laughing at my jokes or what seems like me not willing to leave the stage, going on and on and on. The spotlight makes me see nothing in the dark room, including the host of the open mic somewhere there in the audience who is giving me a bunch of signals, as I'm told later. And probably a couple of middle fingers too.

Luckily, I am the very last one to perform embarrassment, so people start leaving not because of me, but because the show is over. I get back to my table and take a big sip of water.

"I think you're funny," a guy at the next table says.

"Thanks. I didn't have a chance to tell one more joke from the stage."

"Tell it to me," the stranger suggests.

"Oh, okay. I had a massage recently and it was so good and relaxing that if the masseur fingered me, I would not resist. I wonder if there's a place with a happy ending for women besides romantic movies on Hallmark channel."

"Dylan. Comedy lover." He goes for a handshake.

"Mirra, an award-wanting writer." He's a very winsome comedy lover, I note.

He chuckles. "Where are you from, Mirra?"

"I was born in Ukraine. Well, technically, I was born in the country that doesn't exist anymore."

"Which is..."

"USSR. It collapsed, because women wanted to wear foreign lingerie."

"Ha."

"Where are you from, Dylan?"

"I'm Ukrainian too," he says with a typical New York accent. "My great grandparents immigrated to the United Stated in the nineteen thirties."

"Let me guess, that makes you...a jew?"

"Correct. Are you too?"

"You know what they say, there're three drops of Jewish blood in everyone," I reply.

"Who says that? Nazis?"

He makes me laugh.

"Where were you born?" I ask.

"Long Island, unfortunately."

"Why so?"

"We have a reputation."

"You're a member of how many clubs?" I apply the only stereotype I know.

"Exactly!" Dylan says. "My family had matching white Volvo station wagons and a golden retriever. The dog had a sleeping pad with her name embroidered on it. So yeah, I consider myself a badass."

"As a matter of fact, I'm a cosmopolitan—a person of the world and a cocktail. I think it doesn't matter where you were born or what nationality you are as long as you're not an asshole," I say.

"Very interesting. I wonder what your social circle is like."

"I don't know that many people, so it's more of a rectangle...which is really a triangle...that looks like a straight line...and there's a dot somewhere there...and that's my social circle. So basically it's just me. I can introduce you to me if you'd like."

"I'd love that."

"Dylan, I have a very important rhetorical question: if a man could reach his own penis and blow it would it be considered gay? And would he do it?"

"How about we go somewhere else where we can talk? And in the meantime I can come up with a funny answer."

"Deal."

"I also have a question for you," he says. "How come Ukrainian women are so beautiful?"

"Chernobyl."

Dylan laughs out loud and even though I failed on stage this night, I won anyway.

It is not super cold outside but it feels like winter has been on for over thirty-eight years or so. I think people date more in winter—to stay warm snuggling.

"Is this cold gonna be over, like, ever?" I pop my collar.

"You're from Ukraine. It's even colder there."

"Well, it's not like I like it! Bad weather does not make me homesick. Speaking of weather, a while back there was a massive fog over the Verrazano bridge that made Staten Island disappear."

"And no one even noticed," he chuckles. "Are you on Instagram?"

"I don't have Instagram but in case you wonder—I have eggs for breakfast and a spectacular ass."

"I can tell," he winks. "I checked that...but not that I've actually checked that...I mean I saw that...you! I saw you, but not like in a bad way, on stage, you know, while you were walking to it. And you can have any ass you want...I mean...I assume that...but it'd be great if I actually see, I mean if you let me...oh, damn, that's not what I mean. Ugh, forget it," he facepalms.

"You don't seem like a social media junkie who shares his every piss with followers online. Am I right?" I save Dylan from his niceness.

"Correct. But I'm always in vacation mode and happy for real. In case you wonder."

We come to Bobo on West Tenth Street, a cute French country-themed place, where all the girls are wearing red lipstick and all the guys are gay, the waiter recommends chicken for the main course, and chill music sounds like the guitar string torture from Breaking Bad. I like it.

How to distinguish a good place from a really good place? A really good place has the bathroom door from the ceiling to the floor. In just a good place, you can see other people's feet.

"What's this?" Dylan points at my pendant that looks like a tiny ball with a hole.

"It's nothing, just a head of my ex."

"A skull of the defeated enemy?"

"Gold plated."

"Ouch! Dangerous girl. Fun!" Dylan claps his hands.

"I'm a no filter writer. And also no make up, no

games."

"No shit?" he grins.

"How was your weekend? Wrote a lot of inappropriate messages to girls?" I ask him.

"So many inappropriate messages. 'Hey girl.' 'What's up?' 'You registered to vote?'"

"How dare you! Very, very inappropriate."

"What's it like in Ukraine?" he asks me with unhidden wonder.

"It is an amazing place. You can easily hear: 'Be sure to read this book. The author is a terrible anti-semite, but the book is excellent.' Even on a one-way street, you need to look on both sides—safety precautions. And in winter there are days when it can get down to minus twenty-two degrees that spit freezes and becomes a weapon."

"Celsius or Fahrenheit?

"Either is too cold! And also, mini-split systems that produce zero noise are the go-to in Ukraine unlike in New York—typical window air conditioners with the sound level of a tractor. That alone is a good enough reason to love Ukraine," I say.

"Yep, that'll totally do."

While Dylan orders us drinks, I'm caught up in a deep thought.

"Why are you silent? Where did you go? Come back," he says. I'm surprised he can read my resting bitch face.

"Silence is gold."

"I'll join you in your silence. Imagine how much gold we can save together that way."

"This is so Jewish of you."

"Stereotypes? What are you, an anti-Semite?"

"Me? Not at all. I hate everyone equally."

"I don't even know any stereotypes about Ukrainians."

"It's okay. I'm not a typical one. Neither are you."

We give our order: Dylan gets wine and I get seltzer.

"Do you not drink alcohol at all?" Dylan asks.

"That's right. Sex, seltzer, rock 'n' roll, baby! I caught myself thinking that I can't have both business and wine. It is too damn exhausting. Don't get me wrong, I like wine but after I have some, I can't do a thing—everything stops. So it's either wine or everything. Every time you're wasted your time is wasted. Interestingly, this enlightenment happened during the worst hangover and the best business proposal I've ever had. And I liked not being anxious so much that I postponed booze for a while. It's funny how it works: we drink to calm the yelling monster Anxiety and the side effect of alcohol, among others, is anxiety. If I have two or three drinks, I'll get out of my head. But my head stores my reality—it's all I have really."

"Sometimes I think that alcohol is a big lie. It didn't quite replace cigarettes in the movies—only super cool and super bad guys smoke now—it actually filled the hands of characters. One hand for a cigarette, another for a drink. The way they pour that drink, any drink, into the glass, take the first sip and swallow, looking pointedly away..." Dylan sips his wine and acts out what he says.

"Oh yeah. That looks so meaningful! Though no

slurred speech or headache or weakness shown."

"Mystery of art."

"I don't smoke cigarettes, I don't use drugs, I don't drink alcohol. The only thing left is to become vegan and die from happiness," I say.

"No, no, no, no, no, no, no! Don't become vegan. Please, pretty please. If you do, how are you going to be able to have all the deliciousness in the world?" He seems disappointed for a sec.

"Are you kidding me? I eat baby cows, baby lambs, and baby pigs for breakfast. Never can they ever be replaced with tofu."

"I once ate a horse meat burger and if that upsets people I get it. Though they will be glad to know it made me violently ill," Dylan says.

"The levels of hypocrisy in our society fascinate me. Eating cows is fine but horses no no no. Making things from goat leather is okay but from crocodile no no no. If it's equality—it's equality in everything."

"I am fifty percent convinced pigs shouldn't be eaten. They are smarter and more social than horses. Our lines are fuzzy," Dylan says.

"Once I tried shark meat. It was meh. I guess the one I ate was not social enough," I say.

Dylan laughs out loud. It's really the best feeling when someone gets your jokes, when someone just gets you.

"So, wait. Are you not going to drink again, like ever?" he asks.

"Oh, I will drink and smoke cigarettes again and do all possible drugs...when I'm ninety-two. Whiskey with ginger juice and champaign with orange juice.

Bubbles and sugar—what's not to like? And drugs: maybe pills for high blood pressure? Breaking Bad time, baby. It'll mean I have reached my destination point. Until then I'll just enjoy the ride. And hangovers are definitely not a part of it."

"Cheers!" Dylan says. "So what do you do besides wanting an award for writing?"

Ha. A man who listens.

"I'm a fantasyologist. I imagine something and then it comes true. For instance, I created a tool for the Cyrillic world that helps professionals work with information. An all-in-one media intelligence platform. Not only is there competition of people but of information too—you know, likes and shares and views. I still think it's unreal that such a form of demand exists."

"A tech start-up of some sort?"

"That's right. And what do you do?"

"Oh, my business is super real and very estate."

"Nice. Working for yourself or someone else?"

"I have asked repeatedly to be called 'His Royal Awesomeness,' but no one listens to me. So, I settle for managing partner of Ninth Avenue Capital."

"Poor man." I pat him on the shoulder.

I have a sex dress. It is a no-brand, handmade by my design, off-the-shoulder black pencil dress that I've owned for about nine years or so. Anytime I wear it—a good time is guaranteed.

"Would you like to go to my place?" Dylan asks me after our long chit chat that seems to never come to an end, which is very inspiring. No long pauses, no awkward moments, very natural.

I pet my dress.

"Actually, yes. But I should probably warn you, because any women's magazine recommends to..."

"Warn me that you're a strong and independent woman?"

"Yes, that too. Just warning you about the mess we're about to create—I'm on my period."

"It's okay. I'll drink it."

It is the most romantic thing I've ever heard in my life. *Ha, he's interesting.*

The elevator opens right into his apartment in Soho. A huge painting of a girl near the window watching the ocean is the first thing facing the entrance. There is something eye-catching, intriguing, magical about this painting. This same painting I saw in Nikki's apartment in Paris.

Is this like a famous painting that everyone has a replica of? Why is this chick by the ocean following me throughout the world?

Usually, families in New York aren't big, so all of its members can fit into an apartment for Thanksgiving. So I thought. Dylan could fit Port Authority in his place.

"Sorry, my place is a mess," Dylan says.

"No worries. Most importantly, no mess in your head," I say.

Dylan stares at me like he recognized something, or someone.

"I should go to Kiev," he finally says.

"Why? I am right here."

He smiles back.

"So you're tall and bald and make good decisions.

What's the catch?"

"I'd say small penis but it's not. Statistically average. You'll see," he says.

"Well, take off the pants and let's get to know each other thoroughly," is what's really on my mind but instead I say, "Is there anything else I should know?"

"I have a Justin Bieber song on my iPhone and I dance to it in my underwear when I'm alone in my apartment. Do you want anything?"

"Seltzer would be great."

He opens the fridge and I see about a dozen large bottles of Perrier, all sipped and sipped unevenly.

"Oh, there it is—you are crazy!" I point at the bottles. "That explains everything," I smile.

"What, are you judging me?" He grabs a seltzer from the fridge and hands it to me.

"No. I'm making fun of you. That's way worse," I wink.

Dylan stares at me like he's trying to read my mind, but everything he's looking for is written all over my face.

"Oh, by the way, I need to order delivery from the deli."

"More Perrier?" I say.

"Haha. Yes, actually. Some fresh water. I bet they're going to mess up my order again, just like they always do."

"So why don't you change the deli?"

"But this is my deli! This is where I go to, where I order delivery from!"

That is so very much New York.

"Dylan, it doesn't make any sense."

"Oh, shut up," he says kindly—I get goosebumps.

"I heard you. Good point. I know when to shut up."

"Good girl," Dylan says.

"I'm afraid so," I whisper in response.

Dylan takes his phone and turns on Edwin McCain's "I'll Be".

"Seriously? This song?"I'm a bit surprised.

"Big hit in the middle school dance scene," he says. "I've always had success with the ladies dancing to this song."

"But the lyrics are very ambiguous and kind of not very happy," I say.

"Oh, yeah. I don't know why people think it's a romantic song. Some even get married to it walking down the aisle. The lyrics are horrible and their meaning is quite sad."

"I like the music though."

"Dylan still got it with da ladies." He winks, which makes me smile.

Then he lends his hand.

"Dance with me," he says.

Ugh, what a cheesy move, man.

We start dancing in his kitchen as if it's some lame romcom about middle school, where he's been waiting long and she materializes fast. High levels of dopamine turns the brain into wet bread and norepinephrine makes me so energetic that I can easily deconstruct and then construct back the Great Chinese Wall. Houston, total eclipse of the brain in three, two, one...

And I lose it.

Re: Thank you note.

Dear Santa!
First and foremost, I'm sorry I did not believe in you for over thirty years. You know, circumstances. The cynical world of consumption, all the gifts, and your franchise on the global market. And in the Coca-Cola commercial you're sort of disgustingly idealized.

I'll be brief. I am sure you do not have much time to read all this. Thank you for fulfilling my dream. You were crazy fast! My respect. I promise to be a very good girl all year long. For the next year I already have two dreams. Hoping for a long-term, mutually beneficial cooperation.
M.

The key to a successful long-term relationship in New York is treating it like addicts do: one day at a time. Plus, both of you have to know where you're going so you can determine the best way of getting there. To conceal love is even more difficult than to simulate it. Same with orgasms.

Beauty and power—a chance for natural high. Two defiantly gorgeous people who love each other insult everyone around them with the mere fact of their existence.

Dylan and I have an inside joke called "raping promises" where D says he is going to rape me and I respond with disappointment: "Promises, promises."

We can talk for hours, literally, about anything and everything, as if it's a non-stop entertaining podcast live.

A little tired of adventures, I've been looking for a beautiful story; and I think I bagged a good one.

We share the same opinion about most things and happen to not like the same types of people. We both add zip code to a name to create a nickname online, love food and comfort money can buy, plan in advance but not too much, make decisions fast and try to not overthink, find Allbirds sneakers the most comfortable shoes ever made, believe in homogamy, and may throw up after the second cup of Cafe Bustelo Coffee.

He's so easy, psychologically stable and predictable. Knowing what will be tomorrow is not a bad thing at all. And even to his grumbling I listen with pleasure. It's like he's got a limitless amount of my credit. I actually use the word *we* now and it's not just a pronoun.

The way he makes me feel is constant but full of moments. Those moments when someone tells you something beautiful and then that they have never told anyone else that before. Special. Fucking precious.

Before you spend a lifetime with someone, you need to spend summer together. And we do, at a rented house Upstate.

Dylan cuts a watermelon in a pan. He takes the biggest pan that is in the house, almost the size of a bath tub, gets rid of the rinds, cuts the watermelon into large slices, covers the pan with a lid, and puts it in the fridge for an hour. For some reason, the watermelon tastes better if eaten from the ice-cold pan, when the fruit juice flows from the hands to the elbows, while you look at each other, and smile like the happiest people in the world. You are the happiest people in the world.

The fridge is stuffed for the week that we're planning on spending in the house, before going back and forth between the city and Upstate all summer long.

For dinner is pasta with chicken and salad. There's nothing better than food being so good that you dance to it. Dylan has his own method of figuring out if pasta is cooked—a method he's learned from his father. He takes a fork, catches one macaroni in the boiling water and throws it right onto the wall next to the stove. If the macaroni sticks to the wall—it means it's ready. It's adorable and amusing and a little cuckoo. I'm loving it.

I can watch him in the kitchen forever. I can just look at him forever. I've reprogrammed myself and for the first time in my life love does not equal pain. Love is a good thing. It is confident and calm and understanding. One team, no competition required. Things are defined and simple.

Dylan laughs at my jokes and doesn't judge the jokes I laugh at. If I had to sum up our relationship in a few words, I'd choose affection and laughter. Not at the same time or instead of one another. One starts when another finishes, never ending, in circles, like wisdom and nonsense, so that life feels full.

There's a huge window, from ceiling to floor, all around the house. We watch the sunset together and it's the best binge of them all. Then gaze into the stars wondering how silly we must look from up above going on Instagram and liking photos..

"The chocolate cake in the kitchen is yelling 'Eat me!' I'm not sure what's worse: eating a cake at this hour or admitting that food talks to me," I say.

Dylan brings me the cake. He's in a white t-shirt and grey sweatpants and I catch myself thinking that sweatpants are the sexiest clothes ever. Once I found myself at a department store in the men's section where I almost came just by looking at men's sweatpants on hangers. I wanted to save them from their sale, take them with me to bed and cuddle. And here I am, looking at sweatpants, with a man in them; and they're all mine.

"Actually, I want some tea too," I say. "We have...that thing in the house, right? What's the word in English for that thing you boil water in for tea?"

"Tea pot. You don't use it? What do you use to make tea?" Dylan asks me surprised.

"Coffee shop."

I get my tea. And come up with a solution to overcome the fear of missing out: start using a decent cup. Put your goddamned to-go coffee or tea down and spend fifteen minutes at a table enjoying your beverage. You won't miss out on much really. Oh, and also stop saving your precious time texting in acronyms: pgm img wyd ttys ppl afaik cu hth ymmd imo. You won't be able to watch all of Netflix anyway. And by the way, when you say something, don't add that it's in your opinion. Of course it is. Who else's opinion can you express talking from the first person? Perhaps, a FOMO on grammar would have been useful once in a blue moon. I'm done with advice and can go back to my enveloping silence. But the sound of New York catches me even in Upstate.

"With all the virtual reality and artificial intelligence why can't we figure out how to make a powerful air conditioner with less than thirty decibels that doesn't cost a million dollars?" I say.

"The sound doesn't bother me."

"Maybe we can get a new fan or something?"

"It will be expensive this time of year," Dylan says.

"Ugh, I don't like the word expensive. It's very limiting."

"But Mirra, some things are expensive."

"Expensive is not a constant matte—it's all relative. Beside, you're a successful white male businessman in America. You can't complain. What's the worst that can happen to you? Your french fries will be delivered cold? Your legs will go numb if you sit on a toilet for too long? Don't you want to make the world a better place?"

Dylan grins. "When a white American man declares he wants to make the world a better place...he's talking about The United States. That is his world."

"How about making our private world here a little better?" I smile.

"I'll get a quiet one if you want," Dylan agrees.

"Dylan Goode, you really are a good man."

This is how we figure out that Dylan is really good at buying things online and forgetting he ordered them. Later, Dylan falls asleep next to the AC, and we find out that he is a typical man who thinks he can put some dirt on his booboo and it'll heal itself.

"D, how did you get sick? Did you lick the subway

pole again? I thought you were over that," I joke around.

"Mirra! I told you not to bring the subway licks again," Dylan laughs.

Finally, after my multiple caring, life-threatening reminders he sees a doctor and agrees to use the prescribed medicine for his sore throat...and ends up burning the mucous membrane of his throat. As it becomes obvious later, the medical substance first needs to be diluted with water before gargling. This is not the time to write a last will and testament, I assure Dylan, because no one has died from pure stupidity yet. It has to be diluted with water first.

"I want your borsch. It'll help me heal. Will you cook it for me?" Dylan asks with the eyes of Puss in Boots.

I can't refuse the request of a dying-from-sore-throat man. So I go to the supermarket to buy the ingredients for borsch, where I also grab lasagna from the shelf. For some reason I think that it is a pre-made frozen meal but when I come back home and open it, it is actually just the flat pasta box. You can definitely suffer from stupidity. Thank god I'm pretty.

Dylan, brought to the kitchen by all the cooking smells, is hanging out next to me.

"Don't you think it's ridiculous," I say. "We learn so much stuff for years and years, so much information in school and college, we read books and watch documentaries, we build robots and teach gorillas sign language. And nevertheless, most of us have no clue how our own body operates, which should be the number one priority in the learning process."

"It operates on coffee, duh." Dylan clearly feels better. "Well, there's more to that. In New York bodies operate on coffee, alcohol, and the constant fear of missing out."

"And the rest of the world—on coffee and a kind word."

He will get back to the pan with borsch three times during the evening, eating it warm and cold and in a plate and in a pan and with his hands.

I share a story about my favorite sandwiches in my childhood: rye bread with unfiltered sunflower oil and salt, and white bread with butter and sugar. These were the best sandwiches I've ever had. Immediately, Dylan wants them too and I know I can make them.

"The only thing I can't cook is crepes, which is like the easiest thing ever—mixed water and flour. And I love crepes. A couple times that I've tried to make them, I ended up with a scramble."

"Who the fuck eats crepes in New York?" Dylan laughs.

"I do! I mean I would've if I could make them. Or anything of dough."

"I think you're full of crepe." Dylan's got dad jokes prepared for years in advance.

The most ridiculous google search I've ever done that even private mode couldn't hide is can you get sick if someone with a sick throat performs oral sex? Probably even private mode will still pass this info to the head office of the tech giant to add to their collection of the most ridiculous search queries. Ou! There should be a book with just that! I'd call it "The Searchables," like "The Expendables".

One night, after playing chess, while celebrating my defeat, he got so overexcited that he paused, took a deep breathe and said to himself out loud: "Dylan, come down. You're gonna fuck Mirra for a very long time."

"I think from now on we should always play chess naked. This way, I won't lose right away," I say.

"Deal. You can play naked," he says.

Every morning, I wake up to the song Old Time Rock'n'Roll on my alarm and the smell of freshly ground coffee. Some days I stay at the house that becomes my daytime office when Dylan goes to New York. In the evening we play naked chess, because we're two sexy nerds. Sometimes, I walk on his back with my feet instead of massaging it, because he likes it that way. And we have a daily tradition: "five minutes of tenderness"—no matter what we're doing at the moment we drop everything and start hugging.

The first weekend in the country, we just eat, chill, watch Netflix, and avoid ticks—we are on a nap adventure. I'm starting to like the lazy weekend idea. I finally have an excuse to accomplish nothing in life.

"How many hours have you been sitting on the couch today?" Dylan asks me.

"Only like three believe it or not. But it's trending up now."

"I should go to space so work can't find me," Dylan says.

"There's internet in space duh. In fact, it might be the fastest up there thanks to the satellite."

"Dam, good point."

The second weekend I decide I want a bicycle and

gush about how much fun I would have riding it. So I dig into research and get absolutely lost.

"I hate too much variety! It's been two days and I can't choose a bicycle because there's tires and price and brakes and color and speed and cruiser and hybrid and mountain and brand and reviews and delivery fee and assembly service and...fuck it! I'll walk."

"Mirra, why don't you choose a bike of the same color as your nails or something. Easier that way, no?" Dylan suggests.

"There is no colorless bicycle!"

I find a replacement for a bicycle—a pool. My office chair is a pool chair. Basically, I swim and then work, and then swim a little more, and work more. Helps me think better.

Having long, curly hair is like wearing a mink fur coat, in the middle of summer, at all times. Curly-haired people are lucky. Yes, this is us, when we go to bed with wet hair we get up in the morning with a ready hairdo. This is us, who love the rain and hate humidity, because hair triples in volume making us look like Michael Jackson in his "Billie Jean" years (volume, not questionably molesting little boys). This is us, who can have the same haircut for years because it's good and everything sticks out exactly as it should, and not as if a poplar with bangs grow out on your head.

So at the pool my hair is wet, my work is fresh and productive. The best summer for me is feeling my wet hair on my neck from behind and elbows sticky with watermelon juice. Enjoying my life and myself to the full extent equals increased work progress: a constantly growing number of InfoPro.Club users. I'm thinking that maybe if all goes well, three to five years from now I can create an award for journalists and media professionals. There haven't been any decent ones in Ukraine that I can remember. Not even a version of the Emmy's, not to mention the Pulitzer's. And then an actual club, where professionals who work with information could all hang out, mingle and network—a version of Soho House per se.

In New York I can gaze out the window and be inspired by the hustle and bustle of the city. In the country house I can be inspired by a tree leaf. For like an hour. Then I need to maintain the level of craziness to stay inspired. So, every day, for about an hour or a television hour in between work I watch various videos on YouTube and always manage to find all kinds of oddities in them.

Day one.

I stumble upon a talk show of a Dutch national television called *Spuiten en Slikken*, which means *Shoot and Swallow*. In the show, they are talking about drugs and sex. One of the hosts seems to be under the influence—his eyes shine, his moves are sharp. The co-host is pregnant. I guess they did their homework and got prepared really well for this episode's topic. The guest of the show is a gay guy who does porn for work. He is complaining about how hard his job is and what it's actually like to have enemas on a regular basis to look good on camera and what kind of pills he takes daily to increase the amount of sperm, also for the sake of good motion picture and art. In the meantime the video is shown in the background—him at work. Faces in the audience express empathy and compassion. Loud applause. Commercial break.

We're back to the studio. Journalists of the show report about the "Casa Rosso" theater in Amsterdam, where they take a master class from the theater's director and learn how to dance a striptease. The director wants the audience to believe the performance so the actors fuck on the stage for real. The journalists did not take this master class though.

After another break I find out that there's a Yelp version for hookers: customers write reviews, give stars for services, and comment on waiting time, satisfaction level and overall vibe.

Day two.

"We met online. And this will be my first time actually meeting him. I'm expecting a marriage proposal because I feel that he's the one. I'm Christian, he's Muslim. He's very traditional, I do belly dancing for work. I have two children, he doesn't speak English at all. But I'm sure our love will conquer all."

It's *90 Day Fiancé*—the most hilarious reality show I've ever seen. It's terrible—I'm loving it. And all those characters... To be a candidate for any reality show you have to be like a default human before customization and never get customized. It's a special quality so casting producers choose you. In this case you've got to be desperate, believe in soulmates, and be a little nuts. The show is so bad that I'm ashamed to admit how much I'm into it. And there is no direct rhyme with the word fiancé. Well, maybe just one—Beyoncé, but it's illegal to put Beyoncé in one sentence with anything of questionable quality.

Day three.

I watch a short documentary about the political structure of the world, followed by a stand-up comedy, and then end up on the Argentina's version of *Dancing With The Stars*, where the stars actually strip down. During the rehearsal, as they show in the clip, two strippers and their trainer try to decide whether it is necessary to take off a bra on the second minute of their dance or simply showcase the idea of a striptease with facial expressions. Eventually, both dancing partners get topless. Got bless Argentina. Where did it go wrong in the USA?

It's a hilarious show where everybody is a little uncomfortable and half naked. On the stage is a technician from Buenos Aires who takes this competition way too seriously and promises this and that while touching his dance partner all the time. I try not to judge a book by its cover but his dance partner looks like she charges for this affair hourly, or per night. Or maybe Argentina is just a naturally slutty country. Again, where did it go wrong in the USA, the unique country of freedom and prudes?

The judges are typical because the format of the show is international. A bald guy who's always a judge at this type of a show, because he's a part of the TV franchise contract. A lady with straight hair. She might be a singer or a dating coach or something, we don't really know. But she looks beautiful on camera and that's what matters for this show. And also, we need a woman's perspective. A guest star. He doesn't want to be here but doesn't mind getting some extra money for cocaine expenses. And he'll sing at the end of the show. And last but not least...a fourth judge. It doesn't really matter who he is.

The good cop bad cop situation is interchangeable among the four. Tired star hoping for a come back by the means of this show is always a good cop, the lady with straight hair is unpredictable, bald guy does not have a tendency and likes everyone, and the fourth judge is the bad cop and still no one cares because his vote is never final.

Then all summer long Dylan and I play this game: I tell him what kind of craziness I saw today and he tells me what grabbed his attention during the day. Sometimes it is something similar, like the ridiculous copywriting on a pack of nuts.

We also play another game, creating fake band names. So far the list is: Fluffy Skin, Jason's Ears, Kinky Pinkie, Blood Sweat & Tears, Mom Said Cheese, Number Four, Napkin in a Ball, Backpackers.

"Want to watch a movie?" I suggest one night.

"Sure. Which one? I'm kinda sick of movies shot only in New York and Los Angeles. Like, why not move a story to Iowa or Montana for a change?" Dylan says.

"Because some of the stories only make sense in New York. Like *Billions*. If you move it to Iowa, the title won't even be plural," I say. "I haven't seen *Star Wars* and I heard that its parts aren't made chronically. You'll guide me through so I won't have to search online what it's about."

"Mirra, if you have trouble figuring out what *Star Wars* is about I'd be worried for you."

Dylan likes scary movies. He's a little neurotic New Yorker after all.

We end up watching a scary movie that I make fun of. A scary movie is always shot in a suburban area, which adds about fifty percent of fear with just that.

"Mirra, look. This is a great scene," he says pointing at the TV set.

I mentally facepalm. Thank god he's hot.

"Are you scared?" he asks me.

"Oh yeah, you're right, babe. We're watching a scary movie so you can protect me. I'm all scared... starting now, right?"

"Russian bitch!" He laughs and then adds, "O-oh. No response? At all? Are you okay?"

"Shush. I'm busy producing oxytocin. When I'm done, how about we watch *Columbo* instead?"

"I love that show! I didn't know you like it too. And I had no idea you watched American classics. What do you like about Columbo?"

"He's not the oaf people think he is, that he's got tacky moves and is not taken seriously and thus wins. I like his character in general, especially the little detail about him when he brings a hard-boiled egg to a crime scene all the time. There's something very naive about a hard boiled egg, yet it's hard-boiled, hard, you know. And my favorite line is when he's on the phone with his wife and goes, 'Okay, I'm gonna hang up now.' Mrs Columbo says something and Columbo smiles and replies, 'You can keep talking but I'm gonna hang up now.'"

"If I were with you, I'd enjoy even the shittiest film festival that has only movies with subtitles," Dylan tells me and I awww because it's a very sweet moment.

"You just love me."

"Mirra, you love that I love you."

"Of course. Everyone loves being loved, duh. And o-oh, what a coincidence! I love you too."

Sometimes it seems to me that our society is so fucked that I wouldn't be surprised if in twenty years or so new movements of emotionally handicapped people, brought up by superficial success and false happiness, will ban the word "love," will proclaim it offensive to certain groups and will make us call it the L word.

Today, everything is going great in my professional and personal life and it scares the shit out of me. I am not afraid that things will fall apart, no. No matter how comfortable you sit, your butt goes numb anyway. I am afraid of being bored within time and sabotaging everything myself.

Fortnight into the Upstate living, we invite our friends for the Memorial Day weekend. Thankfully, there's enough of rooms in the house for everyone.

After coming back from Paris in January, my closest social circle completely changes, my whole life changes; or maybe because I've changed, or my attitude, I don't know. It happens so. People choose different paths and go different ways with different companions. Only a few stay with you in the long run. Those are the real ones; they meet you at the airport, pull you out of blue, and rejoice at your success. And you do the same for them. Simple, engaging conversations define a good relationship, when talking you don't notice that four hours have passed and there is still something to be friends about. The main point of any friendship overall is to have as much fun as possible.

Frank Ellis, my long-time honest friend who I've known for a decade at this point. We met on Tinder—it was the only positive thing about that cloaca. Everything was great about him except he had a child, which was my no-no requirement. He suggested to introduce me to his friend who was also a good guy, single, with no kids. That obviously didn't work out, because real life is not a Hallmark's channel Christmas movie. But Frank and I became friends ever since. He's a thirty-eight-year-old native New Yorker born and raised on Manhattan, who's like an older brother that I never had. He's a radio host at the national station, sort of a celebrity himself who interviews celebrities daily. We get along well because he's snobbish too.

Nora Sparks, she who brings light, my relatively new friend. We met at a French language meet up group that I joined after coming back from Paris to not lose my vocabulary. She recently moved to the city from Chicago and didn't know a lot of people so we kind of hit it off. She is a thirty-one-year-old doctor killing it at the hospital (okay, that may be a poor choice of words). We have a mini tradition: once a month we share a dozen of Krispy Cream doughnuts when we start craving crap food and willing to punch someone in the face for their annoying fact of mere breathing. PMS in your thirties gets brutal, sans exaggeration. Obviously, our period is in sync since we're friends. Her sense of humor is rather dark yet she's kind and compassionate. Early into our friendship, we were having dinner and the waitress was so inattentive and ignored us for forty minutes after we were done eating that it took us one eye contact to mutually agree upon walking out of the restaurant without paying, which we did: no guilt. This is how I knew we'd be friends. Later on, Nora was at my place and we were talking and then I went to the bathroom, because I was dying to pee, and she kept talking so I left the door a bit open to continue the conversation. I think that itself makes us officially married. We get along well because we both are suckers for good comedy.

Mason Reeve, my relatively new friend as of January too. Brooklyn-native Italian boy. We met at a chess club on Thompson Street, where I started going to stay awake because in winter midnight starts at about five o'clock in the evening. His brother gave him a membership as a part of his Christmas gift. Mason was persuaded he was decent at chess but decided to give it a try only to discover I could beat him multiple times. He is a thirty-nine-year-old FBI agent who travels internationally for work a lot and is rather cagey about his plans, though understandably. It only means that FBI does its job well so we civilians won't know what's being taken care of. Know less—sleep better. Mason is single, obviously. He could beat anyone at eating Starburst in a world record speed. He's the kind of person who keeps his umbrella at the welcome door rug outside the apartment. "This way I always know where my umbrella is," he says. He is very straightforward and easy. We get along well because we both like chess and don't play games.

Every single one of my friends is a particularly good person with the qualities one would hope for in a dear friend. Media, medicine, authority—my social force, my essential group. Ironically, all of them have some sort of power in one form or another, so we all get along well since we have a lot in common. The four of us have so much fun and always have a story to tell. I now have a group of decent friends who are all adults and behave accordingly. I cherish time spent together. It's like I'm living in a sitcom, except my apartment entrance door is not unlocked all the time and I have no crazy neighbor coming in whenever and eating my food from the fridge.

And there's Dylan's best friend Emery Zeman with his wife Kylie, whom he married very recently. Emery is a typical thirty-six-year-old white boy from New England, whose family basically owns the region. Dylan and Emery met at NYU, where they both studied, and have been friends ever since. And ever since, Emery's father is a backup plan for Dylan's projects—owning New England is not the limit. Emery is a spoiled child from the family dynamic that made him fear commitment and have lack in trusting people, and spend a lot on therapy—a clear example of what money can't buy. He's been unavailable to all the rabid females due to his engagement to a girl he's been with for four years. And then, right before the wedding, he chickened out. All the rabid females got excited in anticipation of a sweet pie. Being also the type who can't be alone, he met Kylie at her restaurant the same night he called off the engagement and stayed with Kylie ever since. Therapy had absolutely nothing to do with it. And it is a freaking once-in-a-lifetime one-night stand ending in marriage that people keep referring to seeking true romance. So all the rabid females went back to Wall Street bros.

Kylie could invade countries with those brows! She is a twenty-nine-year-old Australian who moved to New York a little over a year ago, got a job as a restaurant manager, and soon enough met Emery. These type of women have always amazed me. Men in their lives are like projects that they create and use to achieve other perks in life. Everything they have—thanks to their boyfriends or husbands. Alone they are worth zilch. It's like their only skill is seduction, manipulating their way onto the ladder of a married life. They could not care less about their careers or personal development; their biggest achievement is planning a vacation where they can show off new outfits that their men paid for. These women are like high class sugar babies but with a marriage certificate. Kylie is extremely feminine, to the point that it looks fake. She's got too much of Marline Monroe in her. Only other women can see this game. I suppose smart men see it too, but they agree to play it anyway. Kylie quit her job after the wedding and started decorating everything she sees: the apartment, flowers, her nails, food they eat, Emery's wardrobe. He's got family money, she's got zest for spending it. I get it. I really do. Constantly saving on something to survive in New York City can be very tiring. My prediction is Kylie will try all possible methods to get pregnant very soon. Erh...being just a trophy wife is so so boring.

It is a beautiful sunny afternoon. While others are in the house taking Dylan's tour and talking business (never stops), Frank, Nora and I go outside, where there's a pool with lounges, patio sofa with a fire pit, and a dining table.

"Frank, how are you doing? What's new?" I ask and lean my back onto the glassy fence that divides the territory of the house with the rest of the hill that goes steeply down.

"I had two wisdom teeth pulled out recently." He sits on a chaise lounge.

"So you lost half of your wisdom?" Nora says and joins Frank at the chaise next to him.

"Sounds right. Getting ready for Alzheimer's that way. First you lose your wisdom, then you lose your mind and you're lost." He is such a goof. "What's up with you, Mirra?"

"I had a dream last night in Spanish language."

"Horror?" Frank says.

"It's hard to tell. I've only been learning it for about a month, so I didn't quite understand whether the dream was scary or not," I say.

"When I'm drunk, I can explain myself in any foreign language, even in Burgundian. And if the other person is in the same state, we'll have a dialogue better than at the United Nations," Frank says.

"Ethanol. Connecting people," I rephrase the famous Nokia commercial.

"I am so glad we all gathered," Nora says. "Otherwise I'd be stuck in the city alone."

"Why? What happened to that guy you were seeing, the one who lives on Roosevelt Island?" I ask.

"That's already a major red flag," Frank grins.

"I don't know how many times I have to suck a guy off until he invites me to spend a Memorial Day weekend with him and his friends. I think he ghosted me," Nora shrugs.

"You think?" Frank asks.

"Well, he hasn't texted back since yesterday so I'm pretty sure he ghosted me. No more sucking for him."

"Maybe he wasn't sure about getting exclusive sucking yet," Frank adds.

"Different rules should be applied when you're in your thirties. Less of 'OMG, what will this mean if we spend a weekend together' and more of 'Okay, you're not crazy, let's enjoy our time together and see where this goes'," I say.

"But if you don't know where you want to go you won't get there," Nora says.

"Most people don't know what they want thus they get nothing," Frank concludes.

"I don't want to take things slowly and see where it goes. If it's not going towards the City Hall then I'm not going!" Nora exclaims.

"Fair." I agree.

"You met on Tinder, right?" Frank asks.

"Yeah."

"The problem with online dating is that people swipe in hopes of getting what they want and not what they need," I say.

"C'mon! Why does it have to be so complicated? I really don't get it. Why not have a weekend full of booze, sex, dance, beach, fun?" Nora says. "Otherwise, why not just tell the truth?"

"Sometimes kindness is wiser than truth," Frank says.

"Are you saying that was kind of him to stop talking to me?"

"No, the guy is a dick. Nobody has the balls to tell you the truth that they don't like you enough to spend the weekend together. All I'm saying is would you rather read a text with a lame excuse knowing it's a lame excuse or be ghosted?"

"Good point," Nora says.

"I personally don't mind ghosting. Ghosting itself is an answer. Although, I do mind when it's inconsistent: answer, no answer, answer no answer, no answer, answer. Just make up your mind! Every lie has consequences. So it is important to give people an opportunity to be silent, meaning not to lie," I add.

"Mimosa?" Frank suggests.

"Make it French 75!" Nora says.

"You got it!" Frank walks towards the house bar.

"I've got something to outcrazy your craziness that will instantly make you feel better," I say.

"What can that possibly be?" Nora sighs and joins me at the glassy fence.

"My ex told me he loved me and then the next day took it back. A year later I gave him one last chance; he said he loved me and wanted to be with me and then ghosted me the next day. Again."

"You were right: it does make me feel better. Your craziness wins," she says.

"There you go!"

"Do you think he regrets it?" Nora asks.

"Oh yeah, he is very much contrite that he hasn't

done it to me, ninny, three times, because third time is a charm," I sneer.

"A man should protect you from drama, not create one. The rest is bad scenery." That's Nora's essence—always ready to give and care.

For a while, we both stare at the hill that seems to have no end.

"How's life besides sucking?" I break the silence.

She smirks. Or squints against the sun, I'm not sure.

Frank makes the rest of the group join us outside and Dylan brings food to start the barbecue. This is the first time our friends meet each other, all of them. And of course it takes some time for everyone to remember names. Nobody remembers a person's name right away when introduced, unless you want to have sex with them. But even then there are exceptions.

"Need help?" Nora nods towards the table.

"Nah, just relax." I start setting it. "Although, I'll need your help at eating—I definitely nailed potato salad today. It is so tasty."

"I want some," Nora says.

"There's celery in it. You like celery, right?"

"I guess so. It's fun." She shrugs and takes her cocktail from Frank.

"Fun is a very strong word for celery," Dylan says.

"Girl, we've got to change your definition of fun for this weekend," Mason says, then quickly picks up Nora and jumps into the pool with her.

After the dive she looks surprised because her drink is now mixed with pool water which makes it barely French 7, but she's laughing.

"I'll make you a fresh one," Frank says.

"And I'll wait for another one," Mason winks.

"Don't! Don't even!" Nora points at Mason, then gets out of the pool and rushes to the house to change the wet clothes.

"Sounds like a great book title: 'Don't Even!'," Dylan says, turning the steaks and sausages, and an eggplant for Nora.

I suggest we play a game "I don't understand" throughout the day. The beauty of this game is that it lets you speak your mind without being thought of as rude or politically incorrect; it lets you express what you really think about anything. This way you can get to know one another, making the small talk actually interesting. And the game is basically complaining about minor random things, which always brings New Yorkers together.

"I'll start," Mason says from the pool. "I don't understand how you can sue a stranger for minor physical violence and your partner for domestic violence not."

"Oof. That's a serious one. Have nothing to add, really," Emery says, walking around the area.

"Somebody pour Mason a drink!" Kylie says and sets the chaise in a sit position.

"I got you." Frank becomes a self-proclaimed bartender, filling up drinks every now and then and collecting tips in smiles and winks from the crowd. "And I don't understand why customer support is so unsupportive most of the time. I've been trying to cancel my hosting provider account and instead they're sending me tons of useless emails. Some companies really have a problem with letting their customers go. They wanted me to confirm the pre-approved confirmed confirmation to delete my account. So I had to call them. Seriously, guys, they kept calling me back two days in a row," Frank says and sits next to the table.

"I can cum faster than the waiting time on a one eight hundred number," Nora adds, getting back into the pool, in a swimming suit now.

"There should be an option to kill one customer support representative per hour if no request is fulfilled," Frank facepalms.

"Today people don't do their jobs, but they write blogs on how to do their jobs," I say.

"Meaning?" Dylan asks.

"I guess this is my 'I don't understand' turn. I don't understand why bloggers think of their readers as morons. Every time I try to search any information on the internet, unavoidably I have to scroll through blogs that are first written for SEO robots and then for humans. Besides, there's never just one paragraph with an actual answer to the question. Usually, the title is a listicle that starts with a stupid number. Even significant numbers have changed. Before, it was five, ten, and twenty. Now it's seven, fourteen, and twenty two (things you're missing out on every day to succeed in life). Or whatever the crap they write about. I can understand number seven—the lucky number. But twenty two? Who cares about twenty two?"

"Yeah, for sure," Mason says.

And I continue.

"The first paragraph starts with an introduction to

the author's life because the author of a blog always has to validate why their opinion matters. None of the information in the intro proves that but anyway... They promise to reveal a secret at the end of the post, or an answer to your question. Just keep reading till the end. Pretty please. It's only ten minutes of your life you're never getting back."

"Ladies and gentlemen, Mirra the grandma," Nora teases me.

"My retirement surely won't be boring. I can always make myself laugh. And I'd finally be able to call everyone *hun* then. Now the only person who can pull *hun* without it sounding diminishing is a big black lady at Target; other than that—nope," I say.

"That is so true!" Emery says nodding along.

"Mirra, please go on," Kylie says.

"So the next paragraph of a blog post briefly tells you how the author got into blogging and making insane money on it. But wait for it before they reveal their secret to success. They've been working nine to five in accounting or something boring like that, always maxed up their credit cards (an accountant who is bad at managing their own finance—that's a reliable opinion, isn't it? Same for a fat dietitian and a convicted criminal lawyer). Then one day enlightenment hit: they decided to write about their problems and thus created a blog. The next paragraph explains how to get a domain and hosting and WordPress. The first affiliate link is here. It's already been at least five hundred words at this point. The author reminds you that you're doing great reading their blog and they are about to tell you the answer to the question you searched for. Don't go anywhere. Remember you searched for something? You're a little annoyed but you keep reading."

"Is there an end to this story?" Frank snickers.

"Exactly! There comes the remaining five hundred words about nothing and a couple more external and internal links, but those aren't bringing any money—just for SEO purposes. Sure, you could simply scroll down and see the answer to your question but none of that is available and this is where they offer you to buy their ebook. Worse if they offer to download their ebook for free because that way they will have your email so get ready for endless aggressive campaigns in your inbox. Congratulations! You have waisted twenty minutes of you time that's never coming back," I say.

"I should start a blog," Kylie says.

"Just don't do it with Namecheap hosting. It'll take you longer to leave them than to divorce," Frank says. "Believe you me. I've done both."

"If a service makes me use their customer support for one reason or another, I stop using that service. It's just so time and nerve consuming to get tortured by AI. No thanks," I say.

"Sounds like you don't use much of anything tech," Emery says.

"And you know what? Never been happier," I say and mean it.

"I don't understand why people read self-help books. Why would you need anyone to tell you what to do?" Emery says while putting sunscreen on Kylie.

"I like him," I tell Dylan quietly.

"In Barnes & Noble, on the shelf were two books

right next to each other: *F*ck Feelings* and *Unfu*k Yourself*. Something about positivity and managing problems. Who would read whose?" Emery continues.

"To fuck or to unfuck? That is the question," I say, holding the plates while Dylan puts grilled veggies onto them.

"The real question is what were you doing in a self-help section?" Dylan ask.

"It was a humor section there before," Emery shrugs.

"Books how to get better..." Nora says. "I never wanted to get better. I'm a pretty decent person as is." She gets off the pool and sits on its edge.

"It's because you're awesome as is," Mason comments. "You don't need books to tell you that."

"Oh, romance..." Kylie peeks out from under her sunglasses.

"We aren't together," Nora says fast.

"We're friends but that's it," Mason immediately adds.

Did I just see him flush? Or is it the sun laying onto his cheeks?

"Mirra, can I ask you a question?" Dylan says.

"Always." I redirect my attention fully to Dylan and forget about what I almost saw just now.

"Is there ever a time when humans don't want pizza?"

"When we're sleeping. But even then—we're dreaming about it," I say.

"You know how you can call a fatty and still be polite? Professional Pizza Model," Frank says.

"As long as pizza is not with pineapple. Speaking of

which. Ladies, does pineapple really make cum taste different?" Mason says.

"I keep hearing that," Nora says.

"Pineapple specifically on pizza or in general?" Kylie clarifies.

"Mason, I like how you put the words ladies and cum in one sentence," Frank says.

None of the ladies answer Mason. Instead the barbecue smells make the group slowly, one by one, move closer to the dining table. And as I'm in charge of everything potato (I don't know how that happened), I make sure that the wood burns out so I can put potatoes into the ash to make them charcoal roasted. And just like "if it's not on Instagram it didn't happen," no barbecue counts without this meal. It doesn't take long until all the food is ready, the table is set, people are hungry. And the birds are so boisterous that it feels like a New York party; and no one freaks out that it's too quiet.

"Recently something weird has been going on with me," Nora says, putting a little bit of vegetarian everything on her plate.

"Oh-oh, do tell," I say.

"Is it another French 75 situation?" Frank asks.

"It's always a French 75 situation, baby," Nora winks. "But nothing to worry about. A New Jersey housewife must have sneezed on me on the subway and I caught the virus. Otherwise I have ho explanation why I've been recently enjoying crochet so much."

"Oh geez, I thought something horrible happened and I left my gun at home," Mason breathes out relieved. He's always the protector.

"Crochet, huh? Were you on edibles or something?" Emery says.

"Edibles are the worst," Kylie says.

"If by worst you mean best," Frank winks.

"It's all good—I'll always eat yours," Emery says to Kylie.

"I've tried once and hated it because it made me paranoid and lazy at the same time. Not the best mix to be honest. I was so high that I heard someone getting into my apartment (or so I thought), but was too tired to get off bed and go check," Kylie giggles.

"So now you're going to open a handmade crochet store?" Mason says.

"No-no, my career goal is to rise high enough to the wealth level between not shopping at TJ Maxx and having private minions. Oh, and I now have a cat!" Nora says. "His name's Oxymoron. I call him Oxy for short, but sometimes I call him Moron when, you know, he's a moron."

"Show me the picture," Mason says.

"I don't really have his pictures," Nora says.

"What? How come? Not a single cat picture in your phone?" Kylie says.

"It's not like my cat calls me," Nora replies.

Dylan cracks, and everyone else too. Nora does have a point.

"I'd be funny to get a dog and call him Wag so that introducing him I'd be like: ladies and gentlemen, please meet Wag. Wag the Dog," I say.

"Or call her Macarena, if it's a girl. But her full name would be He-ey Macarena," Frank says and pauses for a second.

Everybody glances at Frank.

"Okay, I heard me. That just made me so old," he smiles. "You remember Macarena, right?" He looks at me looking for support.

"He-ey, I don't remember," I sing the tune and partly do the dance.

"Oh god, please don't remind me of the time when I had zero understanding of what was going on with literally everything," Emery says.

"You mean your past weekend?" Dylan jokes.

"Once you get a pet, and health insurance for it—you're officially a grown up," Mason says.

"Any pet?" Kylie asks. "Maybe it's only applicable to cats and dogs."

"Right. Cause piggies are delish!" Mason says.

"Mason!" Nora exclaims and pushes him on the shoulder.

"Well what?" He laughs and then adds quietly, "They are!"

"And rabbits too," Emery whispers.

"What?" Nora says.

"Nothing." Emery dampens the vegetarian rage without its commence, and makes an eye contact with Mason.

"I have a guy friend who has two hamsters for pets. I don't understand who would care about hamsters besides eleven-year-olds and pharmaceutical companies that do research," Kylie says.

"It can be considered cruel?" Dylan tries to object but not very confidently.

"Would you prefer your medicine to be researched

on hamsters first before putting it inside of you and dealing with side effects that could have been eliminated?" Kylie asks.

"Don't they do the research on rats?" Frank says.

"Either way" Kylie says.

"Eh, okay, good point. I don't care about hamsters. Screw them," Dylan says.

"There's also something else that defines you as a grown up: piling up unread *New Yorker*," Frank says.

"I think you're right, Frank," I say. "After I got my subscription I never read a single story; except cartoons of course—for the child in me."

"No! I read mine from cover to cover!"Emery exclaims.

"You're my adultie," Kylie pats Emery on the head.

"Somebody, pass the water please," Dylan says and Mason does without lingering a minute. His reaction is impeccable.

"I don't understand why Americans buy so much toilet paper whenever it's a crisis." Kylie says.

"Please, let me," I say and stand up. It is one of my favorite topics of all times. "Because any instability scares the shit out of people, literally. That's why in movies they say, "Let's save our asses." And what do you usually save? Your most precious thing. Thank you, thank you very much," I bow down and sit.

"You should be a writer," Dylan pokes me.

"That's a great idea! Do you think I should plan it out or write by the seat of my pants?" I smile.

"I don't understand why people keep congratulating with Happy New Year on like January eighth. There should be a rule: it is only acceptable up to

January second, considering all time zones. Other than that it's like congratulating with Independence day in August," Dylan says.

"I heard this same New Year joke on *Curb*," Emery says.

"It's not something new. Everyone's thinking about it every holiday season and only Larry David put a copyright to it," Dylan says.

"*Seinfeld* is probably the best bromance on the screen," I say.

"The greatest bromantic comedy of all time is *Dumb and Dumber*. I'm dead serious," Emery says.

"Oh, I love the nineteens movies!" Dylan's face lights up in pleasant nostalgia.

"They should do a reality show where people live the nineties lifestyle but today," Mason says.

"I want to be on a reality show about being better about watching reality shows," Frank says.

"I'd watch that," Nora says.

"These days we'd watch anything," Frank says.

"Not anything. A show still has to be popcorn worthy," Dylan says.

"*Crown* makes me fall asleep so fast," Emery says.

"Yeah that doesn't look like it's for me. Though, good to know, in case I can't sleep," Dylan says.

"Is it just English people pontificating and glorifying their royal bloodline?" Kylie says.

"There are other royalties in the world but nobody cares about them," I say.

"I care. I support royal people," Frank says.

"You do? Okay, name at least one without googling," Nora says.

"Simba, Fiona, Princess Peach, King T'Challa of Wakanda, Sir Mix-A-Lot," Frank says.

"The rapper?" Emery says.

"Yeah but he's still a sir so he's royal," Frank concludes.

"I found this amazing Stanford professor Robert Sapolsky on YouTube and have been listening to lectures about behavioral biology. Did you know that the only child's IQ is lower than the first born's child of two and more? Or that if there's a gay child in the family, the heterosexual child is biologically more reproductive? I also found out that female stripers make more money when they're ovulating. Can you image someone actually researched that, most likely with a state grant?" I say.

"So I just got a new state grant to research strippers," Dylan says.

"Yay! Let's party! As many lap dances as you want." I wink.

"Fine Mirra, I'll take a lap dance but under protest," Dylan says.

"As in 'I don't want it but fine, okay fine, I'll take the lap dance'?" I say.

"Pfff. You are so logical." Dylan rolls his eyes and smiles.

"It's my sexiest trait," I say.

"Has anyone ever seen Porn Awards? It is so funny!" Mason says.

"I saw it once. It's hilarious," Kylie adds.

"I'm going to produce one. And will prepare a speech, like MLK— 'I have a cream'," Frank says.

Everyone laughs. Frank is a comedy star after all.

"I heard that most European men are uncircumcised. Is that so in Ukraine?" Kylie addresses that to me.

"Yeah, That is true. Not exactly a lollipop," I explain.

"I did not expect that!" Dylan exclaims.

"I mean, God Bless America!" I smile.

"Amen!" Nora and Kylie say it together.

"Actually, I have a contradicting opinion about pornography. On one hand it was a product of sexual revolution, but on the other hand porn is another way of controlling women after the wave of feminism in nineteen sixties by degrading and objectifying them," I say. "You can even objectify a country. For political purposes, of course."

"A country? How?" Kylie asks.

"You know how they keep calling it the Ukraine on the news?"

"What's wrong with the Ukraine?" Kylie says.

"Not only 'the Ukraine' is grammatically incorrect in English it is also not the official name of the country. It's Ukraine," I explain.

"Isn't Ukraine, Russia all the same?" Emery asks.

"Like America and Canada," I say. But back to talking about sex. Politics is way too dirty."

"Porn is just sex. As simple as that," Mason concludes.

"Nothing is just a simple thing, especially when it comes to a multi-billion dollar industry. There are already a couple of generations raised on the normalcy of cumming on a woman's face," Nora says.

"Cosmopolitan said swallowing cum is very polite,"

Kylie says.

"Great book title: 'Swallowing cum. Etiquette for generations'," Emery says.

"If two people like it, there's nothing wrong with that," Mason says.

"*That* I agree with," I say. "But it has nothing to do with porn, where a guy goes down on a girl. More often than not he's doing it all wrong. Once in a while they should hire a female consultant or something."

"Right?" Nora says. "In reality, it's annoying and totally ruins sex mood. A lot of men use porn as a manual and it's just not right. Not morally, physiologically wrong. There's actually the right way to suck on a clit, people."

"Have you seen this advertisement of underwear for periods that said 'For most women and folks with vaginas'," I address this to girls mostly.

"A clear example when political correctness becomes stupidity," Nora facepalms.

"People created terms for a reason: to stop using long descriptions of every word they want to say; and now we're back to square one—little people, intellectually challenged, people of size, person of material wealth, people of advanced age, people with testicles, folks with vaginas..." I say.

"If it ever happens so that the word *people* becomes offensive, they're going to have to rename the whole dictionary, again," Emery adds.

"Wait, who are those folks with vaginas?" Dylan is confused.

"Probably those bitches who know nothing about a human body. No trans person can menstruate when on hormone replacement therapy. Those born men can't have periods simply because they have no internal organs for that and hormones obviously can't grow them. Those born women stop menstruating after increased levels of testosterone," I say.

"Technically, those born men after surgery do become folks with vaginas but still can't menstruate for obvious reasons," Nora adds. "So the ad is very politically correct but all wrong biologically.

"Without menstruation, underwear with a pad becomes a diaper," Frank says and smiles.

"Guys, I don't mean to offend anyone and I apologize in advance if anyone takes offense anyway, but can we please stop talking about menstruation while we're still eating?" Emery says.

"Don't call us guys. Call us people born with vaginas who identify with their reproductive organs!" Nora grins.

"So what's right and what's wrong in life, doc?" Mason asks Nora.

"Everything and nothing? Nora shrugs. "Whatever makes the two happy?" she looks at Mason.

"Mirra, is it weird that I think your emoji cartoon thing in iMessages is hot?" Dylan asks.

"Nothing is weird anymore," I say.

"Okay, now I know that two of my female friends are pretty dominant and always have an opinion," Mason points at me and Nora.

"An opinion doesn't equal dominance. Women have always had an opinion. We just recently started to express it publicly and now actually want to be taken seriously. We want to be treated as an equal, and not as your younger autistic sibling. Pardon me, as your younger person who can't have an eye contact sibling," Nora says.

"We are more than just pretty objects that neither fart nor poop," I say and then add, "Actually, we do. It's just white women poop Skittles."

"Taste the rainbow," Frank says.

"Yam!" Dylan says.

"Ew!" Kylie says.

"Now I'm down with eating ass," Mason says.

"Catholic women poop candy in the form of Jesus. Black women poop with some jazz tunes. Asian women are the toughest because they poop wasabi and that, as you may know, burns a little," I continue.

"That's why I'm cautious to do anal with the Japanese woman across the hall in my building," Frank says.

"You just don't like it spicy," I say.

"Genders, no genders, norms, no norms. Why can't we all just get along?" Dylan says.

"Sometimes we aren't supposed to. It's okay to have different opinions, don't you think? This way we progress, hopefully? Mason says.

"Evolution needs conflict," I say. "Unfortunately."

"It's like putting on high heels and velvet sweatpants: technically can be worn together but not looking good at all," Kylie says.

"High heels and velvet sweatpants sounds like an outfit to me. Or at least the start of one," Emery says.

"The start of an outfit is underwear. At least that's the way I start my outfit with," Kylie.

"And heels, right?" Emery says.

"That, or lipstick," Kylie says.

"Both work," Emery says.

Emery and Kylie are still in that phase.

"You all know the tragedy of Calvin Klein's daughter? Every time she goes to bed with some guy, she's looking at her dad's name," I say.

While everyone is giggling, Dylan leans to me and whispers into my ear, "There are only two people who constantly make me laugh: Louis CK and you."

That is the nicest thing someone has said to me.

And as it usually happens, the conversation eventually flows into talking about relationships, as well as moves us onto comfortable patio sofas around the fire pit after the sunset.

"I want to wear mustaches with you and every time someone asks us a question about them—we furl our eyebrows at them," Emery says, looking at Kylie.

"It's New York! Who's going to question your looks? Even if you yell, no one will react, unless you yell 'taxi!', but even then no guarantees," Kylie replies.

"Only Freddy Mercury and Hitler could wear mustaches. And now they're dead. So should mustaches. And long beards. They always kinda look like pubic hair," I say.

"I'm so glad we agree on the most important styling matters in life." Dylan makes fun of me.

"I've noticed that women talking to their girlfriends call a penis dick and a pussy vagina, while men talking to their friends call a dick penis and a vagina pussy," Nora says and sits down close to the fire pit.

"Yeah, I do that too," Kylie adds.

"If the vagina could speak, I imagine it'd have a British accent," I say.

"What?!" Mason is surprised or confused or both.

"Well, cause you never know what she actually means when she says something, how she actually feels when she says she feels in a certain way; whether it orgasms or not. But it'd be very polite: 'Oh hello, dear gentleman, please proceed'." I try to do the accent.

"And when the gentleman is doing it wrong, the vagina, like in maps app, would insist: please, proceed to the route," Kylie says.

"The penis would have an Italian accent. Because it's always showing off and trying to impress and all that. 'Scusi signora per favore, over here, I'm right here, mia bella'," Frank says.

"Now I want to go to Italy, rent a car and just drive there visiting all kinds of towns, eating and cooking, sit outside and gossip about neighbors. That could be my retirement plan," I say.

"Did you know that you two have literally the same shape of a lower lip and a shape of a face?" Kylie nods at me and Dylan.

"You mean good bone structure?" Dylan grins.

"It's astonishing how people from different parts of the world can have similar face features," Kylie says.

I stare at Dylan for a bit. "Oh yeah, he does look familiar. Like I know him or something," I ironize.

Kylie's right. I see it now and wow.

"I have a question," Mason says. "If a missionary is sent to persuade and convert others to his religion, what does a missionary sex position convert us into?"

"Married people," Emery blurbs and starts laughing.

"It's unfair. It's like the whole world is meant for two people: meals, computer games, even townhouses are for two families." Nora almost flips out. "I'm sincerely happy for all of you, but I don't understand why it's almost impossible to date a decent, well-educated gent."

"I thought we stoped playing the 'I don't understand' game," Frank says.

"We have?" Nora is surprised. "That doesn't make me suddenly understand everything." She's well tipsy at this point.

"Tough break up," I point at Nora, which explains without details what she's going through.

"The concentration of weirdos in the pool of normal men is so unexpectedly high that I'm keeping social dickstance," Nora continues. "And you all have no idea how many people are just not clever."

"Oh, Nora, we know," Emery says.

"There's a possibility that we're turning into *Idiocracy* movie," Frank says.

"We already did," Dylan says.

"What?! Starbucks started serving blowjobs?" Frank says.

"Yep," Dylan says.

"Do they deliver?" Frank says.

"Nope. Non essential," Dylan says.

"It'd be so nice to hear 'I got you covered' not only from my insurance moto," Nora says. "That should be essential."

"Nora, I got you," Mason says and hugs her.

"Everybody, this is Mason—the sweetest gun owner and the softest elbows in the Tri-State area," Nora wheedles.

"Hey-hey! It's not easy for men either. You girls don't show up with an Instagram filter for a date. And some of you are weird too. Once, I liked a girl but she turned out to be a witch," Mason says.

"Mason, long fake nails don't necessarily mean that. Maybe she's just from Oklahoma," I say.

"If you want to live in coma, come to us to Oklahoma," Frank says.

"Ha! They've got oil, so it's not all that awful there," Dylan adds.

"Mason, can I take your sweatshirt? I'm a little cold," Nora says.

"Sure. I don't need it." Mason grabs it from the chair and hands it to Nora. "Don't complain about it being big on you."

"Pffft, the whole point of a sweatshirt is for it to be big." Nora rolls her eyes.

Is something going on between these two?

"I guess I've been unlucky in general. The other day I saw grapes on ice cream. Aha! Grape ice cream, so I thought. I bought it, opened it, tried it—raisins. The story of my life," Mason sighs.

"Welcome to adulthood," Frank says.

"I feel like some men should have their bar mitzvah at thirty-nine because this is when they truly enter adulthood," Nora says.

"Oh, c'mon!" Dylan exclaims. "Don't generalize. When I turned twenty-six, I threw a big house party and called it 'the bar mitzvah deuce'. Should I do 'the bar mitzvah thrice' when I turn thirty-nine?"

"Totally! It'd be a great party!" I say. "You know this famous joke? A summary of every jewish holiday: they tried to kill us, we won, let's eat!"

"Yeah people always be trying to kill Jews. Although we pretend we won and eat but to be fair there's very few of us left," Emery says.

"You should reproduce like tomorrow to fulfill the gap," Kylie says.

"Yeah I'll put a Craigslist up. I'm sure that will go over well," Emery smiles.

"Of course! It's Craigslist. You can even find a business partner there," Dylan adds.

"So hey I had to ask you something. I have an exciting opportunity. How would you like to further the Jewish faith? And before you say no, it's not about the sex it's about the tribe," Emery tells Kylie.

She nods.

"You guys are all free next weekend for my bar mitzvah?" Emery says. "I will be saying goodbye to my fear of commitment." He kisses Kylie.

"Does that mean you'll finally share your Amazon password?" Kylie asks.

"Babe, I don't know if I'm ready for *that* kind of commitment yet," Emery says.

"That't more significant than sharing lives together. You will love me even more!" Kylie says.

"I'm already at my full capacity," Emery grins.

"Divorce!" Kylie jokes.

Emery kisses Kylie and says: "So to be clear you didn't divorce me?" Emery asks.

"Have I taken half of your assets?" Kylie laughs.

"Ugh, you men and your fears. At first men fear that somebody wants them and then that nobody takes them," Nora says.

"It's because there's too much choice in New York, and chasing is like our nature," Emery says.

"Na-hah! Too much choice in New York is an illusion. A lot of people in New York—sure, but your options are pretty limited. You know when you have too much choice in the New York dating pool? When you're fine with dating just anybody," I say.

"Elaborate," Frank says.

"There's eight million people in New York, right? Approximately the same amount of men and women. Do the math: four million minus already married, minus not ready for a relationship, minus gays, minus crazies, minus morons. Then, you want your person to have specific qualities, and looks and height, you want to be attracted to them sexually and have commonalities so you can talk and have fun together, maybe share hobbies and religious views, and definitely share the same level of affection and same sexual temperament, understand each other's sense of humor, be ok with their mental conditions if any and with genetic diseases if you plan on having children. And most importantly, you want a person who won't annoy you in the long run. Because it only gets worse within time. So being in love is crucially important. Without love—what's the point?" I say.

"That's quite poetic," Dylan says and kisses me on the cheek, which makes me sort of zoom out.

While I stare at the fire I hear Nora saying "I've got about a thousand people as a result of that equation," and Frank saying "That's a doable number," and Mason saying "I started the second round of dating people I had already dated before," and Emery almost agreeing to share his Amazon password with Kylie after hearing the statistics.

The statistics no longer applies to me. This feeling is relatively new to me because it hasn't been a regular one in my collection of feelings, at least this long for sure.

I am frightened by happiness. I stress out about the fact that I don't stress out. Wait a second, I'm fine? Everything's suddenly fine? That can't be true! What's wrong? This is so typical for a New Yorker—to stress out that you haven't done enough.

Ironically, it is Juneteenth, the slavery abolition day when I find my inner peace: freedom from myself. And it is just a very good summer. Me likey. Oh, there it is. I kind of get my friends from Westchester with their Pizza 2000 and all the tranquility now.

Then one day along the close of summer I feel incredible tension. My leftovers of nervousness chase me slowly and hit unexpectedly, like an edible.

In the late afternoon, even after having swam in the pool for twenty minutes non-stop—still no relief. I'm cranky and just can't find my place. I pick on every little detail, making caustic remarks—every adjective is full of venom. Herbal tea and cartoons—my personal magic recipe from stress—isn't helping.

"What's going on? Are you okay?" Dylan asks.

"Yeah, I guess..." I sound like frosty snow does when you step on it.

"Hey. Hey! What's wrong? Mirra, you don't have to

defend yourself—I'm not attacking. Talk to me."

I need things to be defined. I have to know what's gonna happen next. And if it's not meant to be—it's not meant to be and oh well and you'll be missed. A lot. If it's not you, it's going to be someone else. But I really hope it's you. I want it to be you. Well, because it is you.

What I want is we move in together and watch Woody Allen movies. Then we get both a red Poodle dog and ginger Tabby cat. But they will probably have to be naked because I don't want you to die from allergies. And I'll probably be the only one of the two of us who has the privilege of going to the beach because you're the whitest person even of all gingers and being in the sun with your pale skin equals suicide.

You know what defines a family? Family, where the same goofy shit makes you giggle like a ticklish chimpanzee. People not laughing at your jokes is like people not cumming to your moves. What's the point of anything with them. Sex is great and important and all that, but it's totally overrated, because at the end of the day you want to have a conversation and laugh. And anytime we socialize, I'll be able to say: 'This is my husband. Obviously I'm his better half,' kissing you on the cheek. No one can kiss on the cheek the way a loving woman does. We'd be this couple terrible to write a book or a movie about be-cause there'd be no misunderstanding, no climax scene, no dramatic premise at all. Our kids will be all cute; bold like me and bald like you. I joke about you using Pantene Pro V shampoo because you're still hopeful and you say it's good for your scalp. I know you like talking with me. And isn't that the whole point? And we've got to have the attic to keep old family films there. I have no idea how we're going to get the attic in New York City...but I'll figure something out. I always do.

"Do you want to be together?" I say instead. "Any thoughts on that? Panic attack?"

"Phew. I thought something bad happened. Mirra, of course I want to be together. Aren't we already?" Dylan looks surprised and relieved. "I want to make you happy," he says calmly and kisses me. "Except just one thing."

"What is it?" I'm the one to almost have a panic attack instead.

"When you do your breaking bad at ninety-two, rather than high blood pressure drugs we should do heroin together. It seems weirdly romantic."

"By that time there'll probably be a heroin subscription service delivered to your door monthly. Satisfaction guaranteed. Cancel any time, aha."

He wants to make me happy? He wants to make me happy! Did I just get myself into a committed relationship? How do I do this? Should I from now on wear an apron or something?

"So, you're mine?" Dylan asks.

"I'm no one's. I am on my own, my own whole unit. 'Only a pill, a brain and an ass have a second half. I'm originally whole,' as my favorite Russian actress Faina Ranevskaya used to say. You're your whole unit too. And we're a team now."

"Understood. That's the way I like it." He embraces

me and then adds, "There's one more thing."

"What's that?"

"I just want you to know that by the time of your retirement plan in Italy all hair I'll have left will only be a mustache," Dylan says.

"Hey!" I try to object. "Eh, you're probably right. By that time I'll probably have a mustache too. You can call me Fredy then," I tell Dylan.

It is always more pleasant in man's hands than outside of them. With Dylan, I don't have to think about my behavior every single moment, I can be myself and he hugs me and comforts me even when I am unfair, wrong and angry. Probably, in order for someone to kiss you when you are at your worst, it is necessary that this someone loves you very much.

I get to know a different New York with him—a happy New York. Until now I either had a good time or a good story. With Dylan I don't have to choose. Apparently, you can break patterns. It's like basic obedience training but for humans: you need information, sometimes a professional, and some time. A masochist that I was, addicted to emotional pain, I now get my high from power: having it, being around it, creating it, taking it over, giving it, even watching it in movies and shows. Love is a form of power too, whether you give it or receive it.

Love is not the question—love is the answer. And I finally stop being annoyed with my own thoughts so I am able to live without earphones in. It took me a lot of walking to make peace with myself and find harmony within, which usually helps enjoy the big world outside your doorstep. Walking is the best: it helps me think...and not think, whichever I need the most at that moment. And never will I ever lie to myself again. Now I even have the easy gait of a chill person. Though, I don't have the need to write long forms anymore, only short stories and four-page long comedy sketches. Do I like it? Who cares! I am happy! I am living the creation, not creating the fictional living. In books, my alter ego went through things and always got it all in the end. Now I'm living the reality I create. I appear in my own reality, which I invent myself. The best things in life are a good joke, a rock 'n' roll song that gives you chills, and time in the morning when you already woke up and don't have to rush anywhere and can bask in bed. Still, something I could never do without is somewhere to walk to and someone to love. As well as fresh air, laughter, storytelling, passion and coziness on all levels of life.

Little do I know I created a reality where pregnant me will escape the country of my origin right before things get out of control and messy—like imposed martial law messy. I always wanted to experience a spy movie, because it seemed super-duper fun and exciting. "Be careful what you wish for because you might just get it". They're damn right about that. There! I fucking got it.

1 YEAR LATER

Well, what? They do it like that in movies!

BACK TO BASICS

We all would love to have an account on just one website, where we could laugh and masturbate and buy shit; a place where you go to for seltzer and end up with a bicycle and moral support. That is the dream of a person with a smartphone. Wait a minute! Isn't that Amazon's concept?

InfoPro.Club is a place like that but for all information Cyrillic.

They say that information is the most important thing at all times and that he who owns the information, owns the world. Information is power, but if it's in hands of idiots—it becomes dangerous.

News is a product that's well marketed and sold to its consumer. It's all nothing but artificially significant trash, a toy, because anything and everything is relative. Even the strongest edifice crumbles, ideals change, the Institute of Strength of Materials burns (Quite literally. Kiev has seen that one on the news, twice).

Since the principles of journalism have changed drastically with the social media boom anyway, I caught the flow and sort of did the impossible. When I started, everyone told me that I wouldn't change the way information is produced and consumed in Ukraine, but I did it anyway. Journalists and experts have been exchanging information within the Club, and not just on Facebook like they used to. InfoPro.-Club is a favor for both and actually a very useful tool where they have an opportunity to sell their story.

A while back there was a long-lasting attempt to bring Esquire magazine to the Ukrainian market. The dilemma was the following: the terms and conditions of the publisher's franchise demanded the imprint to be in the official national language of the country. Here's the thing: the official language is Ukrainian but the majority speak Russian. People who read Esquire magazine don't read in Ukrainian. And people who read in Ukrainian don't read Esquire. They later published the magazine anyway, in Russian. That being said, some things can never be changed, and some things absolutely can—it's only a matter of negotiations. You can make arrangements with everyone about everything. And make people do it your way. It takes time, like training a dog, creating patterns and conditioned reflexes. Books like "How to Win Friends and Influence People" are written to identify manipulators. Or you can actually avoid all the complications—work only with those who you like and who want to work with you too.

The new media season starts in September.

Reading the daily news in Ukraine, I have a feeling that something huge is about to happen, and it's not something good. Having déjà vu feels like you're going crazy for a moment. Though, it is not far from the truth—the news I mean. The presidential election is scheduled for November first and that means only one thing: promo campaigns have already aggressively started. And as far as I remember, something bad always happens in Ukraine in November.

One group of analytics is saying that it is about the right time to build the new democracy (because the old one had expired, apparently). The other group of analytics is suggesting they build an Ikea shelf first and see how that goes. Democracy only works when you're engaged. The media broadcasts both sides but not because of freedom of speech, lack of censorship, or objectivity of facts. The two main media corporations in Ukraine are owned by two major Ukrainian oligarchs who are in opposition to each other and thus their political minions and fosterlings are too.

The European Union's fundamental values are respect for human dignity and human rights, freedom, democracy, equality and the rule of law. These values unite all the member states—no country that does not recognize these values can belong to the Union. No country is also strategically located in the center of Europe, in between two worlds, two languages, two visions of the future, except Ukraine.

Everyone wants to express their opinion. Not everyone should, but luckily (or not), social media lets you do that, anytime, anywhere, anyhow. Everyone wants to be an influencer, an expert, someone whose words matter. InfoPro.Club gives them this opportunity, and the possibility that the media will value their opinion. Surprisingly to all, it does.

Together with the new media season starts the new era for InfoPro.Club. Gar Jafarov expresses his interest in my Club. It is very possible that I'll have more work with it, perhaps, with the new investments, expand the Club to InfoAwards and a physical club. All just like I wanted.

Gar Jafarov, a.k.a. Nose, is a Ukrainian oligarch of fifty-seven years of age, whose assets include Maximum Bank, N Airlines, the asset management company Wellmen, and Media One Group, which operates six Ukrainian TV channels and two newspapers.

His appearance indicates that men really don't bother and don't mind looking like Santa Claus who lost his propriety and can't even be sold on eBay.

Nose is an extraordinary person: you can tell him to go fuck himself, so he goes, then comes back refreshed and with a new business venture. Overall, Nose has the power to do good, but always ends up making things even worse, intentionally or not. He's an old conservative brick.

Sooner or later any businessman enters the big game of thrones by either investing in politics or becoming a part of it himself. Nose has always liked to pry, which is quite ironic because there's an idiom that literally says "to stick your nose into someone's affairs" meaning "to not mind your own business."

Gar earned his nickname because of his enormous nose. It is so significant that it could have its own social security number. It fascinates with just one look. If Nose sold vacuum cleaners or knives going from house to house, people would buy them all because the nose makes you speechless. It hypnotizes you with its existence. After looking at it you become like a zombie on ketamine.

He has three major cons: all three of them work with the dad. Recently, he married a model, a trophy, thirty-five-years younger than him. And soon enough, she became a typical Singing Panties—an artist whose husband invests in her singing career. Her name's Marika—such a beautiful name for such an unattractive female. Marika is a victim of human tuning. Her cheekbones, sculptured with fillers, are so sharp they can be used instead of a cheese knife. Her breasts are so big and fake that they look like a butt, her butt is so naturally small that it looks like one of her "before" breasts. Apparently, the era when women inject gummy bears all over their bodies is not over. The result—she has beautiful ears and that's it, but I will not talk about this. Body positive, ugly positive, all that, you know. Peace.

Regrettably, she released a couple of songs, some lyrics of which did not follow the rules of grammar or common sense: "how I stroke your hair with my voice," "and draw the earth in through the nostrils," and beyond any competition, "I swallow passers-by with my eyes." Regrettably enough, she released one more song "Flip-flops" and all of the country all summer long, up until I come to Kiev, sang along flop-flop, flop-flop, flop-flop. It is as corrosive as the "Mah Nà Mah Nà" song from The Muppets. You sing it for days before it fades away from your memory only until you hear it again. Lobotomy won't help. I don't even know why I'm talking about her—it's all a bad taste.

Anyway, Gar a.k.a. Nose invited me and my team. He actually said that: "you and your team." Ha. My team is really just a web developer, a lawyer, a sales pro and an SMM consultant who are all paid per gig. Nose said he wanted to talk about InfoPro.Club and invited me to Kiev for a meeting. I could not say no to that.

"Dylan, I need you to come with me to Ukraine," I say packing the furriest of my coats.

"I'm always down for traveling, babe, but how about in spring instead?"

"You don't understand. I have to go there now. Gar Jafarov suggested we have a meeting about InfoPro.-Club.

"Who's Gar Jafarov?"

"He's a Ukrainian oligarch."

"Really?"

"Don't act like you're surprised. Once I was somebody back there," I shrug.

"I sort of suspected you'd know someone like that." Dylan winks like he figured out The Mystery of the Century.

"Yeah, though that is not why I act like I have powerful friends, krysha, who are ready to provide an "umbrella of protection." No, that's my natural personality type mixed with a slutty ego seasoned with confidence. But people believe it."

"You're cute. Pretty lady-member of organized crime."

"Organized? Schedule, early morning wake-up alarm, crime workweek from nine to five? Hell no," I giggle. "So anyway, Gar invited me and my team."

"Your team?"

"Exactly. Not only do I not have a team, I also don't

have a penis which is required just to be there."

"Mirra, whatever that means just please don't get yourself a penis, use mine instead."

"That's exactly why I need you to come with me. You'll just sit there next to me, be present, that's all I want. Gar will treat me differently if there's a man with me and on my team at once."

"Why would he treat you differently?"

"Says someone who's a little bit of a sexist himself. Oh, Dylan, come on. Equality is a funny fairytale so let's just agree on that and save some time on a debate. Men in business treat women in business like they are their younger brother smoked up on weed."

"Mirra, I disagree."

"Okay, you can. But Gar is a misogynist and in his world all broads are stupid."

"What are you talking about, woman!" Dylan ironizes.

"Uh-huh, very funny. Are you coming with me? Can I count on you?"

"Of course you can count on me. I have a dick but I'm not a dick."

"Thank you."

"And even if they're not on payroll, they're still your team," Dylan adds.

"You're right. They all are very good. I should do like a team-building vacation or something," I say.

"Now tell me, exactly how cold does it get there so I'm prepared?" Dylan raises an eyebrow.

"Relax, the weather there is almost like in New York. But you can pack all of your silly sweaters, just for me. It'll be fun."

A plane becomes the method to go to an interesting performance, catch up with your favorite band on tour, share experiences with friends. A hug is enough of an occasion to come visit someone you miss. And business travel always comes with pleasure—pleasure of freedom to make decisions, and leg space in first class.

I always take the aisle seat on the plane. This way I don't have to bother bothering anyone next to me. A man in the front row smells like an opium stick, which makes me nauseous. Imagine if a skunk vomited. My sense of smell has always been so sensitive that I could beat pregnant women all together, if there was a contest of being annoyed with scents. The man also makes a weird noise about every thirty minutes—as if he oinks and sneezes at the same time. Happy trip for Mirra. Dylan next to me sleeps since take off—lucky bastard.

My good friend Knez Sandro meets us at the airport. He insisted actually. The situation seems like a Brazilian soap opera: my ex-boyfriend meets me and my current boyfriend at the airport because, quote, "why not meet good people?" The only element missing in this show is someone secretly blood-related to their significant other and someone falling down the stairs, who is typically the same person. Back in the day when autocorrection didn't know the word autocorrection and underlined itself, Knez Sandro and I dated. And then I hated him for about six months. Though, Knez Sandro did not even notice it. Now that we're over a decade past all the drama, we warmly care about each other. Turns out you really can be friends with your ex. For me, as a man he's terrible, but as a person he's terrific. He's like a relative. Not like a relative from a small town who arrives with a basket of stinky sausages for a two-day stay, throws his stuff around the house and stays for a month instead. And you feel uncomfortable kicking him out because, you know, he's a relative. Not like that. Relative is a good word. It's family.

Once, when my mom had an accident and was in a hospital and my father wasn't around, I called Knez Sandro for help. He was the only one I could call late at night and he'd pick up and actually help. That night he was out of town on vacation but he sent his older son instead, also a reliable fellow. If that's not the definition of caring then I don't know what is.

Knez Sandro is Georgian, so whatever he says sounds like a toast. If he worked as passionately as he likes toasts, feasts, singing, and chatting, he'd probably be the leader of the world. Also, he's knez for real, as in royalty of the Georgian Tavadi. The title was first applied in the Late Middle Ages and translates as prince or, less commonly, as duke. So, yeah, technically, I dated a prince. And I'm friends with a prince, no biggie.

"Did you bring me some Californian wine?" Knez Sandro asks as he drives us to the city.

"I did. I wrapped it in my sweater for safety, but if the bottle's broken, I'll squeeze the sweater into a glass."

"Yeah, I can degustate a sweater. Fine by me," Knez Sandro says.

Meanwhile, Dylan is occupied with the view of the

city through the car window: the color is a mixture of rotten plums and gasoline blurred in a puddle.

Any man would strain from the fact that I am friends with my ex. Dylan is a grown up, mentally mature man who is confident and self aware and simply trusts me. Besides, he sees the way I talk to Knez Sandro and that's enough said.

A song by the band called Boombox is playing in the car. I like Boombox. I listened to their songs many times although hear them only now. And then it is another song on the radio, and another one, and one more. I don't even know these new singers but they all have the same thing in common. It is unusual, a little stupid, and just weird. They randomly use English words in their Ukrainian and Russian lyrics all the time! The approach in the Ukrainian show business hasn't changed.

You can't possibly imagine Eminem going:
Hi! My name is (what?)
My name is (who?)
My name is
Худышка
The same way Russian-speaking people in New York talk. They just mix up two languages, sometime creating non-existing grammar constructions. When I hear this fictional language, my ears hurt. I want to take this person's head with my both hands and shake it well. Perhaps this way, the two beautiful languages spoken by Wilde and Bulgakov, Hemingway and Dovlatov, Miller and Chekhov can be placed back separately, like East Coast and West Coast. Beauty is also about the way you speak.

"By the way, tomorrow is the day I moved to Kiev fifteen years ago," Knez Sandro says.

"As far as I remember, it's already the third first day this year when you moved to Kiev. Thirty second of May, right? Or was it in Junetember?" I grin.

"No-e, it's tomorrow," Knez Sandro insists. "We should celebrate."

"Sounds like a plan," I reply.

"Mirra, I mean, let's have a party," Knez Sandro says. "I haven't had fun in a very long time, being busy with work and everyday responsibilities. I feel like I'm being covered in moss! Let's have so much fun that even atheists will burn in hell."

"Man, I think you got the whole atheism idea wrong," I laugh. "But I hear you. We're here for a while, so we'll party," I say when we arrive home.

So many homes... In the modern world, home is where you poop in the morning.

My building is built in an L shape, forming a courtyard with a garden, which gives a sort of privacy of entrance. It's not like in New York: you leave the building and you're literally in a street full of passer-by.

I see my neighbors, Gennady and Ilusha, men in their mid-forties and it looks like they are about to fight. One of them is holding a rotten tree branch—the other is standing ready to defend.

"Oh, hi Mirra, Haven't seen you in like forever. How are you doing?" Gennady says, letting down the tree branch.

Ilusha waves at me.

"I'm doing fine. Are you?" I point at the tree

branch. "Why are you guys fighting? What happened?"

"Oh, no-no!" Ilusha says. "We had a bet."

"Ilusha thinks I can't break this tree branch on his belly. I think the opposite," Gennady says.

"How much is the bet," Dylan asks me after I translate Gennady's words.

"Guys, how much did you bet?" I translate back to Ilusha and Gennady.

"Ten dollars," they both reply.

"They bet in dollars and not in Ukrainian currency?" Dylan asks me.

"Dollar is a legit currency, unlike Hryvnia," I reply.

"You can't break it," Dylan concludes.

"You want to participate in the bet?" I ask Dylan.

"I'll see you and raise you," Dylan takes a twenty out of his wallet.

"You guys are insane," I say.

"What? We're curious!" Gennady says and hands me two twenties, one for each of my neighbors. Now I'm a stake holder of this incorporated silliness.

This scene illustrates well that East Slavs are actually not as aggressive as Hollywood portrays or as they might seem at first glance from afar; and definitely aren't that sullen—it's the sleet at dusk to blame.

Dylan wins his twenty back and an extra ten. He can make money on anything, even internationally.

Nothing has changed here. Gennady hasn't changed except he shaved off the mustache. Ilusha hasn't changed—he's still like a dog chasing his own tail.

Since my Mickey pajama days, in the courtyard has been a creaking swing that's concreted into the ground for protection from theft. Later, in the days of me wearing leggings the color of a rabid leopard and singing Backstreet Boys into a comb, an apple tree growing above the swing started to bear fruit. Its apples were wildly sour as if they absorbed the creak from the swing. I know the apples haven't changed either. I'm the only one that has changed, the only one different, for the most part because I don't live here anymore—an occasional visitor, a tourist of my native country.

The doorman of my building in Kiev is actually a senior lady, babushka, who is there for god knows what reason but protection and security. She's there to create and guard the public opinion of who's a whore in the building, who's a sick narco, and whose children are bastards. Not that there're any mentioned actually living in the building. But Lida Lvovna, doorman babushka, in her place, twelve hours a day, guarding, like an old dog who uncontrollably farts but is already a family member.

Lida Lvovna believes that her mobile phone is the source of major radiation so she keeps it in a three-liter glass can. I sometimes miss all the craziness of my native people. She still remembers me and hugs me as if she were my blood babushka. She thumbs up looking at Dylan and then asks us:

"Have you eaten yet? Are you hungry? I've got pierogi with potatoes and crispy onions," she enswathes us with true babushka care.

"We'll go eat somewhere at a restaurant later," I

answer.

"Restaurant?" she rolls her eyes. "Why do you eat that dirty food? Come to me, I'll cook meat pie for you."

Dylan is standing in the hallway shocked. I smile like crazy in amusement.

Phenomenal. You can't possibly imagine a doorman in New York concerned about your dinner. Only people in Ukraine. Not that they care to that extent but they for sure interfere. They bother themselves and they bother you. And it feels like love. Is it good or bad? I don't know. It is absolutely inappropriate. I sometimes miss it in New York. It reminds me of home.

"Want a funny story?" Lida Lvovna asks.

"Always!"

"So I'm driving to the Solomensky Cemetery and a policeman stops me for no reason—I wasn't speeding, I wasn't anything. They just have to stop someone occasionally to try to win a little money, like in Fortune Wheel," she says meaning it is easier to give a policemen fifty bucks and continue driving than be bothered by him for some time and then give him a fifty anyway. "So he greeted me, took my driver's license and was standing there silently, looking at me. I was looking at him silently too. My way of beating corruption is to feign ignorance. After about five minutes of silence, he finally spitted out: 'Why aren't you proposing anything?' 'Will you marry me?' I proposed. The policeman started laughing and let me go."

"God I miss bribery. In America it's called networking," I tell Dylan. "Lida Lvovna, you're the best!

By the way, what were you doing at the cemetery? Who died?" I ask.

"No one. I decided to treat myself nicely and buy a place there for my seventieth birthday."

"Wait. Aren't you younger?" I ask.

"Well, Mirrachka," she says my name in a diminutive manner that automatically pushes the button 'home nostalgia'—I haven't been called that in years, "in my passport, it's sixty-two. But that's not the point. I wanted to buy a place at the cemetery in advance—something to look forward to."

"I love her already!" Dylan whispers.

"But they were so rude and wanted so much money that I decided to live, just for spite! Oh, and I also left them a bad review on Google," Lida Lvovna concludes.

"A bad review on Google?" Dylan asks again and I translate. He's been in cultural shock since we landed; it's only the beginning.

"My grandson taught me how to do that. Now that I know how—watch out everyone!" Lida Lvovna says. "Mirra, will you do me a favor?"

"Of course."

"Next time when you come visit, bring me American cigarettes, will you? That way I'll be able to say I have seen it all."

That is so fucking sad that seeing it all still comes down to one—anything American. Ugh...

She finally lets us go. I like Lida Lvovna, unlike her colleague who's also a little cuckoo but not in a fun way. She says she predicts the future and goes under psychic name Madam Zhana. She has also been collecting some documents to sue and punish Mikhail Gorbachev for collapsing the USSR. I guess she doesn't see her own future.

"If Lida Lvovna were a drug dealer, even her drugs would be fresh and homemade," I say after we enter the elevator to go up.

"Edibles would be perfect for her: pierogi with marijuana—something like that."

"Lida Lvovna is one of the few non-typical sixty-something-year-old ladies in Kiev who has a car, still drives it and is more active than just watching afternoon talk shows."

"All this is so freaking awesome! And unusual! And odd," Dylan says when the elevator doors open and we go towards the apartment.

"I know. Your mind must be blown." I start opening the door.

"In a fun way," he replies and then points at the door. "What is that? Two entrance doors?"

"Oh, yes. It's a weird thing that started in the early nineties. Back then there were too many home robberies so people tried to protect their properties this way."

"By installing a wooden door inside of the apartment that looks exactly like the bedroom door?" Dylan points at the bedroom door.

"I too think it is crazy. That is why I'm sort of a fake Ukrainian." I decide not to explain what it was like to glue stripes of paper around window frames to keep more warmth inside the house during cold winter days in my childhood. Window frames were of worse quality and winters were way colder back then.

Climate change is not an illusion. Yeah, you can watch Friends in different parts of the globe but there are this kind of little things that differ you. And the beauty of it is that you might never know what it would be. Differences are the best!

"Mirra, now that you got me thinking about my networking circle, is bribery really that bad in here?"

"It's definitely bad especially if you're on the wrong side of it," I say.

"I sort of sensed you might know these kind of people," Dylan grins.

"I've heard a couple of stories. I know a funny one, that's for sure."

"Just one?" Dylan doesn't believe me.

"Well, how about I tell you just one now?"

"Deal." The child in Dylan gets ready for a fairy tale.

"For a long time one person had been calling our character requesting a render-vous so he could ask for a favor, in exchange for money of course. Bribery is not just an everyday thing—it's still very personal, you have to make a connection, be referred by a mutual friend or someone who's of a higher rank or has more power. In other words, name dropping is valued—it can fasten the execution of a favor, and at times cost you less. Our character responded to calls but was not eager to meet, postponing it as long as he could, as if having a bad feeling about it; eventually he gave up under the pressure of a common friend and agreed to finally meet.

It was a hot summer, full of annoying mosquitoes of a size of an elephant and of a noise of a Concord.

The secretary of our character said she'd put window screens in his office, he agreed and forgot about it. Men underestimate women who decide to care about them.

On the bribery appointment day, the person showed up at our character's office. The windows were wide open, letting the fresh summer heat inside, which made both of the men sweat immensely. The air conditioner was broken or maybe it wasn't even installed, I don't know. The two did a little bit of a "social dance" and got straight to the point of their meet up. As soon as our character took the envelope with money, the authorities swing opened the door with the words "Well well well, bribery while on duty, Mister Character." People do all kinds of stupid things in desperation. Immediately, without thinking, trying to get rid of the obvious evidence, our character threw the envelope out the window. But by that time his secretary had already installed the almost invisible window screens. Chief executive bitch. The envelope flew directly into the open window, bounced back and fell on the floor right next to the police officer. Everyone started laughing hysterically. The person who brought the envelope in the first place tried to escape outside to sweat there, but was stopped and sat back down in a friendly manner. The situation was indeed amusing, so it was decided to not tell this joke to anyone else for the price of two envelopes for the authorities. They also wanted to cheer to that but our character declined to waste his cognac on them. On their way out, one of the policemen said: 'See you around.' Our character knocked on wood and then on the policeman's forehead, just in case, to be sure not to."

When Dylan and I, half-asleep, are unwinding from the flight, Val calls me.

"You're gonna die from laughter!" Val shouts. "I now own a concrete mixer truck!"

"What for? A new photoshoot or something?" I haven't been surprised about anything in years. Why suddenly start now?

"I had a car accident."

"Holy fucking moly! Val, are you all right?"

"Yes, I'm fine. I was pissed at first but it's actually funny. The driver of the concrete mixer truck hit my car. I don't know what his deal is and frankly don't want to know. Sometimes, the less you know the better you tan. He refused to call his insurance and was very persistent in his decision. Attention, attention! I am on my way to the notary, and the concrete mixer goes into my possession as payment for my car damage! If there's no point of even calling the officials— why bother, right? After the notary visit he'll unload the concrete mixer at a paid parking garage and I'm going to have to drain concrete out of it."

"Have fun," I say and yawn.

"No-no, we all will have fun. Tomorrow, I'm throwing a party in that parking garage. And a photoshoot! And serving a cocktail, 'Concrete'. You're invited obviously." And Val hangs up.

"My crazy friend Val just received a big concrete mixer...as a gift... So we're invited to a concrete party tomorrow," I say to Dylan and lie back down to continue napping.

"Who gives a gift like that to a girl?" Dylan says.

"I don't know. It's not the weirdest of all the gifts she has ever received. One of her boyfriends once gave her a dagger and a doll as gifts on special occasions," I say. "How hard can it be: if you're a man and lost in gift options, jewelry is always a good choice. Val shouldn't have really expected much from a guy who surprised her with an aqua park date while she was in a fancy, sexy dress, new heels, bought specifically for this purpose, with make up and hair that took her two hours of her life. Surprises are never good, ever."

"Noted," Dylan says. "Which one is Val again?"

"The one who lives in London. You'll like her."

It's not even surprising that the party is organized within a day, because it's Val—enough said.

Hm... What does concrete taste like?" I drop my hand to my stomach. *"Okay...hold on...uh-oh!*

PUT ME ON LOUD MODE

America is like pain in the ass, but only thanks to it you realize that the ass in the world still exists. My native city, a city of opportunity—there was an opportunity to leave it.

Nose resides outside of Kiev, in the beautiful pine tree area where the air is so clean it can be packed and sold in gallons as rejuvenation serum. The estate was originally founded as a monastery and functioned off-and-on until it closed in nineteen twenty-three and was reconstructed in nineteen thirty-five into a state-government-owned residence, first under the Communist Party of the Soviet Union and then under sovereign Ukraine.

As Dylan and I drive through a five-meter tall fence, we get to see most of what's in the residential property because the house is situated farther from the entrance, right on the banks of the Kiev Reservoir. There is a yacht pier, an equestrian club, a shooting range, a tennis court, a golf course, an ostrich farm, a dog kennel, numerous fountains and man-made lakes, a helicopter pad, and a small church on one hundred and forty hectares.

Buckingham Palace, the official residence of the

British monarch, contains over seven and a half hectares of total floor space. The total area of Monaco is two hundred and eight hectares. Central Park in New York has an area of three hundred and forty-one hectares. Tribeca is eighty six hectares in total.

According to the press, not the one Nose owns, a one hectare lease costs him thirteen dollars. And they say thirteen is not a lucky number. Imagine paying a monthly rent of less than two thousand dollars for the whole Tribeca area. (Ha! You can't even find an apartment in Tribeca for that price.) Not that the land in Ukraine is that cheap, no. The rent agreement for a period of forty-nine years states the purpose of "implementation of measures for the promotion of national and international programs aimed at improving the socio-economic status." Whatever the heck that means.

"How do you know all this?" Dylan asks me.

"It's not like I live on a cloud. Besides, I've been working with information my whole life."

"This is amazing!" Dylan exclaims. "I've got a hundred grand that I'm willing to spend. I can just buy Ukraine, right?"

"You have to be a governor and also a friend of someone who's in charge in order to lease land on such terms."

"Bummer. I guess I'll stick to only owning the Lower East Side of Manhattan then," Dylan says as I ring the bell at the front door.

Nose meets us and we go to his office which seems like another hectare away from the house entrance. Overcompensation is screaming out loud. The air in

the room is very stuffy, as if it has never been venti-
lated and almost makes me want to leave right away.
But I don't, obviously, because of the opportunity for
business growth.

"I like what you did with InfoPro.Club. It can be a
very useful and powerful media tool if used properly,"
Nose says, sitting down at his desk that's so long it
can easily replace a runaway for a small airport.

"Thank you. I agree. It is pretty good and it's only
getting better and more expensive with time."

"I'd like to buy it," he goes straight to the point,
skipping the social chat.

"Pardon me?" *(Surprisingly, it's never the non-
sense-saying person who says pardon.)*

"I want to buy it," Nose repeats.

"Gar, I'm flattered but the Club is not for sale," I
reply sweetly.

"Everything's for sale. It's only a matter of price."
He takes my indifference for a challenge. His balls
must be growing bigger and bigger with each word he
says.

"You can invest in it and be a partner," I suggest.
"There's a potential to turn InfoPro.Club into an actual club. This way, we'll get in HoReCa industry, too."

"You play chess?" Nose ignores me and asks Dylan
pointing at the board on his desk.

"I do, actually. Mirra and I play chess all the time,"
Dylan replies.

"Oh, she can play..." Nose either states or asks; his
intonation is unclear. The only thing that's clear is
that nothing has really changed in Ukraine except the
currency exchange rate.

"She is ready to play, if you'd like," I get worked up, rankled by his assertion.

Usually, I play chess for the sake of playing it. But I will always remember two things my grandpa taught me: your opponent will make a mistake—use it; when you're about to lose your piece anyway, take anything down with you, even if it's just a pawn.

It is time to start winning the game. I am not as foolish as Nose wants me to be. Right when I think I'll lose and accept that though continue my moves, Nose makes a mistake and I win, which only makes him angrier. Dylan tries to hide the excitement on his face and almost fails. I am as proud of myself as if I'd won a Pulitzer. Nose congratulates me, shakes my hand and invites me to meet up again in a month. Just when I'm about to come up with an excuse, he says he wants to invest in the future, presumably the info future of Ukraine stored in one Club. I have nothing left but to accept his invitation. After all, it's not everyday an oligarch wants something that I have and he doesn't. Intriguing. When it comes to power, there's always something that even rich people can't afford.

"Thank you for being there for me." I kiss Dylan in the taxi back to the city.

"It was spectacular," Dylan says.

"I think I made a strategic mistake not letting him win."

"Oh, this is nothing," Dylan says.

"Yeah...I'm not sure about that."

"Mirra, chess is a game where the woman rules—the queen can go anywhere and beat anyone. You showed him who's got the balls and that he should respect you."

"Ha. Queen with balls. Thanks a lot. I will not be able to unsee that," I joke, though I know I'm right.

Newton's Third Law of Motion states that for every action there's an equal and opposite reaction. Something tells me that Nose likes to get what he wants no matter what. But I don't have much time to overthink this because we have to get ready for Val's Concrete party.

If Val does something, she does it to the full extent. I guess she thought of concrete party literally and chose a parking garage with concrete walls. Its construction was not finished for years, although completely safe, and the owners started to rent out the building as is. Val's party occupies the whole floor. She took care of everything, including heaters and lights and bartenders and DJs and the good mood. There's two types of people: those who create the mood and those who join it.

New York is a miniature of the whole world, a mix of samples, a buffet of people. The crowd at the party is a little bit New York.

Cities, habits, and currency can differ. But no matter race, nationality, political views, food preferences, and gender there are some things about people that are unified all over the world, in economically developed countries—where iPhones are sold. Human nature is the same for all.

We learn curse words first in any foreign language.

We believe that being able to swear at people in their own language makes us multi-lingual.

We always start talking slower and louder in our

native language if we don't know the language of the country we travel to, which makes us look like we're on amphetamines. As if loudness magically translates into, say, Italian and brings us the meal we actually want from the menu instead of accidentally accusing a server of belonging to the mafia.

We give children unusual names. One called her daughter Madeleine. On one hand it sounds beautiful, but on the other hand she is a small, shell-shaped, French cake "Madeleine" according to her passport. Biscuit for friends and family. Another one's last name is Glove. She named her daughter Cashmere. Cashmere Glove. I kid you not. And in general, as history teaches, it's always a bad idea to name your child Usama or Adolf. Something tells me that people who avoid bios would agree on this one.

We think that neighbors from above move their furniture whenever they produce any disturbing sound.

We always have two plans: plan A—how we want things to turn out, and plan B—how they will most likely turn out but we're not ready to accept that yet.

We decide to start a new life on Monday and postpone it until next week if suddenly overslept.

We read articles about how to find motivation to lose weight while eating a slice of pizza, or how to break sugar addiction while eating three tres leches cakes in a row.

We ride with taxi drivers that are never real taxi drivers. They all are entrepreneurs, who either think of driving Uber as freelance with a flexible schedule they create for themselves or as a temporary occupation until their startup launches very soon, like next week soon.

We want to look impressive and glamorous and at the same time piss on the toilet seat and don't clean up.

We know which pills to use the morning after to be able to drink all night.

We want freedom and love at the same time.

We ask a stranger right next to us to look after our stuff in a coffee shop or at the beach so other strangers won't steel it. As if a proximity of a stranger automatically guaranties safety of possessions.

We wear tights with open toe sandals and socks with flip-flops, because some of us are cosmopolitans who come from the village. It happens so: a person can be taken out of the village, but the village out of a person—not necessarily. Although, it depends on education, upbringing, environment and a will to learn and change, of course.

We take only the most important and valued with us when moving. Someone hauls a china cabinet with ceramic statuettes across the ocean, someone packs books, someone makes a choice in favor of a credit card and a stamp in your passport, and not in a marriage certificate as a major life-changer.

As Dylan and I dance, I keep thinking about Nose and what he could possibly suggest at our next meeting that I wouldn't say no to.

"You know, I just don't get it: is Nose really such a blockhead?" I ask Dylan. "I mean, Nose is not a fool. Did he start the game and I just don't notice the alignment of all his pieces on the chessboard? What is really going on here?"

"You have to act calculatingly," Dylan says.

"That's the problem! I can't calculate what his next move is."

"Want me to get involved?" Dylan says and I know he means it. He likes me so much he's ready to give me his kidney.

"Nah, I'm just thinking out loud. No idea where this is coming from: he's just so unpleasant that every time I think of him I want to kick him in the face."

"Well, that's always a nice way to come to a consensus," Dylan concludes.

"He would easily invest in the Club if I were a man. All I would have to do is go to banya with him, drink lots of cognac together, maybe get him a hooker. And then we would sign an agreement. Doing business as a man is exhausting. If this was the case, I'd have to eat butter briquette beforehand of course."

"What? Why would you do that?" Dylan's confused.

"Cause it'd help to not get too drunk right away. Butter would at least postpone fast intoxication for a while," I reply. "But the trick is you can actually die of alcohol poisoning: when the butter digests, the full amount of drinks hits you at once."

"I am so glad you don't have to go through this. No one should. It's unhealthy," Dylan says.

"Well, duh. Dying is unhealthy indeed," I say.

Next to us there's a girl in a T-shirt with the print on it that reads "I'm yours for a pair of good shoes." A guy, after having read the message, decides to joke around. He takes off his shoes, comes to the girl in the

T-shirt and hands her the shoes saying: "Here. Shall we?"

"But these are not new, and for men!" She exclaims.

"Your T-shirt did not specify the details," he smirks, takes his shoes back and goes away.

He got her. He totally got her. She was stupid enough to wear a T-shirt like that. Or was she? Someone is getting some tonight. She will be following him in five...four...three...two...there it goes.

As the party continues, everyone gets sloshed with Concrete cocktail and goes wild, adoring someone they wouldn't in the morning. Later on I, as the only sober person, encourage everybody to go to Odessa like right now.

"I need a life partner...for the time of our trip to Odessa," Val says.

"I think I know a perfect guy for you," I wink.

Knez Sandro is an "I love you but I'm not in love" kind of guy. Val is a "Fall in love? Not possible...lust maybe" kind of gal. They both cause the good and run away.

"What's he like?" Val asks.

"He's like a women-forming enterprise. He loves to seek love, not find it—he likes the search process itself."

"Terrified of commitment?"

"Oh yeah. I don't know when he'll want a committed relationship. Nobody is getting any younger. The older you get the more likely you are to actually die on one day together. But he is so much fun if he's just for fun." I show a picture to Val.

"Fine by me," Val says and glances at the picture. "Oh, he's cute. I'll take him. Wrap him up!"

And I text Knez Sandro, since it's his moving to Kiev day today. Of course he joins us and we all head to the city on the Black Sea shore.

Odessa for Kiev is like Miami Beach for New York; a couple hours away can completely change your life for the weekend. Even though in New York the ocean is still the same, maybe it's the palms or the increased humidity that changes the mood to a festive one. Kiev's Dnieper river is perfect for morning fog and sadness, because it crosses the territories of three countries—Ukraine, Russia and Belarus—and collects all the sorrows of the Slavic peoples. But Odessa's Black Sea is for fun! Besides, Dylan's grandmother was born in Odessa so it is my responsibility to introduce Dylan to a very special city that's truly one of a kind. You can't explain it—you can only experience it.

Odessa...

It always has a reason to come visit. No reason at all is a good enough reason to go to Odessa.

It doesn't let bad people in with you. You travel only with people you love—as it always should be.

It meets you in the darkness of an early, pre-sunrise morning, gives you freshly squeezed orange juice, and accompanies you to newly cleaned streets to take pictures.

It brews crappy coffee. But this is nothing. It's nothing. Sugar will make everything better.

It photographs your silly faces and frozen poses pretending to be cheese saying "humans".

It can't stop you from dancing in the middle of an

empty street to Bon Jovi's "It's My Life".

It is just like New York: people are either irritated or amazed with it. But you can't deny it.

It makes you tired but in a foolishly pleasant, enjoyable way.

It lets you nap for a couple of hours and this nap feels like a twelve-hour night's sleep. Maybe there's something in the seaweed of the Black Sea that vaporizes as energy.

It might think that something is over. It just doesn't end there. This is the beginning. Everything has already begun.

In Odessa I find out I'm actually pregnant. So I tell Dylan. He's excited to have a sample of both of us. I, on the other hand, have no idea how to react to the news. I guess my maternal instinct doesn't come in one package with a pregnancy test.

"Having children is expensive. It's like buying a Mercedes convertible for twenty-one years in a row," I tell Dylan.

He looks happy and dumb.

"So let's have a Jaguar for twenty-one years in a row instead. Big deal. Or maybe two Jaguars," he says.

"What am I, a garage for your sperm vehicles?"

"Yes please."

Here I am, a smart woman smiling stupidly. He loves when I smile. With Dylan I smile a lot.

The hotel we're staying at is a beautiful historic building reconstructed the Ukrainian way. It means that something is definitely fucked up. They made panoramic windows the American sky scraper style.

That is, they are walled up tightly—you can't open them; even window handles are not provided. The building is only five floors. (Long-lasting facepalm). The central air system is carefully turned on in advance for the convenience of visitors, blowing heat. Of course there's no thermostat. The room is exceptionally warm, so warm that I feel like I'm in a sauna, and about to die of suffocation and a heart attack combined. Perhaps so many people in Ukraine are gloomy and dismal because they lack of fresh air in public spaces?

The receptionist replies that they've already switched the heat on for winter. God bless America and its freakishly cold Starbucks all year round.

"I need fresh air! People need fresh air!" I say despairingly.

"Me too, actually," Dylan says. "Let's go for a walk. You can walk, right?" he points at my stomach.

"Yeah, since I was like two."

"Okay, you can definitely walk." Dylan stops being overprotective, grabs my hand and heads towards the exit door. "Come on, what am I sightseeing in this city today?"

"Everything! Are you ready for everything?"

Everything means exploring Odessa with a professional tour guide, a very funny lady Rosa. When Dylan, Val, Knez Sandro and I board the minivan, the first thing Rosa says is, "Alright, everyone's here, the door is closed. We're all ready. From A spot to G spot pleasure starts its journey."

"God I love Odessa!" Val says and we all burst out laughing.

Little Odessa in Brooklyn is nothing like the real Odessa. It's like comparing sushi in Japan to sushi in any European town that has no access to the ocean. The authentic Odessa is about Derybasovskaya Street, Potemkin Stairs, and of course Privoz Market. It was founded in eighteen twenty-seven and operates as a mix of a department store, farmers' market, and live Craigslist. Privoz is not just for fresh food, it is also for communication, city news, and vulgar gossip. No wonder that Privoz is mentioned in The Odessa Tales by Isaak Babel—the market itself is full of funny characters.

Dylan says he's going to stay in Odessa forever after he tries brynza cheese, dried and salted taran fish, and kiziloviy kompot—a kousa dogwood fruit sweet beverage. Greenhouse tomatoes stand out tremendously; they actually taste like tomatoes and not rubber foam. I'm not surprised with Dylan's reaction. There's a food cult in Odessa. So he's having multiple gastronomic orgasms and here comes one more when we head to a family style restaurant called At Angels' for a very special treat bichki and their entertaining parrot who has been taught to say the word "ass."

In the early two thousands, this same restaurant used to be called Pharaoh. It had bison testicles on the menu. They cost about three hundred dollars and you had to order the meal three weeks in advance before making dinner reservations. Pharaoh's bartenders were so hot that you wanted to embalm and drag them into your pyramid. And girls dressed up so vulgar they looked ridiculous, like palm trees in Siberia. But ever since then it was rebranded to be a cozy place with delicious and non-pretentious food.

All year long East Slavs eat the traditional New Year's Eve salad with a French name "Olivier"—salad the French have no idea about. When East Slavs make this salad—it's always enough to fill a bathtub. Same with borsch. They eat until they roll out of the dinner table sweating of exhausting digestion. Everyone is supposed to be full. That is why there're so many neurotics: it's not good to waste food by leaving it on the plate: consequences of the Second World War still in action. I still don't like to waste food either—my fridge is full of leftovers and I detest it because I'm a foodie and like variety and freshness. And when I cook this soup, it can easily feed a family of three people for about a week. No matter how hard I try to adjust the amount of ingredients, I always somehow end up with a fish tank of borsch. Some things just don't change. My father eats borsch for breakfast—yep, he's that tough. Native land inheritance.

We walk a lot in the historic parts of town. The courtyards of old Odessa kind of look like the ones in California, minus pool and chic. The final part of exploring the city is a show at the National Academic Theater of Opera and Ballet, which Dylan calls the Royal Palace due to its architecture. On our way there we see a priest in a cassock and a girl in a mini skirt next to him. They are talking to each other rather coquettishly. Then the priest hugs her waist, his hand sliding down, and spanks the girl on her buttocks— must be letting go of her sins.

At the theater tonight is operetta—a show similar to a musical, that combines both music and subject matter. After it is finished, Dylan tells me we should from now on communicate like we're in an operetta—in a comic, amusing manner with sudden singing in between. I sing oh yes, baby, yes in A major. Outside the opera house an old man is feeding a pigeon, carefully, to not scare the bird away. And the other two pigeons are racing towards the bread crumbs. Same goes for the media. You've got to give them some bread crumbs and they all will run towards you, and all the mediums will want the crumbs too. Something is about to happen. I don't know, maybe it's the fish in my stomach, but my guts scream that it's the calm before the storm. Big change is coming up next—good or bad we'll only know after it's done. Thus far, there has always been two options.

As our spontaneous trip to Odessa is over, Dylan, full of experiences, goes back to New York to do his work. I stay at the epicenter of my work in Kiev and in the meantime decide to sell my apartment and take care of that before the next meeting with Gar. I already have something good, something fad, something goofy, something frank. All of it and the people I love, my family and my chosen family—friends, all are in New York now. And family is everything. It's people that define you because they create places of love, regardless of zip code. I come to the point that I can visit Kiev and Odessa anytime if I want to and stay at a hotel with room service.

A month doesn't seem like a long period of time, but surprisingly so much can happen. Things go so haywire.

BULLHORN SHOUTS—HERD MOOS

"The grant for the title of the President of the country goes to..." drumroll sounds, finalists of the presidential contest show *Ukraine's Got Talent* hold their breaths, the audience in the TV studio retains absolute silence, ready to explode in applause at any moment at the instant command of the show director.

The host puts off the results—the moment of truth —to his best ability, taking a commercial break three times. The judges have already spoken their opinion about every contestant and the coaches revealed obstacles and funny moments that happened to the contestants during this season of the national voting race. Then it is a flashback on contestants who left the reality show before the semi-finals and how life is treating them now. Unfortunately one of them is dead—a minute of silence in his favor breaks with a cherry beer commercial for younger millennials.

The host once again announces the list of sponsors of the show and expresses gratitude on behalf of each candidate to their patrons. Among them are shampoo for alopecia, cognac, and woven designer suits for men with bellies.

The main prize for the winner: the certificate for the presidential office, redeemed only for five years, plus the pin-code to the state budget and the book "Constitution," but the last prize is not that meaningful, just to honor the tradition of the show that's been on the air for six seasons. The TV channel that has the exclusive rights broadcasts this show twenty-four seven. The ratings are phenomenal with each new season and the success is unbeatable. Besides, it's also daily news about the contestants, the talk show, the reality show part, the voting itself—audition round, semi-finals, the grand finale. Once every ten years a change of positions is launched. It's called crisis. And the crisis is the most popular period of giving political characters their roles, new or old. Sometimes characters leave the race altogether, sometimes they go to prison, sometimes they have a heart attack.

No one ever asks questions, no one is surprised why everything good suddenly becomes bad. Very convenient. Citizens just keep watching the show, sending text messages to support their favorite contestant; text message rates apply.

Here's how the show would go in the United States.

THE PRESIDENT FACTOR

INT. TV STUDIO. NIGHT.

The studio is like a typical talent show. 4 judges sit in front of the stage. A host is on the stage with a microphone. There're 2 stands on the stage like at a political debate.

HOST

> Ladies and gentlemen. Welcome to the finales of the show The President Factor. Today, we are going to choose the next President of the country. Get your phones ready for sms voting. Your vote matters!

Audience applauses.

> HOST
> Please welcome our judges. A bald guy, who's always a judge at this type of a show, because he's a part of the franchise contract.

BALD GUY stands up and waves to the audience and the host.

> HOST
> A lady with straight hair. She might be a singer or a dating coach or something, we don't really know. But she looks beautiful on the camera and that's what matters for this show.

LADY WITH STRAIGHT HAIR stands up and sends an air kiss to the camera.

> HOST

> Please give it up for a
> guest star! He doesn't
> want to be here but
> doesn't mind getting some
> extra money for cocaine
> expenses. And, he'll sing
> for us at the end. So
> don't you dare go any-
> where.
>
> (to himself)
> Oh, that rhymed. I'm good!

Audience applauses.

> HOST
> And last but not least a
> fourth judge.

FORTH JUDGE stands up to greet the audience but the Host doesn't pay attention to him and continues.

> HOST
> Now that all of our judges
> are introduced, let's get
> to know the contestants of
> The President Factor! The
> finale!

Contestants show up on the stage.

> HOST
> (reads his notes)

Contestant number one. Two years ago she graduated from college with a degree in English language and literature.

(theatrically whispers to the camera)

I think she definitely has a plan how to beat unemployment in this country. According to her one and only official Instagram account she is, quote, student, author, motivational speaker, dating expert, dog lover, coffee junkie, everyday cuddler, wrist watch wearer and an empathic little bitch heart emoji, heart emoji, heart emoji. End of quote. Please give it up for…

(looks in his notes)

…empathic little bitch.

CONTESTANT NUMBER ONE smiles and dances on the stage for the camera. Audience applauses.

HOST

Contestant number two. He

has shown up on such shows
as "Late Night with John
Smith," "Get Some Sleep,
Dude" on CNBJFM-MC channel
in 2001, "I'm Your Queen,
No, You Are Not" in Great
Britain - the English version of our show, and
"23rd Street Station of R
train" on…

(looks in his notes)
Oh, not on TV, an actual
23rd Street subway sta-
tion. Okay, then.

(to the camera)
Now that you all know our
finalists and their fac-
tors, let's choose the
next Prrrresideeent!

CONTESTANT NUMBER TWO waves. Audience
applauses.

HOST
And the first round is
called Presidential debate
a.k.a. talent battle.

Contestant number two starts juggling
and dancing and singing and finishes
his routine with an acrobatic element.

Audience applauses.

HOST
Now, that's what I call a
good debate. Let's see
what Contestant number one
has prepared for us.
Ready. Set. Go.

CONTESTANT NUMBER ONE
(comes to her stand)
Actually, my therapist
says I shouldn't take part
in anything that can put
down my self-esteem. And
this seems like such a
stressful activity right
now.

HOST
That's the rule of the
first round. You have to
show us your talent.
There's a country at
stake.

CONTESTANT NUMBER ONE
Only when we can give up
the concepts of our limited self can we attain en-
lightenment and libera-
tion.

                    HOST
          Oh, my god! Her talent is
          motivation of others!

Audience applauses.

                    HOST
          For the next round you
          have to answer one ques-
          tion: does Western consti-
          tutional law engage with
          Jean-Paul Sartre and exis-
          tentialism?

Contestants look at Host confused.

                    HOST
          I'm joking, obviously!
          It's a bikini round. Let
          the country see if you're
          hot enough to be the Pres-
          ident.

Contestants take off their clothes and
stay in bikinis. Audience applauses.

                    HOST
          You know what? I fully
          support you guys so I'll
          stay with you in a bikini
          too.

Takes off his clothes and stays in
Speedo. Audience applauses and cheers.

                    HOST
          Let's hear what our judges
          have to say, their finale
          thoughts and comments and
          words of support before
          the results.

          LADY WITH STRAIGHT HAIR
          I think that Contestant
          number one is so worth to
          be the winner. I totally
          dig her because I'm a cof-
          fee junkie too, just like
          her. You go girl!

                    BALD GUY
          I fully support Contestant
          number two. Have you seen
          him juggling? How does he
          do that? Amazing! Abso-
          lutely amazing! He's my
          President for sure.

                    GUEST STAR
          Thank you for coming to
          see me. I love you all.
          You are the best.

                    FORTH JUDGE
          What's interesting about
          this season is…

Host interrupts Forth judge and doesn't

let him talk

>   HOST
>   Thank you for your bril-
>   liant comments, as usual.
>   And finally it is time to
>   find out who is going to
>   be our next President!

Host opens an envelope and pauses.

>   HOST
>   You wouldn't believe it. I
>   guess the bikini round
>   changed the whole contest
>   dynamics because the win-
>   ner is…me! Thank you,
>   thank you so much for your
>   trust and support.

Host looks at both contestants.

>   HOST
>   As the newly elected Pres-
>   ident I promise to learn
>   how to juggle and motivate
>   others. And also answer
>   the crucial question: does
>   Western constitutional law
>   engage with Jean-Paul
>   Sartre and existentialism?
>
>   (pauses)
>   I'm joking obviously! Top-

```
less six-pack pictures for
the White House website
everyday, of course!
```

Blackout.

In Ukraine a six-pack is not essential, so the show goes slightly differently.

The finalists of this season are the following:

Candidate number one. Arse. His political slogan is "Arse will fight corruption."

Candidate number two. HE. Yeah, just that, not even a name. His political slogan: "Only HE is worth being the President."

Candidate number three. Larissa. "No time to rest."

Candidate number four. A female troll of Larissa with the slogan "I win, she'll rest."

Candidate number five. Sergey. His political slogan: "I will hear everyone."

All of the candidates promise a lot. They don't know that the human brain relies on action. If you lie a lot, dementia will develop.

Lastly, the results of the online voting are ready to be announced. All of the prizes are already in the TV studio awaiting the new President.

The way it has always been in Ukraine is when the sugar is taken away, people are ready to tear and toss. But when the right to vote is taken away—everyone shrugs their shoulders and silently lowers their eyes. It is called the adjustment process. If you call a person a pig long enough, eventually they will oink. Ukrainians have been taught well to adjust to all sorts of

messy, monopolistic bedlam and lawlessness hulla-
baloo. All the government needs to do is to give a sop
once in a while and everyone will calm down for a
handout.

Surprisingly, this is not the case here. This time a
different approach is taken. After the results of the
show are announced, the audience boos the winner.
The audience boos Arse and it's quite surprising because butt is in trend today. Sergey is number two according to the results. Instead, Arse should be in his
place, Sergey declares, because Arse and number two
always go together.

Just when people get used to their happiness—
bam! It's a new revolution. It's a new day, it's a new
life. And you're feeling good? You sure? A revolution
in Ukraine is like a litmus test—a test to determine
someone's true intentions or beliefs. The only thing is
that the Ukrainian economics can't afford the swank
of constant change.

The voting results are claimed to be fabricated.
People go out in the streets. The servers of InfoPro.-
Club hardly manage to fulfill all the news queries—
there are so many of them. Daytime protest turns into
a legalized nighttime one with tents, hot tea, and
someone bringing cookies. Then it continues for three
days, with people in the street twenty-four seven.

The demand is only one. Have one more show—
another, third round of elections with the two candidates in first and second place. It's Sergey who is the
face and the voice and the official leader of the
protest. Who would've thought. A sponsor, unre-
vealed in the media, is clearly in charge of the mass

protests against unsatisfactory voting results. Now, it's either Sergey or Arse who is supposed to make the country great again. I'm kidding. They don't even fake promise that.

Sergey is like Kevin—a Kevin can't become the President. You never expect a Kevin to be a leader. Relying on Arse is always doubtful. Quite a choice.

Sergey is very active. During his political promotions he promised EU membership and now declares that people of Ukraine couldn't have declined this opportunity and therefore the voting results must be fake. Just another redistribution of government seats yet again. He gets in the media headlines with his civil grief and gets out with a new credit tranche from IMF.

Paucity can't form a change. A week later, to prove the seriousness of their demand to approve the third round of elections, the quantity of protesters is strengthened with Actors Anonymous—folks that go in the streets for any political purpose. They are paid daily and don't really have their own opinion except the one told to them. Some do it for a good reason and some for no reason at all. They are morons that do not bother to follow the law. The law is not written for idiots, if it is written it's not read, if it is read it's not understood, if it is understood—not the right way.

In the meantime, the news talks about another fight in parliament. A member of one political party kicked the shit out of a member of another political party; in the name of the better future I suppose. The very fact there was a fight means only one thing: in the coming years no one is going to change anything. Change the economy, comply with laws, improve the standard of living—none of this interests the deputies. All that matters is political PR and ratings. And fights, as well as politicians sniffing lines right in parliament as if it's a Hollywood party scene, apparently seem civilized. Journalists report on events, rather than reporting on unacceptable behavior. Why aren't shaming rituals and cancel culture applicable here? Street protests, now angry, escalate to the point of occupying a government building, aided by Actors Anonymous— the self-proclaimed special forces of the revolution.

A rule of three—if three people in the street stop walking and look up in the sky, most of the street will do the same. It is almost impossible to resist. Same with other things too: everyone laughs—you laugh, everyone breaks the windows and crashes things—you do the same. It is hard to resist the majority when you are in the epicenter of it. When absurdity is happening the only way to handle it is to be absurd too. The basic principle of building a new democracy is to create a series of events so that people do not guess how they're being played. And then everything goes on, increasing tolerance to anything that's fucked up. How is it done? You start up stupid nonsense, launch a promo saying that it's cool and let it flow into the masses. Some will accept it, some will not. People can be organized according to a required level of craziness. Those who pick it up are a herd that can be controlled. Make the loudest one its horn, not a speaker. The horn yells so he must have important things to say, right? None of the yelling can possibly happen without the media coverage and constant content updates.

Watching the news I can't believe it. Everything looks like insanity. Sometimes I never know for sure whether events occur on purpose or accidentally. Though, in politics even "accidentally" is a press release written by someone.

Consuming news in the morning seems like a crazy idea, very exhausting. However, I sign into InfoPro.-Club, wondering what news to expect in the following days. On the back end of the Club, the access to all info queries is available to me without any subscription fee, obviously. I see all updates: who submits a query, who accepts it, where it's published afterwards, and the statistics of all kinds of metrics. As I keep browsing, I find out that the same journalist accepted most of the queries about the political development of the country. I click on his name and open analytics that lead to the online version of Gar Jafarov's newspaper. Digging for more, I set up a search for the current year with the tag "politics" and see multiple journalists who covered this topic. They have been very active users for the past year and have one thing in common: they all are employed by the media outlets of another oligarch—Gar Jafarov's political opponent. But there have to be experts who created the press releases to distribute. I then check the queries submitted within the current year. PR One company, a division of Jafarov's Media One Group, and its specialist Bogdan Zima is the verified expert source in the Club. In other words, one company of Gar Jafarov working in the public relations sector has been creating news to be distributed through Jafarov's other media companies and, most importantly, picked by its competitors. The metrics show that mentions in Jafarov opponent's media covered the topic significantly as opposed to Media One Group. Technically, they were winning the news race. Or have they been diddled? There's always someone who creates the news before they're broadcasted. Gar Jafarov is already in charge of half of the information flows in the country. Apparently he decided to use InfoPro.Club as a tool to influence the media corporation of his concurrent oligarch. Sneaky, sleazy reprobate.

It all finally makes sense to me! But I decide to check it anyway, looking for the one. As they say, one who's looking will always find. There it is, that one specific press-release posted on InfoPro.Club two days before the first street protests started. The main message is a call-to-action to all citizens to go in the streets and protest. "It is now or never. The President is the servant of the people and not vice versa. Those who have chosen the President should have the ability to overthrow him anytime, as well as the government and parliament..." And blah blah blah, yada yada yada, so on and so forth in that aggressive style. Yep. It was submitted by Bodgan Zima, picked up by all Ukrainian media outlets nationwide and then trending for forty-eight hours. InfoPro.Club has been used as the media source to force a state revolution.

Sometimes things just cannot be foreseen.

Only now I start to acknowledge that the rehearsal of this insanity started about a year ago and climaxed with the debates about new democracy. As I read the news for the previous Tuesday and a week before that and last month, as well as weekly digests of the year, I see the development of the main subject just like in bad fiction. Amid all stories there is a tendency to a certain opinion forming—the government needs to be changed, that's the only way, and there's no turning back.

The development of the brand of the national revolution is happening so fast and is so well-directed, informationally, that for just a second even I believe that this revolution is needed and will really change the life and consciousness of the people, who will have essentially fought for nothing. As a result, of course, the people won't get anything, except for more credit from IMF, and more, and more, and then more again that will have to be paid back by this generation, and the next generation, and the next generation after that. Hours of broadcasting on world television channels and in the press about the country that no one knows the exact location of on the map ain't worth it. The Ministry of Culture and Tourism could have simply bought broadcasting minutes to advertise the country. It's somewhere there on the map. Come visit. Welcome.

As with any brand, the revolution has its own logo and a slogan and a soundtrack—the collection of regrets. The principles of branding and marketing are pretty much the same for sausages and pop stars and political revolutions.

At this point, the Boulevard of Young Corruptionists—the central boulevard of the Ukrainian capital—is filled with tents and citizens of all ages. They bond and talk about the bright future and believe in it. The next step must be the sacrifice of a life or lives to push the limits and make a significant amount of people come out into the streets in fear of being the next one killed by the government. Publicly, eighty people will have been killed overall. Not publicly? The amount yet unknown.

Which is worse: burning books or burning flags? First comes the flag, then the books; what happens next is on the news.

Because of the instability and political mess happening in the country, there isn't much happening on the real estate market either. People are waiting for what's going to happen next, what direction of development the winner will take. Therefore I have only one offer for my apartment which is on the lower borderline of my expectations. I am not exactly in a rush but going back and forth transatlantic for more offers is not my preference. Suspense is the worst. Moreover, I don't feel safe in Kiev anymore. I do not know what to expect next and it scares me. You can't protect yourself from instability. There's no condom for revolution. Though, even condoms break. Predictions are hard: it can go anywhere from high inflation level to the imposition of martial law. Within a month that I've been here it's both.

It is the day when I go see Gar Jafarov at his home office again. But it takes a while to even leave my building because the adorable craziness is happening in the lobby. One of the two elevators is completely blocked by a cat in labor.

The homeless ginger cat with smart eyes and long whiskers has been living on the ground floor of my building for a couple years. All female residents have been taking care of the cat, brining her treats, toys, and blankets. Women are especially happy to be friends with other women if the latter have whiskers, even if it's a feline.

Lida Lvovna was opening the entrance door to start her work day when she saw the cat. She thought that the cat was brought by the smell of her home-made fish for lunch coming out of her bag. This cat is the most well-mannered cat that can possibly exist. So Lida Lvovna let the cat come inside to give her some food. But the cat ran straight to the elevator and immediately laid down inside of it. A second later the cat started screaming like she was tortured. Lida Lvovna ran after her. Residents started gathering in the lobby, asking what was happening; some complained that they had to take the stairs. And then the cat started giving birth. "How dare you, you red stupid slut!" Lida Lvovna yelled at the cat, taking her lunch box out of the bag and trying to block the elevator doors from closing with it. "I haven't slept well and have to work a full day today and my god-damned steamed fish has smeared everything in my purse! I said stop screaming! I do not have epidural anyway, you ginger cunt with ears!" But the cat could not un-born the kittens; and the elevator doors kept smashing the lunch box and the buttocks of Lida Lvovna a little bit until the miracle of life was over. She would have insured it, like Jennifer Lopez, had she known she'd get hit so hard by the elevator doors.

"And now," Lida Lvovna finishes the story, "this ginger slut is a mother and we have to move her somewhere away from the elevator, but she's being overprotective and isn't letting just anybody touch her kittens except me."

My neighbors start to calm down, some of them have already used the situation as an excuse to get a drink and calm the nerves, congratulations to the new mother etcetera etcetera.

Then the father cat shows up in the lobby, but not alone: he's got a mouse in his mouth, which is not even dead yet. It moves, it blinks, it's fresh—whole foods organic. I'm not sure whether it is for the cat lady, or a gesture as a thank you to Lida Lvovna. All women start screaming, me included. All men start laughing (ugh). They will take care of the mouse and the rest of this furry fauna. Time to do business.

The taxi driver turns on music and I hear classical, one of those flirty sonatas for the piano in a major tone that sets a good mood. My mood is already good enough for a person who throws up for breakfast. Today, I threw up oatmeal with honey and berries. Classical music is also the best choice for an incredibly violent scene in a thriller movie.

Gar is talking to me pleasantly as we're drinking tea. This is the most social chat that has ever existed—*People* magazine would go broke not being able to write anything scandalous about it. He then opens a safe, takes out a gun, dumps it out on the desk, and drops a stack of papers next to it. "Business Purchase Agreement" it reads. On the first page, in the paragraph about the price, I see a blank gap. Only then do I begin to grasp the significance of what I had contributed. I feel like I'm in the *Sopranos*. He threatens me in the best traditions of film mafia—with a smile.

Egads! I opened Pandora's box. Good work, Mirra, good work! Do I really want to slam the door on him and then deal with the consequences of his ill ego or try to get away with minor troubles while I still can?

When I'm stressed to the extreme, I talk like a cold-blooded rationalist before bursting into tears for hours.

"So when you said you wanted to invest in the future you meant..?"

"My future, Mirra, my future. Obviously."

"What will happen to the Club if I sign the papers?" I ask.

"It is no longer your concern," Nose says.

"And if I do it, you won't bother me or..." I suddenly feel nauseous, notice an empty waste paper basket next to the desk, grab it, quickly puke—the vomit of course spreads all over the basket and leaks onto the floor through the chrome wires—and continue like nothing happened, "...you won't bother me or my family and will forget I exist? Is that so?"

"I understand it is hard for you to digest the information but please don't vomit in my house. It is disgusting," he says beastly.

"Well, I'm gonna throw up anywhere and anytime I want." I imagine how I'll barf cuss words on his exit door. If he lets me out, of course, and won't shove those cuss words back down my throat, or whatever it is that these people usually shove up into someone in cases like these, under these circumstances.

"You're going to make the right decision?"

"You're robbing me!" I say and barf, yarf, blargh—

another vomit spasm, which goes away as fast as a sneeze so I don't pay much attention.

"I'm taking what I want," he says looking at me in disgust.

"By threatening me? You took out that gun for what? All right, kill me. And you won't get the Club ever. You think that you can put this gun to my head and make me sign the papers? Ha! No. That's not how it is going to work," I retort.

Gar is a leg bouncer. It freaks me out and makes me want to puke again. I hate it. Leg shakes are a symptom of anxiety or a sign of feeling stressed. At least I can continue talking to him when he sits. Because then he stands up, comes very close and stands over me, morally pushing me down so that my spine momentarily gets scoliosis curvature. This is the only way he can taste the success and enjoy it.

"Mirra, why all the drama? Calm down."

Never in the history of calming down has anyone calmed down after being told to calm down.

"You must have misunderstood me," Gar continues. "Don't you remember I offered to buy the Club from you when we met? My offer is still on. I will give you twenty thousand dollars for this website."

"Website? Are you kidding me? The value of the Club is now two million. And I'm tired of repeating: it is not for sale, Gar. I'm leaving." I stand up, head to the exit, and open the door.

Gar's security guy, his personal jackal, who has apparently been behind the door all this time, is standing in the way not letting me go. Gar follows me with the face of an annoyed but patient parent, touches my shoulders, and steers me across the office back into the chair.

Touching someone's shoulders is trying to mess with their confidence.

"Mirra, don't leave yet. I haven't finished talking," he leers and swaggers back to his chair.

Gar Jafarov is not the type of man capable of both cruelty and integrity. Rumor has it, his reputation rests on forceful methods of influence. I really don't want to check whether he will chew me up and spit me out. It's not a game anymore. I can't deal with this sincere enormity. I am way too keen to escape from that. When worst comes to worst—safety is what matters. This fight is not worth fighting. He keeps the pressure and I am almost at the point of signing anything so he just lets me go and all this madness stops. I want to cut it off like a scene during montage. Apparently, Gar is enjoying himself a lot because he suggests we play chess. Although, it's clearly an order rather than a suggestion—to prolong the moral execution so to speak. If you're going through Hell, keep going. Right, Churchill?

Gar slides the board to the center of his desk like it's a magic trick. He chooses to play white without asking and opens with the King's Pawn Game.

If I created the problem, I will be able to find a solution to it. All I have to do is look for it... Think, Mirra, think! My mind is racing to the point that I almost feel the cells moving inside my brain in search for the information. I ask to use the bathroom or else I'll throw up all over again so of course they let me.

It is a masterclass in opulent excess—rumors were

right. Nota bene! Watch out for someone who flushes in a golden toilet. And that's in a guest bathroom. I wonder what he has in his master one, a golden throne?

Best ideas come in the bathroom indeed. It's like a knee-jerk reaction. Once some shit comes out of you, an idea comes into your head instead. This is when I remember Nikki's story.

Usually, I'm pretty tight-lipped when it comes to information, especially if it's delicate, especially if it's not mine. Going through other people's dirty linen is not my life principle. Neither is walking over their heads. Though in an attempt to avoid being robbed and potentially beaten, not only have I to defend myself, but also attack. If there's demand there's market—a simple rule of economics. I do not have a maternal instinct for my fetus yet but I do have the maternal instinct for my business baby. So I am going to protect it at all cost. Especially since it wasn't so easy for me to have it in the first place.

"Gar," I say after having come back from the bathroom and do the Queen's Pawn move. "I personally think that people can use their bodies as they please. Unfortunately, Ukraine is a country more tolerant to Crocs than sexual minorities, or any sorts of sexual experiments, leastways publicly, leastways when you're a governor."

"So?" he says, annoyed, and uses his bishop.

"And I'm sure, Gar," I continue with a knight, "that you were young and needed money or whatever when...um...you accepted a movie role. An adult movie role."

"What are you talking about?" Gar looks irritated.

"Why don't you go to this website address and search this keyword." I write it down on a post-it, bend over the desk to hand it to Gar and pronounce slowly and clearly, "Pinocchio."

He makes a couple of typos on his computer and it takes him forever to open that specific video, which is available publicly at no cost. I'm just waiting for his reaction. My strategy is working.

"Blackmail?! You're blackmailing me?!" Gar is angry and surprised. His nostrils expand, heavily breathing, making his nose seem twice as big as it already is. And he can't even castle.

"Self-defense, Gar. Self-defense. I don't wish to sell the Club. But you want it anyway and won't stop, will you?"

Gar nods. His eyes glow with malevolence.

"That's what I thought." The ball is in my court. Strength is not muscles only. I breathe out—it's my move. "You could easily erase me, but unluckily this way you still don't get the Club—you need my signature and access. You could beat me or shoot me to get that but you see, Gar, Dylan, that man who was with me at our first meeting, he wouldn't let it go. If you cause me any sort of physical damage—there will be consequences. You're a smart man, Gar, you know that for every action there's always a reaction." I do royal fork and then lose my queen too in a very stupid way.

I really, really want to stomp away. But it's either people tell you what to do or you tell them what to do.

"So here's the deal, Gar, a compromise for both if

you wish. I keep my mouth shut about what I've seen in that video. And oh, by the way, there's more of those videos, on different websites. But I'm sure you can recall starring in them. You buy the Club for what it's actually worth—this way you have it so you leave me alone. And we part ways." It's better that way or he won't let the business grow or even be anyways after this.

"How do I know I can trust you?" Gar says.

"You don't. All you have is my word. I wasn't the one who started all this. I just wanted an investor for my business, which you have successfully used because the tool I created is working very well."

He looks at me a bit surprised.

"Of course I know you're behind the revolution and the informational mess that's going on now. You should be thankful the Club only costs two million, and not twenty; which would've been possible have I stayed in charge. But no-oh! You ruin everything others create. Everything becomes disposable in your hands."

He opens his mouth to say something but I interrupt him instead.

"I don't want to hear any of your chauvinistic comments." I raise my hand to shut him down. "This ends now. And believe you me, Gar, I do not want to see you again, neither in videos nor in person. Ever."

His face looks exhausted and he has got black circles under his eyes. The leg shaking starts again. The thinking doesn't take long—the shaking stops in a matter of seconds.

"Let's meet two days from now for the transaction.

I need all the web addresses."

"Gar, when I said I didn't want to see your face again I meant it. You already have the Agreement right in front of you; and the time for price negotiations is over. All that is left is to write down the number into the blank gap, just like you planned it beforehand. And if anytime in the future you decide that this is not over, there will still be consequences. It ends here, now. Let's finish everything before I get nauseous again. It's a draw, by the way." I point at the chess board. "Unless you want to pointlessly continue moving the remaining pieces around."

Gar half-rises to see the full board from above, and falls back into his chair, his body slumping, losing its stiff posture. Then Gar's chair rocks back and forth, lulling.

"Fine," Gar says after a short pause and nods. "Fine! Just... Do me a favor, shut your mouth, will you?" Jafarov, exasperated, clicks his tongue and lets out a huge breath.

And we cut to the chase in complete silence. I'm from Ukraine—I don't trust the government. I've lived through too many changes so putting me at risk again is off limits. I sign the papers and give Gar the addresses to all of his porn videos—it is now his headache dealing with privacy; he transfers funds to my offshore account in Cyprus. I would have used cryptocurrency, as a light version of offshores, but Gar is too old to understand how it works. Two million later, I take my powers out the door. InfoPro.-Club is no longer mine.

In the taxi back to the city, I cry all ride long. This

is too fucking much for me!

"Are you okay?" the frightened driver asks.

"Yes, I'm alright. Hormones," I answer. The word hormones scares most men worldwide because they have no clue how to react to that. And so they shut up.

When I search for a compact mirror in my purse to freshen up, or better say, clean off the mascara from all over my face, I find my ten-euro casino chip. I still take it with me everywhere I go.

Yes, I'll definitely be alright. Thanks, lucky ten.

This is when I realize that I'm done with Kiev. Nothing awaits me here anymore. Fuck it. Fuck the Club. People can do whatever they want as long as I'm not there for it.

Nothing mobilizes like the sudden decision of a woman. I call my real estate agent and tell her that I accept the offer and am willing to sell the apartment on these terms right now before the end of the work day. Because after that I will no longer be in the country. She calls me back in literally ten minutes saying that the buyers agreed. I sell my apartment in a matter of two hours and hand over the keys—my keys. I don't even bother to pack and leave everything for the new owners as is.

Decisions, decisions... It is official—nothing awaits me in Kiev anymore for real.

I call Val.

"Hi. Let's have dinner? My treat."

"I'm totally in," Val replies. "How about Italian?"

"Let's have Ukrainian. It's been a while since I've had it. I missed it."

"Consider it done. We are going to be fat and happy. And maybe have a cocktail," Val says.

"As long as it's not a Molotov Cocktail," I add.

We eat, go to a live music show, then to the movies and end up at a twenty-four seven cafe, drinking numerous cups of chamomile tea, where I briefly bring down the news about Nose and the Club. Everything works in the capital as if nothing is even happening in the whole country.

"Val, can you stay with me till my flight in the morning? I've had a very exhausting day and I know I won't be able to sleep tonight anyway. And also I don't want to be alone tonight. Can we just hang out?"

"Of course! You can stay at my place," she replies. I call her my friend for a reason.

There's one more place left to visit.

Cold morning sunrise is a beautiful thing. Gosh that is some strong wind. On the foggy, frosty, gray morning, I'm waiting for the sun to appear and brighten all around with its warm rays. Right in front of me is the Boulevard of Young Corruptionists, where the tires are on fire, creating a smoky black wall all the way up. It is like burning art at the Burning Man festival. First they create, and then they destroy it themselves, also at sunrise—preparations for the new season. I hope that after burning tires the new season will be better.

Val stands next to me taking pictures of this beautiful mess of mind. The Boulevard is Wonderland and the crowd is Alice. "How do you know I'm mad?" "You must be or you wouldn't have come here." To complete the scene, "Beethoven's Silence" by Ernesto Cortázar would be the best soundtrack to showcase sadness and resentment—feelings in the commodity bundle.

"See, when I wanted to do InfoPro.Club I just wanted to do it because I was persuaded I could. But I didn't give a damn about it, I did it for the sake of doing it, so it succeeded." I take a deep breath. "I guess this is how it all really works in life..."

"Um, yeah, pretty much," Val nods. "Devalue what you want and you'll get it."

"And this," I point at the Boulevard of Young Corruptionists, "was not really in my business plan. Should I take the fall for the revolution?"

"Mirra, don't dramatize. This is not your game." Val puts me back to reality.

"I still feel like I lost something very big and significant, you know. It's a very shitty feeling. I can't even explain and I'm the one good with words. Like, the level is passed. The very last level. And then what?"

"You signed the documents for selling the Club, huh?" Val asks.

"He made me. Now I can freely leave Kiev."

"Whoa. Freely? What do you mean."

"Nose wanted to buy the Club and he did."

"And if you said no?"

"This wasn't even an option."

"Fu-u-ck."

"Yeah...two lives is too much to jeopardize for this bullshit. You and I will figure out the financials when I'm already in New York, okay?"

"Sure, no worries. Wait, two? Who's two?"

"I'm pregnant."

"Fu-u-ck. I mean, congratulations!"

I am so grateful I know Val that no words can describe it.

"Thank you for saving me then in London, and believing in me," I say.

"Yeah, I figured you needed it. Also you had a pretty damn good business idea and you were right about the control of the information flows. So I did the double investment really," Val says. and then adds, "Maybe I should work with Gar."

"Want an unwanted advice?" I say.

"It's fine. I know how to deal with oligarchs and have my own methods," Val winks. "Do I have any whores with genital herpes in my catalogue?"

Kiev, the city of my college years, with lots of parties and friends who are now famous and successful, one of which is the President of the state. Ukrainian politics has always been a circus. Finally, things are in the right order now in this chapiteau: a clown is the head of the circus, not the trained puppies. It is a very unstable yet interesting media era in Ukraine. A war that needs no winner. It lasts as long as harmony of hatred is maintained. Although, the best way to win a war is to never wage war. They, the new people in power, want to know right away who is friend and who is foe. How ironic it is: fight for democracy and true freedom of speech, win, and put in prison or simply eradicate anyone who has got a different opinion. But the story unfolds without me seeing it. All I want to watch is my washing machine spinning. Unlike any political news, it is actually clean.

ROOK MOVE

The largest number on a phone calculator is nine hundred ninety-nine million nine hundred ninety-nine thousand nine hundred ninety-nine. No place left for zeros. After that they become virtuality. If you stare at them long enough, the numbers start looking like calligraphic commas—signifying it's still not the end.

It's a wonderful feeling. The best part of owning money is not knowing what to do with it, which experience you wish to have now, how to power it up next. It makes you think a lot about what you really want.

This is how you know you have zero financial problems: you don't reheat your food. And you cook not because it's cheaper than going out, but because you simply want to cook; and because it's healthier. The power of doing what you want. No compromise, no lying to yourself.

I had an idea to go to a casino and waste the money from the Club sale. Put everything on zero—reset, start from scratch, check the luck of fate again. But I didn't do it. I believe neither in luck nor fate—I believe in me. Fucking finally! Most people think it's obnoxious. Most people also suck. The majority doesn't mean quality. Snobbish? Absolutely!

Money and sex are enough for enjoying life; and then more money and more sex, and then even more money and even more sex—a lot of people live their lives not knowing it's actually not enough. Neither money nor your title on a business card will please you.

Chasing money, I never had it. Being engaged in what is really important to me, I feel a lot of joy and satisfaction, and the money inexplicably appears in my life. I just somehow always have it. And this is when "Je veux" by Zaz starts playing as one of the main soundtracks, should this be a movie. "Oubliez donc tous vos clichés. Bienvenue dans ma réalité."

For the last thirty-three years I've been going through puberty. At least that's what it felt like. *Oh, that's what it means, nope, don't go there, bad idea Mirra, but maybe? Ouch, that hurt*..and all that stuff, you know. Then it was a year of bad haircut decisions. The only regrets in life so far? Bangs at thirty-five. And here I am—thirty-six years of age. I am a grown up, which essentially means three things: kids smoking vape anywhere indoors are annoying; there are now prices for parents—about seventy percent reduced cost of the actual price of anything that you lie about so your parents won't get a heart attack; and I'm very much into a new porn category. It's called real estate listings. I can just open one of those websites and enjoy my night. I usually start with a prelude: co-ops in Washington Heights for tree hundred and fifty thousand. Then I move to condos in midtown to spice it up. And when I'm ready to finish:

houses in California for eighteen million dollars give me instant pleasure. Yeah, adulthood! I've also spent two hundred dollars on chocolate milk this month so judge away. What I should have done earlier is use the most expensive dating app instead of Tinder to filter preferred search options—Zillow.

When I was a kid, there were these tall scary thirty-something-year-old grown ups who made decisions and ran big businesses and ruled the world. And now I have to deal with them and do business with them and...o-oh, wait a minute—I am one of them! Even now I sometimes feel like a child, thinking how can I even compete with them or dare to express my opinion; that there's someone "bigger' and older than me, and how can I beat them if they are the gurus and...I keep forgetting, I am one of them! I don't have to please anyone or seek appreciation or be that go-getter girl.

Everything has changed. The rain, the traffic, the people, the title, the attitude: it all stops to wait for me, to listen to what I have to say, to engage with my musings, to be ready to immediately suggest a solution to a problem that hasn't even arisen yet. And I can just be what I want. I can just do what I want. I am what I want. There was a time when I wanted to be a mix of Laima Vaikule style and Angelica Varum grace. The truth is I am a mix of Pamela Adlon style and Fran Leibowitz sarcasm. And you know what? That's me and I love it.

And I've also learned that it's actually easy to make new friends, at any age. You talk to strangers, you bother them, you participate in their lives. They want that too. In New York people are desperate for meaningful connections and true friendships yet afraid to seem intrusive and needy, so nobody texts more than once suggesting to hang out. They are overly busy with work, yoga, volunteering, hobbies, binge-watching, running, going out, gossiping, traveling, dating until they stop and reflect on what's going on in their head, surroundings, life only to realize that they are in fact lonely too. And extremely busy schedules on purpose is a way to cope. This is when you become friends. Those who are meant to will stay.

With every plus one number to an iPhone we lose minus one friend, but care about strangers liking and following our lives instead. Facebook still gives you an impression that you have a lot. Followers slowly replace friends. Though, knowing what some of them had for dinner last night won't make them closer to you, will it? It's the proverbial double-edged sword: you feel out of touch when not on social media but you're worse at being in touch because social media exists.

As a grown up you have to learn how to deal with your pain alone. You're also one-on-one with your fears. There is no more your favorite person in the world, grandpa, who will run to you the second you cry to blow on your emotional booboo. Fears, baseless and not the instinctive ones meant to save your life, make no sense and tremendously reduce the quality of life. Grandpa said "Be happy!" instead of goodbye all the time. I am, I am grandpa! I know you see me!

Being in your thirties is the time when stupidity can no longer be justified by youth. Maturity is when you stop being embarrassed that you find some tracks of Eminem quite melodic. I too just don't give a fuck. If your society pressures you—change the society. If you have to yell to be heard you're doing something wrong. Don't pretend to be interested in a conversation when you're not. Just leave. There's no need to wait till your mid-sixties to be able to do that. Or ignore invitations to boring conversations in the first place. Life is way too short to tolerate all that. Stop fulfilling other peoples comments, likes, and shares. Stop caring what people think. At the end of the day no one is thinking of you at all. Peer pressure can't be your motivation. The only motivation that pushes you forward is your will. "I want it" is the only motivation that actually works. No books, no speakers, no pills can. If there is a will there is a way. I find it ironic when time management coaches are late. The question I still don't know the answer to is who's motivating motivational speakers when they're not motivated enough? I still wonder if hysterical laughter as a defense mechanism to cope with stress existed before the Consumer Era too. Following trends is so wearing.

Who of us girls hasn't bowed to Louis Vuitton bag, right? Especially when using a backpack. Personally, I've done both and I've had both. Actually, my preference for caring stuff is pockets, especially when all the stuff I carry around is a phone, a passport, and a credit card.

Everyone and everything's a brand. And you're paying for the brand's marketing expenses. When you live with no idols, no brands—there's a completely different life you might not even know exists. All you have to care about is what it is that you want. Life on your terms, by your rules.

Right now. Today. Not tomorrow. No what ifs, no anxiety, no depression, no extreme ups and steep downs, no unpredictable worries or regrets. The most unexpected thing that's waiting for you is when you give an effort to really think about what you want.

Here's what might happen along the way: you might lose money, you might even lose people, you'll be over neurotic relationships and compromises; life will change drastically. You'll get everything new. Decent. And it's totally worth it.

Give up the concept of your limited self and...you'll be surprised.

You're the creator of your reality. Not obstacles, vicious powers, governments, currency exchange rates, weather forecasts, Putin, Trump, neighborhoods, boyfriends, etcetera...it's you. Create it yourself. It's the only fun way to live it.

The worst vice is advice, as they say. I'm not giving you advice. I'm giving myself advice, my future self. Remember who you are. Tattoo it if you tend to forget. Fucking remember who you are!

During my unplanned chaotic trip to London and Paris and then Monaco, I was having a dialogue with myself, discussing important topics and questions, the answers to which I had been looking for. I wrote down everything that bothered me and the things I wanted to solve. It wasn't unusual for me to write— I'm still a writer and will always identify as one—but when I read what I wrote down, it all made sense to me. Surprisingly, it all just made sense on the paper.

So I applied it. The result turned out not exactly the way I planned or wanted, though I'm not a control freak either. I can't and frankly don't want to be in the spotlight. I'm a behind-the-scenes kind of a person.

I rent the impressions I'm looking for, and I always find that next adventure. Sort of a nomad, but not to the extreme—I have the need for a place I can always come back to and so I have this place, the place to re-set, the place to think next, my place for three seconds of silence. No matter how comfortable you lie down, after a while your body goes numb anyway.

Being a cosmopolitan, a citizen of the world, is when the importance of citizenship fades and you understand that the globe has become much smaller and the differences between cultures and mentality are gradually erasing and human nature is really the same everywhere. People are awesome!

At any given moment I know I can go anywhere in the world and for this I don't need to sacrifice my life saving for a private jet. I can live in any house of any style and decor without being tightened with mort-gage obligations. I need it bright. I want it bright because I hate longing and darkness and never blush with timidity or embarrassment. I'm a writer, who used to do journalism—I feel at home everywhere.

Well, I can't go anywhere in the world right now, and most importantly don't even want to. But it's nice to have an option. Just like living in New York City: you don't need a Snickers delivery at two in the morn-ing but it's awesome to know you can. I have found all I was looking for and I am not going anywhere. Be-sides, traveling with an extra carry-on in your tummy is not fun. I should really sue Sir Richard condom company—two percent risk of a completely protected sex is a hell of a chance. Sir Richard is not a gentleman at all. Usually I'm not a big planner but I'd like an opportunity to plan a life inside my body.

My state wasn't thought through in advance and I'm not quite ready for all this and the time is not right, but also I might not ever be ready so the right time is always now. It's meow or never. And frankly, it's such a huge relief! No more pressure about the biological fertility clock ticking, which makes you feel like the only right time to have a baby was yesterday. Phew. Now I can just deal with it and only time will show whether this cycle of life has been worth it.

I got myself visibly huge short-term boobs. They come with multiple side effects: mood swings, and experimental nutrition choices like strawberries with macadam powder. And not because of hormones, but because I'm a foodie.

We all get what we want.

The Brands, Sonia and Ricky, now host a bi-weekly get together dinner. Food is still bad.

Molly and Felix Acker continue smoking cigarettes.

Anton now has a long-term girlfriend, which proves that everyone can find a pair, even those who smell bad.

The homeless guy at Macy's. I got him a warm blanket and a chicken broccoli meal. Also, I gifted him my old umbrella that I was trying to lose for so long—something to cover his masturbation sessions with. As it turns out, he used to work on the futures market but then life happened.

Guy on the plane to London. I hope you stopped lying to yourself and people.

Dwight Hale is in prison for fraud and embezzlement.

Kellen Watz was diagnosed with severe OCD, Val tells me.

Ange Lanvin lives in Los Angeles now and does not drink. He was obsessed with a six-pack and got himself one, I mean six, I mean one pack of six of his own. But I love him in all sizes and shapes. One day he was having Chinese for dinner and the fortune cookie said, "You should talk to your friend today." Ange took it for a guide to action (I would too, if in search for a reason) and finally texted that actor on Instagram. Soon after that they met and since recently are a living-together couple. He killed two birds with one stone: he is happy as hell and a trending artist among the rich and famous, because acting can open doors to movies—or perhaps dick sucking does, but that's not the point. Anyway, I have a reason to actually go to LA. Ange proved that people can change if they want to and I'm very proud of him.

Nikki, whose information basically saved my life and I don't even know her last name, gets back into the sex business, because not all art sells well.

Guy in Monaco's casino. Thank you.

Loris Monti is still persona non grata in the United States yet most of his businesses are here.

Frank Ellis keeps making tons of jokes, entertaining America and beyond in his radio show every morning.

Emery and Kylie Zeman are expecting a baby boy.

It's the first boy since Emery was born so his family is happily crazy and praise Kylie, because "it's a boy, a boy!" Never be late to your Sexists Club meeting in the twenty-first century, aha. Good luck, girl.

Renat Novak, my genius web developer, keeps writing code. Something tells me we'll work together again soon.

Lada Lembas, my sales pro, moves to New York and we're friends now.

Paul Triggs, my lawyer, continues working hard— his shirt gets even more wrinkled.

Victor Maly, my SMM pro, continues working for the Club, because the kid's only motivation is money and no principles whatsoever.

Lida Lvovna receives a package with Marlboro Lights and American Spirits. All kinds of them.

Gennady and Ilusha, my neighbors, continue getting into trouble even after one of them broke both of his legs and another one lost a pinky. Their wives got life insurances and started a YouTube channel to monetize on their husbands' "What if" ideas.

Gar Jafarov is being investigated. I kind of wonder whose money will win.

Jafarov's wife no longer sings. At least some good news for the country.

Jafarov's bodyguard gets killed doing his job. Oh well.

Rosa, the tour guide in Odessa, opens her own travel agency.

Bogdan Zima, a PR guy whose press release made the revolution a trending topic in the world, joins an ultranationalistic party.

There's nothing more permanent than something temporary. Val Zironka and Knez Sandro are together now. Well, sort of...as together as a long-distance relationship can be. Even Mission Impossible is always possible.

Nora Sparks and Mason Reeve fall in love with each other too. It started on Memorial Day; and lots of French 75 cocktails to blame, or thank. And that makes it four of my friends who couple up with each other. My mission as a matchmaker has been completed. Nora and Mason are the perfect match—they both are so busy with their crazy work schedules that they truly enjoy spending time together. They live in once mine Tribeca apartment.

I think something happened at that house Upstate that made us all think about the future then. An unspoken, invisible, indescribable, metaphorical kick in the head, that made us ask ourselves some serious questions. What are you doing? What do you want from life? Who do you want in your life? Who do you want to be? What makes you smile everyday? Finally, who makes you laugh, because at the end of the day this is what truly matters—I'm in earnest.

Needless to say that Dylan is my best friend. He has all the qualities I have ever wanted in a man. Most importantly, he's got moxie; and a sharp wit. Wits never sag. I created him in my thoughts and then he just showed up for real. I want to tell him all my odd night dreams and hear all of his. Sharing a dream is always a very intimate moment. Love prefers sameness.

Oh, and we're married, live in Soho and store unevenly sipped bottles of Perrier in the fridge. All together. MD—we're almost medicinal to each other. Mirra Vladi and Dylan Goode. The power of peace. The power's in peace. It's nice to know that my vladi is goode.

The girl near the window watching the ocean in the beautiful painting by Vicente Romero Redondo still affects me. When I look at it, it gives me the feeling of stability, security, home.

Dylan brings me my favorite flowers. "Double Chocolate" Irises smell like a mix of toffee and caramel. Ecstasy in a vase. They awaken an appetite for fried dumplings and sauerkraut and condensed milk and pickles and Nutella with bacon.

"These flowers smell so good. Do you think I can eat them?"

"Babe, you can do anything you want," Dylan says and then adds, "you might throw up afterwards but I'll hold your hair."

And he does. But not because of flowers. When I open a new soap bar that has an apricot scent, I can't stop thinking about it and try a little piece.

Sunday—the fun day. We're having a lazy chill day with no plans whatsoever, except brunch at one of my favorite places in the city. A true NYC diner called Coffee Shop on Union Square West has an amazing scene morning through late night and delicious sandwiches. Especially their barbecued chicken sandwich with cilantro-lime sauce. Yam!

"What do you want to do now?" Dylan asks me.

"My current goal is hitting snooze only once," I reply.

"Ha. I mean for work or whatever."

"I used to live life as a project, with deadlines for micro achievements approved by society. Is this okay that all I think about now is 'nesting'? Also, I want to be that girl in the painting: stand near the window and stare at the ocean."

"Certainly. But just this is not enough for you. You'll be bored within a couple of months tops," Dylan says.

"Ah, you know me too damn well. You're right."

"Think about what you want to do."

"Well, for starters, I'll purposefully Google dildos, guns, and drugs and will look forward to all the contextual ads. It'll be the same dildos, guns, and drugs but starting at eight hundred ninety-nine dollars, because it's targeted for millennials."

"Mirra, you're such a nerd!"

"Well, what? I've been jobless for months. Again! I have to entertain myself for a while somehow," I say. "D, I don't know. Maybe it's the pregnancy thing. But I am so tired of all the buzz and people around constantly talking, talking, talking. Who the fuck cares how your day was, stranger. Shut up! It'd be great to have a silent hotel with an organic foods farm, somewhere in Big Sur, where you could escape to for a month, you know, to chill. No schedule, no speeding, no FOMO, but caprese, flax linen oversized shirts, barefoot walks. Detox from social bullshit. No movies, no shows, no books, no music, no content of any form, except your own thoughts; no distraction whatsoever—just you and you. Learn how to deal with yourself again and not get annoyed with own thoughts; learn to sit with your feelings, not run from them; learn who you are and start loving you. I'd call it Awesome Month. Imagine, a person who'd come stay at my retreat hotel, could say: 'I had an Awesome Month'!"

"Well, that can be arranged."

"Oh?"

"I mean, this is literally what I do. Ninth Avenue Capital invests in hospitality and real estate," Dylan says and then adds, "wait a minute, what are we, moving to California now?"

"Dylan, you don't move everywhere your company invests in, do you?"

"Question answered."

"Unless just for summer," I add. "But we need a good summer house. Although, all houses in Cali are technically summer houses..."

"You mean for winter," Dylan says.

"There! That's the reason I love you! Yes, of course I mean winter!"

"You know how in some movies they try to depict hell; and it's like this huge mass of naked bodies wailing and screaming and crying on top of each other. And they are in flames or submerged in red bloody water or something; countless arms reaching up towards you. You know the scene?"

"Yes. That's also what New York beaches look like in July."

"Right on the money. And that's also how I feel about winters in New York, wearing layers of clothes," Dylan says. "So maybe we should think about getting a summer house, for real. I mean winter house, just somewhere in warmth. You'd be perfect for the position of CEO of laying on the beach."

I love Sundays. Sundays are the best days to think. And pancakes, obviously!

In the booth, I lean closer to Dylan and take a picture of us. I've noticed that people only take pictures when they're feeling good, content, happy. It's explainable: we only want to remember the good. But it's the crisis that moves us forward—it would make sense to remember the starting point too, no?

"Hey, what would you do if money was no concern?" Dylan asks me, finishing up his sandwich.

"Money *is* no concern." I give him a smile. "It never has been. You know that like no one else."

"Okay, okay, call it limitless, never ending income, billions, zeros that they don't even have a word for."

"I'd open a wish foundation, where I'd make wishes of people come true. They don't have to be sick or dying or under the borderline of poverty. I'd make wishes come true for anyone. The only requirement would be an original wish that the person for one reason or another can't make it true themself. A trip to Disneyland or a helicopter ride can easily be arranged, they wouldn't need me for that. I think I'd be surprised to find out that not so many people can dream big. What would you do?"

"I'd write non-fiction and start with a book about decent restrooms in New York City and would call it 'What's That Smell?'," Dylan replies.

"Ha. Okay, something to look forward to," I say.

My phone rings. It is Loris Monti calling.

"Loris!" I pick up the phone. "How are you?

Haven't heard from you in like forever."

"Mirra, ciao! I've got good news: I'm ready."

"That's wonderful. What are you ready for?" I ask.

"The book. I'm ready to write my book. With your help of course. And then I want a movie. Can you write a screenplay too? Ah, why am I asking this?" Loris says it like he's rolling his eyes in the meantime. "Of course you can. You'd be perfect for it. I read your books. And I definitely want you to write for me!"

I immediately think of Ange and who he might know and maybe by this time he already knows someone in Hollywood. There's always someone who knows someone who knows someone—six degrees of separations. There's always a friend of a friend of a friend who belongs to a particular circle. There's nine of them in the movie industry, as in nine circles of hell. But it's okay. People break into the industry all the time.

"My old friend has a production company in Los Angeles and New York and is waiting for the screenplay," Loris says and we talk the details and schedule a series of interviews over the phone to dig into his story.

There is another, different life, a life full of pretty people who only cry effectively, wear Fedora hats and look good in them, fight and run in high heels, give hysterical speeches with applause at the end, publicly confess to lying at a meaningless event that is always broadcasted live worldwide, drink triple double scotch at midday and not fall down like broken wood furniture, start a road trip with a stranger and end it with the best friend, talk not the way they ever would dare and love not the way they should. Movies. One needs no truth. One who tells the truth is always inappropriate, seems stupid and angry. Even if people accept the truth—it still annoys. That is true. And all about such matter..

"I think I just got a writing gig," I tell Dylan after having talked to Loris Monti.

"But you won't have time to...deliver," Dylan reasonably notes.

"I'll give birth during a lunch break."

"I meant the writing, silly," Dylan laughs.

"It's okay, D. I'll figure something out. I always do." I wink.

"I thought you couldn't write long forms anymore."

"I don't have the need to experience the dramatic premise myself to be able to write about it."

Oh yeah, as it turns out, I can be happy and write at the same time. That's what it means to be a professional writer, and not fucking aspiring. God, I hate that word.

"In any case, you're a brilliant writer and I'm glad that you still write, doesn't much matter whose story it is," Dylan says. He is my biggest inspiration. "What I don't get is why don't you even consider writing as your only full time career?"

"I've never taken it seriously that you can actually make a living off of it. There's no decent money in book publishing, or at least not the kind of money I want," I smile condescendingly but not to Dylan—to the publishing industry. "Besides, I want other things to be going on in life, somewhere close to me, so I can reflect and get inspired."

"Shall we grab some seltzer and go throw bread-crumbs at tourists on Chelsea Pier?" he says.

"D, I have a better idea. Let's go to Apple Store and do the most insidious evil prank—switch all iPhones and iPads to Russian language there."

Dylan laughs out loud but I'm dead serious.

"I'm never bored around you. One lifetime with Mirra please." He lifts his hand a little as if making an order. "I love you so much."

"You better. Otherwise what's the point of it all?"

We then go to the Whitney Museum. Almost right away, on the second floor, Dylan goes to the restroom and I sit down on a bench in front of a painting to wait. A man sits next to me.

"I've been watching you," he says.

"That did not sound creepy at all," I say.

The man grins.

"What I meant to say is I know about InfoPro.Club and what it did," he says almost whispering.

An immediate feeling of fear and anger arises from my gut and comes out as an hyperventilated exhale.

"Who are you?" I think the worst: that Nose sought vengeance and sent this man to me. "Who sent you?" And as I say that I try to get up but can't without help, so I start to sway back and forth like a roly-poly doll. Not helpful. Then I search for keys in my pocket, the sharpest object I have and a second later give up because of the stupidity of the situation. I am so pregnant that a sudden siren in the city or my own sneeze can put me in labor. Can't even get up myself because of the heavy belly. *Dylan! Where are you? Why the hell is it taking you so long?*

"Don't worry. I'm not from Gar Jafarov. He's under control," the man says and smiles in content. "My name's Andrew Dean and I'm here to offer you a job. I apologize if I scared you. That was not my intention at all."

"A job?" *Ugh, I watch way too many spy movies. Wait, what? Whose control is he under?*

"Yes. A job. We need a communications consultant in Washington," he says.

"Jeez, you surely do need a communications consultant since you delivered the good news in the scariest way possible."

"I was told you have a unique perspective. Now I can see that. Bold." He's got the absolute of a poker face—impossible to read at all.

"Couldn't you just have sent an email with the job offer or something?" I say.

He looks at me silently in the way that responds: "better in person." Well, that gets my full attention now—I'm intrigued.

"Exactly what sort of consultancy do you need?"

"Analysis of information flows, in brief. It's an ongoing full-time working process. You might need your team."

"My team... Right." *I need to fake my team again. Or form an actual team from my freelancers for future endeavors.*

"By the way," he continues, "compliments for the good price set for the Club."

"How did you know?" I'm surprised.

"We work with information too."

"Who are we? And who would I hypothetically be

working for? Which party? Or person?"

"Well, neither, actually. An independent consulting firm."

"You do see that I'm pregnant and won't be able to do anything for a little while, right?" *Oh my god oh my god oh my god! Whatever this is, but it's basically real time Wag the Dog movie happening! And it is my favorite movie of all times!*

"The job won't start in a little more than a month anyway so you have time to think," he says.

"But I live in New York..."

"Mirra, let's do the following. You give me a call." He hands me his business card, "So we can meet and have a proper conversation." He pauses. "New York, Washington...things can be arranged. The world's not that big. Congratulations on the baby." And he leaves.

There's never enough of power, there's no absolute power because in democracy lots of people want it. And people in power will always abuse their power, and there will be others who will try to deprive them of power by setting obstacles to fail or by waiting for them to make a mistake on their own. Or both. Lots and lots of people are employed with only one goal: to keep someone from failing, and to provide crisis management in the event when that someone inevitably does fail.

I have discovered that power and love can come together. All you have to do is choose the level of power you want to play at. I don't need to rule the world, just my own world that I create. *Or do I? Nah. Or maybe? Stop. But seriously? Oh, common! Shut up! No, talk to me! The inner voice, where did you go? Ugh, I gotta pee now.*

One day I'll write a comedy movie in the best satirical propaganda style. I already have the logline: "After Russian hackers have invaded every election process in the world, a group of Americans decide to restore justice in the world and create a crisis in Russia by messing up with the market of kasha—their national strategic reserve. But the unexplainable power intrudes. No, not nuclear power—worse; stronger—the power of truth."

At this point Dylan knows what to expect from me but still gets surprised every time like the first time, when I tell him what has happened to me just now while he was in the restroom.

"Mirra, how the fuck do you do this?" Dylan asks.

I have heard the exact same question slash laughter slash engagement from Ange.

"What? You mean go to the museum and get the kind of job offer that I couldn't even dream of? Honestly, D, I have no clue. What do you think I should do?"

"M, it's your choice. Personally, I wouldn't mind making connections in the political scene. But whatever you decide—I'm with you no matter what."

Now that's the man I married.

I've always been a metaphorically do-it-myself, fix-it-myself kind of person but lately all I want to do is just pay people to handle EVERYTHING. I'm so over trying to prove how capable I am. Professionals do it well. Take my money. Solve my problems. And I've always thought of the American Dream as you move here, okay this is America, go dream now. All dreams

I had have come true. Does that make me American now? Eventually, I've got the ten things I wanted: self-identification, happiness, husband, children, screenplay and a book deal, good friends, business, house with the ocean view, and a job offer I can't say no to. There's a little problem though—I'm out of dreams at the moment. This is when people usually get into writing books. But that's what I started with. Well, I do it my way. Now what? Politics? Awesome Month hotel? Both? And what about the city? Now would be the time to continue my career here in New York. Or not? I mean, I'll always have my New York regardless of anything.

I've never dreamed of climbing the classical vertical career ladder; instead, I've always thought of my skills development in a horizontal manner. So much of multidimensional thinking to do.

There's always a choice and a way. Predefined destiny is nonsense. You choose and then you deal with consequences of your decisions, and it rolls like a snowball, getting bigger and further from your initial decision. Ironically, we are always alone when the most important decisions need to be made. If you're lucky, you won't be alone to deal with the consequences.

Looks like without even planning anything, I already have something on my calendar. Though, I still can't believe what has happened to me. Ну не ёб же ж вашу мать! My apologies. When I'm overwhelmed, I swear exclusively in Russian—there aren't enough English words to convey everything I want to say from the bottom of my heart. Dylan even learns a couple of my words to mix in his poor obscene vocabulary of cunts, dicks, and fucks. Most of the time we use the good words. But sometimes when we use the bad words—we use them right.

And even giving birth, I will be swearing—it is the right time. In the hospital, for a long time nobody can understand why one nurse constantly laughs—she simply understands Russian.

Turns out pushing a baby out of a vagina is still less painful than full Brazilian wax. I always say that there's at least two options and two choices and two ways. I give birth to twins, a boy and a girl, one of each. I guess I'm out of options now, in the most adorable way possible. Man, they are disgustingly beautiful in that vaginal discharge. I'm super thankful movies actually lie about that.

Keep pushing, keep going forward. The temptation to perceive life as a continuous forward movement is quite significant. One way or another, life teaches and pushes us: in childhood to take the first steps, in adolescence to fall but get up, in youth to determine the motion vector and set the goal, in adulthood to run as fast as possible, in old age to evaluate the path traveled. We are constantly on the move. There seems to be no more popular topic than time management, skill development, prioritization, increased efficiency, speed of achieving tangible results. Harder, better, faster, stronger. Oh, it's never enough. Perhaps that's why so many people run—they just can't stop and running gives them a feeling of constantly moving forward, like this way they're doing something. Running in place is also running. Technically?

Every day tons of responsibilities, expectations, and comparisons fall upon us. We feel that we simply have to be successful, be number one and the best in everything and always. To survive, I presume. Life turns into a continuous fast forward.

We get a small piece of information meeting new people or seeing new places and then run in fear of not meeting more new people or seeing more new places. How many more new people do you want? How many people do you really know? Wouldn't it be more interesting to get to know more about the people you already know? What they like, what they don't like, how they drink their coffee and what type of movies they watch, what they like to eat for dinner and what they feel when they wake up in the morning. What is their biggest fear? Or the most embarrassing secret? Do they like to plan everything or be spontaneous? What's their limit of pain? Are they close with their family? What makes them tick? Stand up or sketches? What was their first love like? Do they like talking about politics? Chicken or fish?

Share is more than just a button. All the people you follow on the socials, how well do you think you know the real them? Do they wish you a happy birthday? Do they even bother to know your birthday without a social media reminder? Quantity replaced quality. That's also the primary reason why I don't believe in open relationships, which are more about sharing and not caring. In a non monogamous relationship the significant other ain't that significant. Why even be where they can do without you? They call it ethically non monogamous, as if adding the word ethically changes your naturally installed feelings of posses-siveness, jealousy, and betrayal. I'm too old fash-ioned—I call it ethically asshole. To be fair, when I don't care—I share.

How do polyamorous people do it: constantly look for new people to date? Hell no! It's enough that it takes a while to find one decent person. And I've no-ticed that people who claim to be polyamorous more often than not are people you'd never want to sleep with. I guess they're just maximizing their odds? Overall polyamory seems too complicated whereas relationships are actually pretty simple. People just tend to overcomplicate things; some subliminally look for that. They feel alive this way, they say. They're ac-tually never happy though.

There're people who care and who annoy the shit out of you. There're things that are actually important and that help you feel better for twenty minutes. There's love and there's polyamory.

True love can transform, but it's imperishable. The only love, and not a primary love of your boyfriend's new girlfriend. It's okay, anyone can fuck anyone. Why form a harem for that? Yeah, I haven't yet expe-rienced everything monogamy has to offer. One dick at a time, please. Monogamy gives you a feeling of family. The beauty of a family is you already know they love you.

And I am so very much looking forward to our fiftieth anniversary with Dylan.

Isn't variety the spice of life, they say. In "I want to experience it all" statement from what life has to offer I personally choose all kinds of feelings in different life situations. It is so good to feel everything, the good, the bad, all of it. Because this is the way to know yourself, to be in balance with yourself, to live in a certain reality, until you disagree with it in case you do. Because you can disagree with your reality, did you know that? And you surely can choose a different one. Life is meant to be felt. It's how you know you're alive.

There are now known at least twenty-seven distinct dimensions of feelings, on physiological, cognitive, neurological levels. Admiration, adoration, aesthetic appreciation, amusement, anger, anxiety, awe, awkwardness, boredom, calmness, confusion, craving, disgust, empathetic pain, entrancement, excitement, fear, horror, interest, joy, nostalgia, relief, romance, sadness, satisfaction, sexual desire, surprise. Turn on the light! I want to see it, I want to sniff it, I want to hear it, I want to taste it, I want to touch it. I want to feel it all—this way I am.

It is the beginning of my legacy.

Good communication is key to everything. Three simple rules can make life and communication much easier: tell good people that they are good, tell those who make shit that they make shit, and try not to mix one with another.

We sometimes overcomplicate things that need no attention whatsoever. Here's a super easy way to understand if you've found yourself in something overly complicated: if mom calls, what will you tell her?

We have been taught a lot: to succeed, to be fast and furious, to be the best. But no one taught to slow down, pause, and enjoy the moment. Don't succeed—

experience. We are not taught to really enjoy our own successes. In pursuit of leadership, we simply don't have time to enjoy the ride. Start stopping. Ou, that's a great name for a podcast.

Life is too short to bother about societal pressure. If you do, you simply won't have time to live the way you always wanted. FYI, there's no second, spare life. To avoid seasonal exacerbations of the public opinion malaise use over-the-counter pill "Fuckoffall" every time before socializing.

It is so important to want something, try new things, create experiences to remember. When you don't, you limit yourself to the lifestyle adjusted to less and less. Like living in New York City with so many food options and caring lunch from home with you trying to save a buck or two is a good example of that ugh lifestyle. Your limit is only in your mind. You have to try everything in life! Though some people by "everything" understand promiscuity, drug addiction, and finding unjustifiably dangerous situations and not mountain climbing, chess, and thermodynamics in everyday life. The scariest feeling is when you get used to things and don't want more, to the way things are and don't want change. Life is what you make it so choose to make it fun.

Smile more, and more often. The balance can be disturbed not only by actions, but also by thoughts because thoughts are followed by actions. Rejoice in whatever you have in the moment and adhere to the good mindset. Thoughts radiate energy, so please train your mind to not shit all over like a puppy. Replace fear with confidence, sadness with enthusiasm, irritation with gladness. Let everything positive in—you'll get more good news and opportunities. Laugh at your fears—they dissolve from laughter.

Enjoy the moment of being alone, being just you. Alone does not equal miserable, alone means me time with lots of opportunities and endless possibilities. We want to get to know someone, so why not get to know yourself first? This is the relationship that will last forever, guaranteed.

Enjoy the moment of meeting someone new, having an interesting, deep conversation. Maybe you'll stop searching, you never know. Everyone has a story and it's unique.

Learn to enjoy the moment of rejoicing your victories and achievements, even the small ones. There's no such thing as payment for joy—joy is not a credit line.

Love. Something, anything. Everyday. Love. Someone, anyone. Love enough to share a muffin, or a life.

Life is about these moments. These moments are happiness.

Oh yeah, and books. My books are still my legacy. A literary manager sends me an offer of representation. It's been two years since I emailed the initial query and totally forgot about it and even stopped waiting for a response. Man, it takes a long time to read emails! Now, I have a manager who's already sold the manuscript of my once self-published novel for a hundred thousand dollars plus royalties; and within a month she somehow manages to get me a publishing contract for the prequel, which is my other self-published novel, doubling the money; and there will be a movie. Yay! I watch so many movies I might as well do one.

Invest in a young woman who needs a boost. She will spend the rest of her life giving back and paying it forward.

Most of the time you can predict how things will turn out, mathematically or psychologically—if you know either or both. It ain't that difficult—basic rules plus pertinent probability theory. Sometimes you have no clue what's going to happen and that's the beauty of life. Still, absolutely anything can happen, with no causality whatsoever. It starts with an idea.

Life is cyclic. Today one month is a common cycle: menstrual period, apartment rent, utilities, phone, content subscription, clothes subscription, furniture subscription, bank statement, pool rental subscription, you name it. Time is the most expensive and valued currency. You pay for joy and happiness with time, you pay for healing with time, even for money you pay with your time. Only, you can't buy time.

How many more cycles are you willing to spend on what you don't want? Do you even know what you want?

WHAT DO YOU WANT?

LUCKY ONE

LUCKY TWO

LUCKY THREE

LUCKY FOUR

LUCKY FIVE

LUCKY SIX

LUCKY SEVEN

LUCKY EIGHT

LUCKY NINE

LUCKY TEN